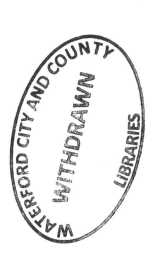

Dead Horsemeat

Dominique Manotti

Dead Horsemeat

Translated by
Amanda Hopkinson & Ros Schwartz

Leabharlanna Chontae Phortláirge

Arcadia Books Ltd.
15-16 Nassau Street
London W1W 7AB

www.arcadiabooks.co.uk

First published in the United Kingdom 2006 by EuroCrime, an imprint of Arcadia Books
This B format edition published 2007
Originally published by Editions Payot & Rivages, Paris, 1997
Copyright © Dominique Manotti 1997

This English translation from the French *A nos chevaux!*
copyright © Amanda Hopkinson & Ros Schwartz

Dominique Manotti has asserted her moral right to be identified as the
author of this work in accordance with the Copyright, Designs and Patents Act, 1988.

A catalogue record for this book is available from the British Library.

ISBN 9781905147359

Typeset in Bembo by Basement Press – London
Printed in Finland by WS Bookwell

Arcadia Books gratefully acknowledges the financial support of Arts Council England.
Publication of this book is supported by the French Ministry for Foreign Affairs,
as part of the Burgess Programme, headed for the French Embassy in London
by the Institut Francais du Royaume-Uni.

Arcadia Books supports English PEN, the fellowship of writers who work together to promote
literature and its understanding. English PEN upholds writers' freedoms in Britain and around
the world, challenging political and cultural limits on free expression.
To find out more, visit www.englishpen.org or contact
English PEN, 6-8 Amwell Street, London EC1R 1UQ.

Arcadia Books distributors are as follows:

in the UK and elsewhere in Europe:
Turnaround Publishers Services
Unit 3, Olympia Trading Estate Coburg Road London N22 6TZ

in the USA and Canada:
Independent Publishers Group
814 N. Franklin St. Chicago, IL 60610

in Australia:
Tower Books
PO Box 213 Brookvale, NSW 2100

in New Zealand:
Addenda
Box 78224 Grey Lynn Auckland

in South Africa:
Quartet Sales and Marketing
PO Box 1218 Northcliffe Johannesburg 2115

Arcadia Books is the *Sunday Times* Small Publisher of the Year

Praise for *Lorraine Connection*:

'A breathtaking parade of graft, corruption and bad business practice. Superior stuff' – Sue Baker, *Publishing News*

'A controversial novel in its native France, examining the shady politics of power and oppression through the eyes of an investigating *policier*' – Maxim Jakubowski, *Bookseller*

Praise for *Dead Horsemeat*:

'Set in French Dick Francis country, it is even better than *Rough Trade*' – *TLS*

'Danquin is an outsider – an openly gay police officer in a rigidly straight organisation. But this brief description does not do justice to the peace and verve of Manotti's writing. She effortlessly handles a fiendishly complicated plot. And is funny' – *Daily Telegraph*

'Packs more into 175 pages than some American or British novels twice its length. Manotti unravels it skilfully and with style' – *Sunday Telegraph*

'Fits together the shady past and present of stop-at-nothing yuppies in a socially acute crime yarn with punch and pace' – Boyd Tonkin, *Independent*

'Highly recommended' – Bob Cornwall, *Tangled Web*

'Apart from the sheer élan of the storytelling, it's the complex picture of a society that affords the real pleasure' – *Good Book Guide*

'Bleak, transgressive, sexy and quite literally unputdownable' – Anne Beech (Pluto Press), *Bookseller*

'A heady brew of drug-trafficking, political and business intrigue and horse racing. Manotti reveals the skulduggery and deadly plots in a new Europe where borders are as national to the business elites as they are impenetrable to refugees' – *New Internationalist*

'A volatile mixture of power, cocaine and horse-flesh – excellent' – Sue Baker, *Publishing News*

'A rare treat, but for the lover of horses it's a little disturbing. You have been warned!' – *Horse* magazine

'EuroCrime at its best . . . this one is a racing certainty'
– Pete Ayrton, Serpent's Tail

Praise for *Rough Trade*:

'The novel I like more this year . . . extraordinarily vivid'
– Joan Smith, *Independent*

'Highly evocative' – *Time Out*

'Manotti has Ellroy's gift for complex plotting, but she has a grip on the economics, politics and social history of Paris which marks her as special . . . *le flair* in abundance' – *TLS*

'A splendid neo-realistic tale of everyday bleakness and transgression'
– Maxim Jakubowski, *Guardian*

'It's difficult to believe that this gripping, politically sophisticated mystery is the author's first novel' – Marcel Berlins, *The Times*

'The complexity and uncompromising tone has drawn comparisons with American writers such as James Ellroy. But Manotti's ability to convey the unique rhythms of a French police investigation distinguishes *Rough Trade*'
– *Daily Telegraph*

'This vivid portrait, with a clever twist, shows a side of Paris that a tourist will rarely see' – *Sunday Times*

'A memorable trip down the mean streets of the 10th arrondissement'
 – *Independent*

'Utterly-convincing realism' – *The Herald* (Glasgow)

'Stopped me in my tracks . . . I've been begging Arcadia to fast-track translations of everything she's written'
– Anne Beech (Pluto Press), *Bookseller*

'Hard-hitting' – Bob Cornwall, *Tangled Web*

'Outstanding . . . the sexual exploitation of Thai children, the unspeakable sadism of zealots and the pornography of the rich are all themes that she uses with total command' – Colin Spencer, *Gay Times*

'First rate' – *Crime Time*

Friday 9 June 1989

A slack sea on a grey day. Annick surveys the little auditorium where Pama's Annual General Meeting is taking place, a windowless room with grey walls and grey seats. Three or four hundred shareholders in dark suits, the soft hum of murmured conversations. Pama handles billions, it is one of France's biggest corporations. But from the shareholders' demeanour, anyone would think that that the slightest splash of colour, the hint of a raised voice would jeopardise the entire edifice.

Pama's communications director for two years, Annick is sitting high up in the auditorium, every nerve taut. Beside her, Nicolas Berger, her childhood friend and loyal assistant, is already bored stiff.

The board of directors enters en masse. A hush falls over the room.

'I always expect the shareholders to stand up at the entrance of the captain and his crew, like we used to do for our teachers at school,' says Nicolas.

No reply. Annick fishes in her bag, sneaks out a cigarette, takes cover behind the row of seats in front, lights it, takes three puffs, then crushes it out on the sole of her shoe.

The directors have taken their seats on the platform. The Chairman's gaze sweeps the room. An elderly, cold and austere man. A lone wolf in the financial tundra. He attempts to smile and his face cracks. He taps his mike and declares the AGM open in an amicable tone, a role that goes against the grain. Then he summarises the Annual Report in a droning voice. Pama is a conglomerate active in nearly every economic sector, and this diversity allows it to limit the risks and ensure the company's stability. The firm has long been part of the French financial establishment, and the Chairman makes no effort to win over or convince. He has no idea, thinks Annick, her hands folded in her lap. She closes her eyes and forces herself to breathe slowly. Nicolas sits lost in thought, his mind freewheeling.

Xavier Jubelin is at one end of the platform, sitting slightly aloof. He listens intently, and even takes notes from time to time. Two years ago, he was at the helm of a thriving, medium-sized insurance company that was taken over by Pama, of which he is now a respected director. Sporty-looking, with a square jaw and astonishingly mobile eyes, he's twenty years younger than the Chairman, who, rumour has it, is grooming Jubelin to be his successor. It is his turn to speak. Annick, her heart in her mouth, feels as if she's leaping into the void. First of all, an even-toned statement of fact. Pama is a holding company, mired by an excessive number of financial interests in an ill-assorted mix of companies. It should gradually shed its investments in industry and refocus on its core business – insurance and property – to revive its flagging energies. In short, contrary to what some people believe and say, the company needs a radical change of direction.

Nicolas jumps and sits bolt upright.

'Did I hear right? Jubelin's declaring war on the Chairman?'

Annick makes no reply. Her eyes still shut, she is listening to her heart pounding. Jubelin continues, a ruthless edge to his voice.

'We have put several motions to this effect to the Board, which has refused to consider them. This is unacceptable. That is why today, we are appealing to the AGM.'

The tension in the auditorium is palpable. Not a sound, all eyes on Jubelin. Nicolas touches Annick's arm.

'Don't fall asleep, things are hotting up.'

Still no reaction.

On the platform, the directors lean towards each other muttering, their hands over their microphones. One of them, Domenico Mori, an Italian, an elegant figure with romantic silver hair, takes the floor. He heads an Italian industrial metallurgy consortium which he built up himself from a family business. His group is Pama's main shareholder, the linchpin on which the Chairman's power relies. And Mori is an old personal friend of the Chairman's, they go pheasant shooting together in Czechoslovakia. The audience listens in silence, in deference to the millions he carries on his shoulders, and there is a sense of relief on the platform: order will be restored.

'We have no reason to oppose Monsieur Jubelin's suggestions.' Hint of an Italian accent.

A tremor runs through the gathering. Pale and drawn, the Chairman murmurs, forgetting to cover the mike: 'Traitor… disgraceful behaviour from an old friend…'. Annick opens her eyes and gnaws her thumb. The platform goes into a huddle, panic is setting in and the audience can clearly sense it. They can't let matters rest there. Counter the attack before rebellion spreads through the ranks. The Chairman proposes an immediate vote by show of hands between the two opposing strategies, his and Jubelin's. The ensuing discussion will depend on the outcome.

Hands raised, a careful count, Jubelin carries the vote. Whistles echo around the room, it's like a football match. The directors get to their feet and talk among themselves. The mike picks up a voice distinctly saying: 'It's a coup d'état'. At opposite ends of the platform are Jubelin and Mori, the only ones still seated, seemingly oblivious to the pandemonium.

Nicolas turns to Annick.

'You knew, and you didn't breathe a word?'

Annick says nothing and brushes his cheek with her fingertips, smiling.

Then things move fast. From the floor, Perrot, a property developer whose business is booming supports Jubelin and requests a proxy vote. They all feverishly do their sums on scraps of paper. Jubelin controls ten per cent of the proxies, the Italian twenty-five. Perrot is a negligible quantity. Who completes the picture? The Parillaud bank representative seconds Perrot's proposal.

Sitting next to Annick is Deluc, a presidential advisor and small shareholder in Pama. He leans towards her:

'The Mass is ended, go forth in peace, sister.'

Annick takes a deep breath and de-stresses.

The directors who are with the Chairman leave the platform, cross the auditorium and exit in silence. The scions of the oldest established French industrial and banking families leave without a word of thanks, like flunkeys.

'They're off to the elephants' graveyard,' mutters Nicolas.

The Chairman, Jubelin and Mori remain alone on the platform. Jubelin wins with seventy per cent of the votes. The choreography of victory. The Chairman frantically gathers his scattered papers, his face grim. The lone wolf is cornered. This is the end.

Annick rises. She thinks she sees patches of congealed blood on the grey wall fabric. I've been waiting for this moment for two years, and now it's happened, but I'm not over the moon as I expected. What I want more than anything else is a hot bath. And now, to work.

Dive into the loo. A quick snort of coke. Check make-up, retouch it slightly. Then Annick steps into the lift and goes up to the twentieth floor. Her secretary greets her with a big smile. News travels fast.

She opens the door to her office. Spacious, black wall-to-wall carpet, white walls. To the left, a matt steel desk, and on the wall, a triptych by Soulages. To the right, a lounge area, two low tables, black leather sofas and armchairs. And facing the door, a vast bay window looking out over the concrete panorama of La Défense and the Grande Arche.

A dozen journalists are sipping fruit juice, whisky and wine, waiting for her. A perfectly informal meeting between friends prior to tomorrow morning's press conference when Jubelin will report on Pama's AGM. When she walks in, they all raise their glasses, and the room echoes with congratulations.

She pours herself a whisky, perches on the corner of the desk, and gazes at them, radiating confidence and glamour in her tailored bright red dress perfectly suited to her blonde hair, immaculate make-up, golden chignon, kiss curls. And she's in the winning camp.

'Gentlemen, 1989 is an important year for the French economy. Share values are at a peak, the property market is booming, and there's a great future ahead for the new generation of managers.'

Low voice, slightly husky, offbeat. Very seductive. She's on top of her subject and her audience. She raises her glass towards them, and drains it in one gulp. Now, the Q&A game. About Jubelin, who's still a virtual unknown.

'Young, sporty, a self-made man. An excellent huntsman and experienced rider. And extremely skilled at his job. Background in insurance.'

And then about Pama's policy.

'Is Pama really going to sell off its industrial assets, as Jubelin announced at the AGM?'

'Industrial investments are always riskier and less profitable than property investments. If we refocus our activities on property, it is first and foremost to guarantee our insurance customers better returns. But the transition will be smooth.'

Competent. Relaxed. A journalist talks of a 'coup'. Sharp response.

'How can you say that? It all happened at the shareholders' meeting with absolute transparency. Our company is a model of democracy.'

'Apparently you've known the new CEO for a long time…'

Annick leans forward with a radiant smile, her voice heavily ironic:

'I'm perfectly aware of what people are saying, and I couldn't care less.'

'She's brilliant, this communications director,' a journalist whispers to his neighbour.

The free-ranging discussion goes on for another half hour, the audience is entranced. Then it's late, and the journalists leave. Tomorrow, there won't be any awkward questions at the press conference. And no hostile articles on Jubelin in the coming days.

Annick moves over to the window. It's done. The pressure's off. A painfully hollow feeling in her chest. The sun is setting. The occasional patch of light on the facades of the tower blocks. Paris to the left, the first lights glowing in the distance. The Grande Arche, to the right, floodlights, they're working round the clock to finish it for the 14th July. Thick glass panes, not a sound. At last, a kind of peace. At this height, nothing can get to me.

Monday 26 June 1989

Full moon over the stables and the surrounding forest, a coolness rises from the trees. The horses are asleep in their stalls, top barn doors open, some lying down, some standing. Others are idly chewing straw. Little noise, a light rustling. And a few sighs.

A man in white overalls and green Wellingtons gaping around his calves walks the length of a row of stalls. He is carrying a heavy iron cube in one hand, and two reels of cable. He stops in front of one of the loose boxes, puts down his load, and opens the door. A frisky little black horse pushes forward its nostrils and sniffs his hand. The man strokes its neck, scratches the base of its ears, inspects the horse. Then he shuts the door and busies himself with the metal cube. Plugs a cable into an electricity socket, two other cables, one red, one blue, connected to two metal clips. Holding the clips, he goes back into the stall. The horse raises its head. He caresses the animal's neck, talking to it softly. Trusting, the horse lowers its head again and carries on munching straw. A clip inside its ear. It tickles, and the horse tosses its head.

'Easy boy, easy does it.'

The horse quietens down. A clip under the tail, the animal jumps, turns its head, curious now, to stare at the man who checks that the clip is firmly attached, then goes out again. He pulls a lever on the transformer. A giant shudder racks the horse, lifting it off the ground. Its eyes rolling, its entire body desperately tensed is suddenly drenched in sweat, then it sinks noiselessly to the ground, its eyes staring, vacant. The man walks over to the animal, checks that it is dead, removes the clips, neatly rolls up the cables then leaves, taking his paraphernalia with him.

Sunday 9 July 1989

It is nearly 2 p.m. this Sunday afternoon, and Romero has just woken up. He is sitting on the floor of his one-bedroom, eighth-floor apartment, gazing out of the bay window overlooking the Quai de la Loire, with a clear view over Montmartre and the northern suburbs of Paris. He is bare-chested, wearing tight, black-and-white boxer shorts. Sitting beside him is a young woman in a baggy T-shirt, her face lost in a mass of chestnut curls. They're nibbling biscuits and eating coffee ice-cream floating in iced coffee in tall glasses. From time to time, Romero dips a finger in his glass and draws coffee ice-cream lines on the young woman's face, which he then meticulously licks off, and that makes her giggle.

'Take your T-shirt off.'

She does so. Romero draws ice-cream circles on her breasts, then leans towards the taut cool pink nipples. The phone rings. He gets up, cursing.

A woman's voice with a trace of a Spanish accent.

'Detective Inspector Romero?'

Romero pulls a face and turns his back to the girl to concentrate on the conversation.

'Yes, it's me, Paola. Go on.'

'Please come, I have to point out someone to you, it's important.' Romero hears the murmur of a crowd in the background. 'I'm at Longchamp racecourse, in the betting hall. Window 10.'

'I'll be there in half an hour.'

'Hurry up. It's really urgent.'

He hangs up, turns round. The young woman, still sitting on the floor, leaning against the wall, is playing with her nipples, squeezing them between her fingers.

'You're not rushing off now, are you?'

He goes down on all fours and licks the salty beads of perspiration between her lavender-scented breasts.

'Those are my breasts.'

He yanks her down onto the carpet, no time for preliminaries, and anyway, that's how he likes it, fast and furious, then to collapse feeling utterly spent.

Quick shower, runs a comb through his hair, hesitates, looks at his watch, already 2.45, no time to shave, T-shirt, jeans, trainers. Don't forget the revolver, ID. A linen jacket. Glance in the mirror, tall, slim, dark hair, a handsome fellow, pleased with himself. Everything's just fine.

The girl hasn't moved. Lying on her stomach in a pool of sunshine, she dozes in front of the bay window. He caresses the small of her back.

'I shan't be long. Will you wait for me?'

No reply.

Romero arrives at Longchamp. It is 3.30 when he enters the betting hall. Concrete, grey, the floor strewn with slips of paper. For the time being, it's not crowded, the public is roaring on the stands. A few loners prefer to hang around in front of the TV screens, exchanging dejected comments.

Nobody by window 10.

End of the race, the crowds suddenly surge into the hall heading for the windows. Shouts, crumpled newspapers, the clink of bottles and glasses from the bar. Romero recognises the noise that he'd heard in the background when Paola had phoned him earlier.

But still no Paola at window 10. He wandered around the hall a bit, vaguely worried. A trap? Unlikely. Lean up against a wall to protect his rear, keep his jacket open, glance around the room. The bell, betting's closed. The crowds make their way back to the stands. Still nobody at window 10. Flashback to the face streaked with coffee ice-cream, to the erect pink nipples. And a sense of unease. Glance at his watch, 3.40. And at that moment, a woman rushes screaming from the toilets at the far end of the hall.

Superintendent Daquin contemplates the corpse of a young woman, sitting on the toilet seat, propped up against the cistern, leaning slightly to the left. Her throat has been slit, the carotid artery slashed, a gaping fresh red wound, the trachea severed, cartilage ruptured, white against deep red, a gold cross on a chain on the rim of the wound. Her blood has spurted out, splattering the walls. Her summer dress is stiff, sticky, rust red. And above the mess of flesh and blood, her face, tilted right back, is calm, eyes closed, mouth half-open. A beautiful Amerindian face, high cheekbones, very dark skin, thick mass of black hair brushing the floor. The pool of blood on the tiles seeps under the toilet door.

The Crime Squad is at work. Forensic doctor, photographer, experts. Just one witness, a woman touching up her make-up saw the blood oozing under the toilet door and ran out screaming. It was 3.40 p.m.

Daquin is tall, well over six foot, burly shoulders, powerfully built, possibly on the heavy side. Square, regular face, not particularly good-looking, alert brown eyes that take in every detail of his surroundings, a powerful physical presence. Since the arrival of his chief, Romero has felt more relaxed. Daquin turns to him:

'Well?'

'One of my snouts. She called me at home…', slight hesitation, '…around two thirty, and asked me to meet her here, by window 10. She wanted to point someone out to me. She said it was important and urgent. She was killed before I got here.'

'Where did you come across her?'

'Jail. Fleury-Mérogis. When there was a big to-do about Colombian cocaine, I went in there to do a deal. She was inside, so was her mother. Mules. They were nabbed bringing in a hundred grams of coke each. She spoke French, seemed smart.'

'Extremely pretty too.'

'Yes.' Annoyed. 'I arranged for her to be released, and I promised I'd get her mother out if she tipped me off on the Colombian ring in Paris.' Flashback to the girl's body, lying in the sun in his apartment. He was wasting time. 'I'm not proud of myself.'

Daquin stares at him for a moment.

'So I see.'

Then he goes back to the body and examines it. The dress's right sleeve has remained intact. Daquin leans over and pinches the fabric. Luxurious silk. Gently tugs the collar. Label: Sonia Rykiel. With the tip of his shoe he turns over a sandal lying by the toilet bowl. Two exotic leather straps signed Charles Jourdan.

'And she spoke good French?'

'Yes, fluently, just a hint of an accent.'

'There's something strange about this little mule of yours. Too well dressed for a poor Colombian girl. Romero, you're hopeless. A cop can learn more about a woman from her clothes than from staring at her tits.'

'Nobody's perfect, chief.'

Silence.

'In my opinion, we should go and see her mother. Now, before someone else does.'

When they reach Fleury-Mérogis, Daquin and Romero are told that Madame Jiménez was released yesterday, on judge's orders.

'May we see Paola Jiménez and her mother's files?'

The minute she was arrested, Paola Jiménez had asked for lawyer Maître Larivière to be contacted.

'I've known Larivière for twenty years. He was already wheeling and dealing with the CIA when I was working with the FBI. A mule who dresses in Sonia Rykiel and has the address of a pal of the CIA… But apparently Larivière refused to take the case. That was before your visit, Romero… Let's check out the mother.' Daquin skims two pages. 'Not bad either. A week ago, she received a visit from Maître Astagno, who stated he was her lawyer. Have you heard of Astagno?'

'Of course.'

Romero is distinctly uncomfortable.

'High-flying lawyer, regular defender of the big drug traffickers we sometimes manage to arrest in France. Last year, he got a Medellín cartel treasurer off. The guy was handling huge sums of money placed in nine accounts registered in Luxembourg. It seems it wasn't possible to prove that the money derived directly from drug smuggling. Does it make sense to you for Astagno to take an interest in an ageing Colombian mule? And manages to get her out in three days?'

'No, of course not. Chief, I admit anything you want. I was careless, I trusted a pretty girl. I was slow, and I'm partly to blame for her death. Now what do we do?'

'We drop it as quickly as we can. This case stinks. Probably a coup organised by the Americans, a publicity stunt before the Arche summit which is supposed to be a landmark occasion in the international drugs war. Paola brings in a sample to bait the buyers. For some mysterious reason, the operation goes pear-shaped. She's arrested, perhaps on a tip-off from the Americans themselves, seeing as Larivière refused to get involved. When you put her back in circulation, the prospective buyers talk to the mother, and kill the girl. And to cap it all, there are probably a few French cops mixed up in it. So tread carefully. You open a case and it turns out to be a can of worms.'

Friday 14 July 1989

Annick, Jubelin and Nicolas arrive together at the private Maréchaux mansion bordering on Place de l'Étoile. They had to walk, for the whole district is in a state of siege. In less than half an hour, the 14th July parade will begin, a special extravaganza to celebrate the bicentenary of the French Revolution of 1789. A beaming Perrot greets them on the steps. In the hall, Domenico Mori, elegant as ever, accompanied by three Italians. Perrot makes the introductions: Enzo Ballestrino, Mori's financial advisor, Michele Galliano and Giuseppe Renta, Munich-based directors of subsidiaries of Mori's consortium.

Then he takes them all on a guided tour of the mansion. The first-floor rooms, high ceilings, white oak Versailles floors, huge curved bay windows overlooking Place de l'Étoile, sumptuous walls and ceilings decorated with panelling and plasterwork. No furniture, just several buffet tables laden with food, drink and floral arrangements facing the bay windows. Between the tables are the TV monitors that will relay the procession. On the second floor, more empty rooms with a view of Place de l'Étoile, groaning buffet tables and TV screens.

Perrot turns to the Italians:

'It's thanks to my friend Jubelin and to Pama that I was able to buy this residence a month ago. It has already been sold to a Japanese insurance company, at the highest price per square metre of the entire Golden Triangle. In three months, I've made a net profit of fifteen per cent.'

'And by underwriting the operation,' continues Jubelin, 'Pama gains a foothold in Japan, without spending a cent. Give me plenty of business like that, and we'll remain good friends.' Laughter.

The guests arrive in small clusters. When the parade starts, at around 10 p.m., there are about a hundred people there, businessmen, members of ministerial cabinets, 'and their spouses', jostling at the windows on the two floors. The procession formed in Avenue Foch winds round the Arc de Triomphe, passing beneath the windows of the mansion, then turns into the Champs Élysées to the continuous boom of drums and, from time to time, the whine of bagpipes.

At the head of the procession, under a vast banner 'We fight on', a grey, silent crowd and a float swathed in black symbolise the death of hope in Tiananmen Square.

Deluc throws an arm around Annick and Nicolas.

'The sight of the defeated is always tedious.'

'I can't share your cynicism.'

'I'm not cynical, my friend. Just realistic. And I don't mix entertainment with politics.' He steers them towards the buffet. 'Champagne all round. This magnificent parade to celebrate our anniversary. Do you remember? It's exactly twenty years since we three left Rennes to come to Paris. Something worth celebrating.'

Annick's mind darts back to that last evening in Rennes. Deluc, running away, her stumbling, caught by the cops, dragged to the police station, fucked by a detective inspector... Were they supposed to be toasting that unforgettable night? She glances around the room. Let bygones be bygones, and any excuse to drink champagne is a good one.

The guests amble between the buffet and the windows, up and down the stairs. In the heavily soundproofed rear rooms, a hi-fi plays music and a few couples are dancing.

On the Place de l'Étoile, after the French regions come the Americans, Russians and Scots, parading to the sound of hurdy-gurdies, fifes, bagpipes and the persistent rumble of the drums.

Annick has joined Jubelin and his Italian buddies. Ballestrino touches Renta's arm, and exchanges a look with him. Silent dialogue. Renta bows ceremoniously to Annick:

'May I ask you to dance?'

He's about thirty-five, average height, slicked-back dark hair, dark eyes, and an elegance that is just a little overstated. A close-fitting grey alpaca suit, light grey silk shirt, and a wide, brightly coloured tie. Annick finds there is something slightly vulgar about him. Amused, she takes his arm and they make their way towards the back rooms.

The minute they leave, Mori steers Ballestrino, Galliano and Jubelin over to a slightly isolated corner of the buffet. They attack the cold meats and talk business. A few remarks about the recent AGM. And Pama's future growth prospects. Quick review. They soon come back to Japan. This Maréchaux mansion deal, the first contact with the Pacific region. But they must consolidate in Europe before embarking on strategic interventions in the Far East. Mori agrees.

'By the way,' says Ballestrino, 'my friend Galliano told me about a nice little opportunity in Munich.'

'What's that?'

'A.A. Bayern, a medium-sized insurance company, solid family business, well established in the region. Has business relations with certain East German circles, useful just at the moment with things starting to stir behind the Iron Curtain.'

'Even in East Germany?'

'Much more than they're saying here. Right now, A.A.'s shares are fairly high, but they could plummet in the coming months, if we so wish. And pave the way for a takeover bid that will be both easy and very profitable.' Ambivalent smile. 'It's not a business proposition, it's a favour.'

'Why don't you keep it for yourself, Mori?'

'My group concentrates on industry. Where insurance is concerned, my stake in Pama is enough for me.'

Taking out his diary, Jubelin turns to Galliano:

'Shall we have a meeting before you leave for Munich?'

They move back towards the windows. Jubelin greets an official from the Ministry of Finance, who pumps his hand warmly. Congratulations. A huge float trundles past carrying a 30-metre steam engine, surrounded by the deafening Drums of the Bronx going wild, to the indifference of the crowd.

Annick dances with Renta. Lots of Latino and West Coast beats. He dances well, and flirts a little, as etiquette requires. His tie is Yves Saint Laurent. Actually more of a bore than a hoodlum. A pirouette and a smile. Annick escapes, dives into the toilet, a quick snort, and returns, ravishing, to the windows and the spectacle below.

She bumps into Deluc, cigarette dangling from his mouth, one of those horrid smelly Indian cigarettes he got into the habit of smoking when he was in Beirut, deep in an argument with an opposition deputy about the soaring share prices and rising Paris property values. The deputy ceremoniously kisses Annick's hand and starts explaining what's happening at Pama to her. He's clearly had one too many. Deluc takes advantage to make himself scarce, the bastard.

Jubelin, Nicolas and Ballestrino are sitting in front of one of the TV screens watching Jessye Norman launch into the 'Marseillaise' at Place de la Concorde. Nicolas turns to Ballestrino.

'I've heard you own a stud farm outside Milan.'

He sounds delighted. 'I do. I've raised a few flat racing champions. Two of my colts ran at Longchamp last Sunday.'

Jubelin adds:

'What a coincidence. I'm a great horse lover. I have several in training.'

'Who with?'

'Meirens, at Chantilly.'

'I know him. If you're ever in Milan, I'd be delighted to show you around my stables.'

Having rid herself, not without difficulty, of the inebriated deputy, Annick spots Nicolas and Jubelin in a heated conversation in a corner, slightly away from the others. She makes her way over to them, and they abruptly stop talking. Jubelin, on edge, turns to Nicolas.

'We'll talk about it in my office.'

Nicolas takes Annick's arm.

'Let's go upstairs and watch the end of the procession.'

Now it's the high point of the whole event. Women balanced on pedestals move forward with mechanical movements, revolving to the strains of a waltz. They are high above the ground, wearing huge wide-brimmed hats, crinolines with skirts several metres wide cascading down to the ground, each cradling a baby. Annick gazes at these stylised giants, which she finds threatening. Inexplicable feeling of discomfort.

The procession is winding up. Perrot moves from group to group. The single men are invited to round off the evening in the restaurant he owns, Rue Balzac, with some lady friends. Nicolas accepts, Jubelin, ever cautious, declines.

Tuesday 25 July 1989

Shortly before midnight, a slender crescent moon, clouds, strong winds. The stables are dark, nearly a hundred stalls around a huge square yard, on the edge of the forest. The trees groan in chorus, the buildings creak, the horses are a little restless. A hoof strikes the floor from time to time. On one side of the quadrangle are the grooms' sleeping quarters, just above the horses' stalls. Two windows are still lit.

In a shadowy corner opposite, a little explosion, barely louder than a banger, and a shower of sparks, then a blazing yellow flame, a pool of fire immediately in front of one of the stalls creeps along the ground and climbs around the door with a crackle. The horses whinny and grow restive. Lights come on in the grooms' quarters. A panic-stricken neighing, pounding of hooves, the straw in the stall is now ablaze. The men are at the windows, the wind blows in sharp gusts.

By the time they descend, the fire has reached to the roof and is spreading from stall to stall with a roar. In the yard, half-naked men race to the doors to release the horses from their stalls. Wild with panic, the horses stampede towards the forest. A groom is knocked down and trampled. A horse, its mane on fire, whinnying in terror, hurls itself against a wall and sinks to the ground, its skull shattered. One whole section of the roof collapses amid a cascade of orange sparks. Along with the smell of burning, the wind carries the horrendous smell of scorched flesh and hide.

Soaking wet, blackened, desperate, the men, clutching every available hosepipe, sprinkle everything that is still standing to delay the fire's progress. And the wind is still up.

A second row of stalls catches fire before the fire engine's siren can be heard. The firefighters have to remove two dead horses blocking the path before they can reach the stable yard and turn their hose on the fire. After battling for an hour, they manage to put out the flames. Half of the stables are burnt out, reduced to heaps of charred timber and ashes, exuding a blackish fluid and a few wisps of smoke. A boy, his bare chest smeared black, lies sobbing beside the charred body of a horse, cradling its head in his arms.

Monday 21 August 1989

Agence France Presse despatch:

As part of its crackdown on illegal drug trafficking, OCRTIS, the French antinarcotics department of the Ministry of the Interior, recently seized 53 kilos of cocaine found aboard an abandoned Renault van in a warehouse in the Paris suburb of Aubervilliers. Neither the vendors nor the buyers have been identified.

Saturday 2 September 1989

The curtain comes down on the end of the first act of Berg's *Wozzeck*. The lights come up in the auditorium of the Opera Garnier. Daquin rises, desperate to stretch and yawn. A glance at his lover, walking up the aisle a few metres in front of him. Of course he wouldn't appreciate it. And I have no reason… Rudi, always so polite and distant. German, Prussian even, tall, broad shoulders, slim hips, blond, a romantic forelock, square jaw and blue eyes. Mesmerising. Women nearly always turn their heads to look at him when he walks past. A rather amusing misapprehension, best witnessed from a distance.

The brightly lit foyer is crowded, noisy and stuffy. Daquin pauses by a window and gazes at Place de l'Opéra glistening in the rain, studded with lights and swarming with people and cars. Enticing. Rudi comes back from the bar with two glasses of champagne. And picks up the conversation exactly where he had broken off when the curtain went up.

'Thousands of people are leaving East Germany, through Poland and Czechoslovakia, and still not a word about it in your press. Incredible. My parents wrote and told me that a surgery unit in the biggest hospital in East Berlin has just closed because all the nurses have left the country. Theo, are you listening to me?'

'Not really.' He smiles. 'I'm thinking over the evening.' Drains his glass. 'I hate wearing a tie, the sets are enough to make you weep, the staging is pretentious, I don't like the music and the champagne's lukewarm. I'm going to find a taxi. How about I take you home with me?'

The phone rings insistently. Daquin takes a while to surface. A glance at his watch, it's 2 a.m. He kicks off the duvet. In the vast bed, Rudi's sleeping on his stomach, his face turned to the wall, his arms above his head. Fair hair against the dark green sheet. Straight out of an aftershave ad. Odd thought. It must be exhaustion. The phone keeps ringing. He picks up the receiver.

'Superintendent Daquin?'

'Yes.'

'Superintendent Janneret, 16th arrondissement. I've just had the Drugs Squad on the phone…'

'What do you want?'

'Can you come over to the station?'

'Now?'

'As soon as possible.'

'Send a car for me, 36 Avenue Jean-Moulin in the 14th. In half an hour.'

'Will do, and thank you.'

Getting up is no easy matter, groping around in the dark so as not to wake Rudi. The bathroom, privacy regained: first of all a long shower, hot, then cold, power jets full on, painful awareness of every muscle. Then, naked in front of the big mirror, he shaves meticulously, enjoying the feel of the metal razor on his skin, the pleasure of watching each familiar feature slowly emerge from the lather, the tingle of the aftershave. That's better. Now the wardrobe, to something to slip into quickly. No idea what's in store, an all-purpose outfit: leather jacket, linen trousers. And Daquin leaves. The ivy-covered houses of the Villa des Artistes make the night seem even blacker and more silent. A car driven by a uniformed police officer is already waiting at the entrance to the Villa on Avenue Jean-Moulin.

The superintendent is pacing up and down outside the police station.

'So what's going on?'

'We did one of our routine swoops in the Bois de Boulogne and my men picked up the usual bunch of transvestites. Plus a young man, half naked in a bush. A punter. And in the pocket of his jacket hanging from a tree, six hits of coke. We bring him in, and he kicks up an unbelievable stink, demands that we inform his father, Christian Deluc, presidential advisor. If it had been up to me, I'd have packed him straight off home, I've got my hands full enough, I don't need any additional complications. But he made such a nuisance of himself that the trannies started getting pissed off and threatened to inform the press if we just let him go. Can you imagine the scandal? Anyway, coke's a matter for the Drugs Squad and the duty officer seemed to think you were the best person to sort the matter out quietly.'

'Is the kid a minor?'

'No. He's just turned eighteen.'

'Have you informed his father?'

'No, we were waiting for you.'

'Don't. Select two of your men to help me do a body search and find us some rubber gloves.'

Daquin enters the station. At the back of the duty office is a lockup with three cells. In the first two, ten or so transvestites in their work clothes. They bang on the bars, harangue the cops, yell and sing. Daquin goes over to them, his step purposefully heavy, his gaze expressionless. He raps sharply on the bars of one of the cells.

'Cut it out, girls. Let me work in peace.'

A lull.

Daquin has the third cell opened, brings out a thin, sullen youth, points to the door of the office just opposite and follows him, accompanied by two subordinates assigned to him by the station chief.

'Leave the door open, the girls want to watch the fun.'

One cop at the typewriter. The other perches on the corner of the desk. Daquin stands.

'Name, kid?'

'I insist on being treated with respect.'

A sweep behind his legs, one hand pressing his head down. The boy falls to his knees. Daquin bangs his head on the edge of the desk, not too hard. His skin splits. Drops of blood splash onto the floor.

'Listen, arsehole…' keeping the boy's head down towards the floor with one hand: '…you just don't get it. You haven't fucked Catherine Deneuve. You didn't steal billions. You sold mini-doses of adulterated coke to trannies in the Bois de Boulogne, probably in return for a free trick. Daddy can't get you out of this mess, it's too sordid for the corridors of the Élysée Palace. *Capisce*?'

Daquin grabs him by his collar, jerks him upright, and steps back slightly.

'Now, your name?'

'Olivier Deluc.' Blood trickles down his nose, touches the corner of his mouth, he licks it, to taste.

'Date and place of birth? Address?'

The youth replies.

'Get undressed.'

The boy stares at him open-mouthed.

Daquin moves closer.

'Are you deaf?'

Hesitantly, he starts to undress, the taste of blood in his mouth.

'Faster. Your underpants too.'

He is naked now. Daquin to the cop sitting on the corner of the desk: 'Body search. Put on the gloves.' To the kid. Open your mouth.'

'You can't do that.'

'Can't I?'

Daquin stands behind him, presses on his jaw joints and yanks his head up. Searing pain in the jaw, the boy's mouth drops open. The cop runs a finger between the gums and the lips and under his tongue. Nothing. Daquin relaxes his hold and dictates to the cop sitting at the typewriter:

'A body search was conducted…' To the kid: 'Now, lean forward, hands on the desk, legs spread.' The same cop, still wearing rubber gloves, explores his anus.

'Cough. Perfect.' To the cop at the typewriter: '… and nothing was found. The suspect was therefore arrested in possession of six doses of cocaine.'

Blood runs down his neck, onto his shoulder. The boy, tears in his eyes, reaches for his trousers. Daquin stops him sharply.

'You'll get dressed when I say so. First of all you're going to give me the name of your dealer. If you do, I'll consider you as a consumer. If not, as a pusher. Six doses is more than enough. Do you need me to explain the difference to you?' The boy shakes his head, snivelling. 'Besides, squealing to the cops gives you a high, you'll enjoy it. Go on, we're listening.'

A mumble.

'Louder, I didn't hear, nor did the girls.'

'Senanche. He's a groom at Meirens, a racing stable in Chantilly.'

'How am I going to find him?'

'He's a wrinkled old man who hangs out around the stables every morning around six, when the jockeys arrive.'

'Has he got a lot of customers?'

A glance to the left, a glance to the right, still naked. Get the hell out of here.

'Ten or so, I think.'

'How did you meet him?'

'I sometimes exercise the horses in the morning.'

'You can get dressed. Sign your statement before you leave. And don't set foot on this patch again.'

Daquin quits the office and closes the door. The trannies burst out clapping. A gorgeous creature, muscular shoulders and dizzying plunging neckline, long legs and high heels:

'If you come and see me, Superintendent, it'll be free.'

Daquin brushes the bars with his fingertips, level with her face, and smiles.

'Too beautiful a woman for me.'

In the car taking him home, he lets his mind wander. Racehorses… cocaine…, Paola Jiménez was murdered on a racecourse in July. A coincidence? Maybe not. An opportunity to pick up the thread… Who knows? I'll come back to it. Then abruptly:

'Go via Montrouge, I know a bakery that's open at this time on a Sunday, I fancy croissants.'

Sunday 3 September 1989

The automatic doors slide open with a soft whoosh. Daquin enters the familiar world of the hospital. Lenglet has been re-admitted. And this time, he says, will be the last. Lenglet, his closest friend since their teens. They'd both rebelled against their families, had similar sexual experiences and intellectual tastes, studied the same subjects. Then Lenglet opted for a diplomatic career and the secret service, while Daquin chose the police. For the same reasons. Whenever their paths crossed, there was support and understanding, but it was always tricky as their interests were not the same. However they enjoyed intelligent, stimulating, lively conversations. *Condemned to live without you, my soulmate, my twin.*

In the corridor, a brief exchange with the nurse: Is it really that serious this time? She nods. Daquin remembers how he'd laughed the first time he'd heard of the 'gay cancer'. And then, very quickly, the urge to know, and the decision, once and for all, never to let himself be lured by the fascination of death. Stay alive, out of defiance. He enters the room. Lenglet, lying in the bed, in a sea of white, his eyes closed, face gaunt, contorted. Daquin relives his own childhood, his mother's slow, systematic death from alcohol and drugs. His father stood by and watched. Icy. Relieved. A programmed death. Resignation. I'd never do that. Daquin leans over the bed. I can't forgive you for dying. And to have chosen this death. Lenglet opens his eyes, stares at him. He speaks in a breathless voice, with a sort of hazy self-deprecatory smile.

'Distressed, Theo?'

Daquin looks at his elegant, almost transparent hands. 'Of course I'm distressed. You scare me. Talk about something else.'

'I'm tired. The Drugs Squad's under heavy pressure. American and French politicians are all het up about the drug traffickers, the number one threat to our civilisation…'

'They have to find a substitute for the Communist threat now that's in tatters.'

'…Our chiefs have been thrown out and replaced by supposedly dependable guys. As they have little experience, the Drug Enforcement Agency sent a few agents over to explain how to go about things. And I've just spent the night in a local police station nannying a kid who snorts coke to piss off his father, the son of a certain Deluc, presidential advisor…'

'Christian Deluc?'

Lenglet pauses for a long time, his eyes closed. Silence in the room. Daquin listens to him breathing. Lenglet continues, his eyes still shut.

'I knew him well. In '72 or '73 in Beirut. In those days he was a far-left activist, and he came to visit the Palestinian training camps.' A long silence. 'Not the steady type, like the Germans. More like a French-style political tourist. We still kept an eye on him. Not a very pleasant character.' He reflects for a moment. ' Uptight. A repressed lech, made you think of a fundamentalist Protestant paedophile.'

Lenglet falls silent, opens his eyes and smiles at Daquin.

'You're the only man I know who is able to listen, without rushing.'

'It's a cop's job.'

'Maybe, I don't know.' Lenglet shuts his eyes again. 'In the end, Deluc's political group folded while he was in Beirut. He pitched up at the French embassy and became friendly with an odd character. Foreign Legion, I think, member of the embassy's security team, whose real job was to find men, women and children to put in the beds of French VIP guests.' A pause. ' We called him "the Chamberlain". I heard that he'd made a fortune on his return to Paris thanks to the contacts he made in Beirut.'

'And Deluc made his career with the socialists.'

'Can't for the life of me remember the Chamberlain's name.' Renewed silence. 'I'm exhausted Theo. I've run out of curiosity. Only memories give me pleasure.'

At the arrival of Lenglet's lover, accompanied by two exes, Daquin quits the room and the hospital. He has never been able to stand meeting current partners, exes and exes' exes, even less around a death bed, around Lenglet's deathbed. He makes his way slowly back home, on foot. A humid, oppressive evening. No way can I see Rudi tonight. Don't even feel like eating a proper meal. I'll make do with what I've got at home.

Back to the Villa des Artistes, a haven of peace and cool outside the city centre. The house has a vast ground-floor room and a glass roof fitted with white blinds. Two huge leather armchairs and a sofa, wood panelling and furniture, hi-fi, impressive collection of CDs, and at the back of the room, behind a counter, a well-equipped kitchen tiled in shades of old gold. On the mezzanine, the bedroom is furnished only with an enormous bed and bookshelves along the walls, piled with books several layers deep. Leading off the bedroom, the walk-in wardrobe, mahogany cupboards and drawers filled with clothes, and a white-tiled bathroom with a big bath tub and power shower.

The house is empty. Daquin stretches out on the sofa, his feet up, and lets his mind wander. For quite a while. Seeing Lenglet dying stifles desire, tingeing it with shades of nostalgia.

It was in Harry's Bar, Venice, Arrigo Cipriani, standing by their table, dressed impeccably and waxing lyrical about pasta with butter in his refined Italian, watching the intrigued Rudi who was listening to him without understanding a word, his head cocked on one side with a sort of anxious tension. It was dark over the lagoon. Suddenly Daquin had been overcome with the intensity of desire, and took his breath away. Possess him there, now... Their eyes met. They finished dinner, without a word, and fucked all night... That was last year.

Pasta with butter. Daquin rummages in the kitchen cupboards.

Boil the water in a large stainless steel pot. Melt the butter in the bowl sitting over the pot. When the butter's melted, put the pasta in the boiling water. Quality pasta. The same as the pasta made by Cipriani. Neither dried nor fresh, excellent. Boil for two minutes. Drain the pasta thoroughly in a sieve. Pour some of the melted butter into the pot, then half the pasta, then some more butter and grated Parmesan, and lastly the rest of the pasta, butter and cheese. Mix vigorously. Pour into a hot dish and serve immediately. Drink spring water with the pasta and butter. It's a masterpiece.

For lack of anything better.

Monday 4 September 1989

Meeting of the Drugs Squad section leaders in the office of the new director. Daquin goes up with Dubanchet, they've known each other since training college at Saint-Cyr-au-Mont-d'Or and have a number of shared experiences, plus a sense of complicity between them.

'Well, have you met the new boss yet?'

Pulls a face. 'Careful... wait and see.'

They enter. The director steps forward to greet them, shakes their hands, smiling. Slim, dark suit, hair plastered back, a distinguished air that makes him look more like a prefect than a cop. He's definitely one of them, but he's spent most of his career in ministerial circles.

The five or six superintendents in the office greet each other with silent nods. The director says a few words about how delighted he is to work with them. Daquin senses the unspoken message behind the smile, it's almost tangible. The man is on his guard. And the meeting begins.

From the start, the discussion centres on cocaine. Consumption is soaring in Europe, heroin-cocaine bartering between the Italian and Colombian mafias, the place is awash with dirty money, there must be no compromise with the agents of death. Following the Paris summit and the setting up of the Financial Action Task Force on Money Laundering, we need to see results. The powers that be are counting on us. Our colleagues in the antinarcotics department seized a big haul in August. Fifty-three kilos of cocaine. We have to do better.

'Fifty-three kilos, but no dealers,' says Daquin. 'I'm not sure we want to repeat that kind of operation.'

The director looks miffed and evokes the Drugs Squad's track record over the last two years. Dubanchet leans over to Daquin:

'Do you reckon the DEA supplied the stuff?'

'It's possible, France is crawling with their agents at the moment. Then something went wrong.'

The director mentions the two spectacular hauls made last year. And, three months ago, the arrest of Buffo, the mafia boss, on the Riviera thanks to close teamwork with other police departments and following a lengthy investigation …

'A hasty arrest,' interrupted Dubanchet. 'I was there. Impossible to prove drug trafficking, he's inside for cigarette smuggling. A fiasco, actually.'

'On a tip-off from the DEA,' adds another superintendent.

'We must be thorough and cautious,' concludes Dubanchet.

Daquin watches the chief who's chain smoking. Relations are going to be strained.

Now, let's move on to the case in hand. At the end of the meeting, Daquin speaks:

'According to two of my informers, there's heavy cocaine consumption in horseracing circles. I'd like to take a few days to check out these leads.'

'Fine. Keep me posted.'

Tuesday 5 September 1989

At 7 a.m. Daquin is at work in his office, Quai des Orfèvres. An office shut away at the end of the top-floor corridor with a window overlooking an interior courtyard, where he has total peace and quiet. A light, spacious office which acts as a meeting room for his whole team, furnished in a functional, all-purpose style. Daquin takes some files out of the wooden cupboards lining two of the walls, places them on his desk and leafs through them. A solitary task, needs to refresh his memory, spark ideas, decide which avenues to pursue. Try to be thorough and put two and two together. Cocaine and horses. Not much. The odd reference. The godfather of the Ochoa family in Medellín is a leading Colombian horse breeder. Flimsy... Racecourses as a money-laundering outlet. We know that... Doping racehorses with cocaine and amphetamine derivatives... A jockey... A lot of rumours, but nothing concrete comes to mind. And of course Romero's dossier on the Paola Jiménez murder. Daquin slips in the Agence France Presse despatch dated 21 August 1989 reporting on the seizure of fifty-three kilos of cocaine by the antinarcotics department. Probably the end of the story.

He removes some documents and files them in his drawer, and puts the rest back in the cupboard. Dossiers are the keystones of power. Sitting with his back to the window, his feet resting on the edge of the desk, he reflects for a while.

Facing him, the whole section of wall next to the door is taken up by a cork board. As an investigation progresses, it fills up with addresses, telephone numbers, messages, appointments, maps, sketches. Daquin gets up, sorts, throws away or files information that is out of date, clears a space for the coming days. Just beneath the cork board, a state-of-the-art *espresso* machine stands on top of a cupboard. Inside are stocks of coffee beans and mineral water, cups, glasses, a few bottles of spirits and a plastic tray for dirty cups. All meticulously tidy. Daquin makes himself a coffee. A few moments' quiet. Glances around the room. Familiar space, sense of well-being.

Shortly before 11 a.m., there's a stir in the DIs' office next door. On the dot of eleven, the men troop in noisily through the connecting door, bomber jackets, jeans and trainers, except for Lavorel, who always wears a blazer and dark trousers, or a suit. Romero, the seductive Latin Romeo, has worked with Daquin for nine years, Lavorel joined the team four years ago after several years with the Fraud Squad and a few sporadic joint operations. Podgy, with thinning fair hair and little metal-rimmed spectacles, he looks like a bureaucrat just on the point of fading away. But he and Romero have been accomplices for years. They were both born and bred on tough urban housing estates, one in Marseille, the other outside Paris, flirted with delinquency in their teens and are proud never to have forgotten it. Romero derives a real physical pleasure from his work as a detective inspector. And Lavorel, whose years at the Fraud Squad left him with a penchant for paperwork, sees it as a form of revenge: redressing, as far as he can, the iniquities of a justice system that spares the powerful and crushes the weak, and making the rich pay. The other two DIs, Amelot and Berry, are no more than kids, and this is their first assignment. With degrees in history and political science, unable to find a job, they took various civil service exams and ended up in the police, without really grasping the difference between their profession and that of a postman. Daquin calls them the 'new boys'.

Daquin makes coffee for everyone, then they all sit down. Daquin gives a brief report on his night at the station in the 16th arrondissement, and the meeting with the new chief.

'So we're going to take a little time check out a certain Senanche, at Meirens's place. He may be a small-time dealer who goes shopping in Holland. If that's the case, we'll soon know. You organise this amongst yourselves. Meanwhile, I'll talk to various departments to see whether they're working on any cases that might be of interest to us. We'll have the first review here, in one week.'

Thursday 7 September 1989

Daquin has a job navigating the suburbs and motorway slip roads to find the entrance to La Courneuve Riding Centre. A vast area occupied by stables, indoor and outdoor schools and a few trees, wedged between a motorway, tower blocks and a landscaped garden. An odd sense of greenery without nature. Daquin parks the unmarked car in front of a low timber building housing six loose boxes. In front of them, a man in blue overalls is busy with a bay horse. Daquin stands still and watches him. His gestures are precise, doubtless repeated hundreds of times. The horse cooperates, waggling his ears, anticipating and enjoying the man's every gesture. There is a physical bond between the two of them, they are like a couple, quietly trusting each other. Not something you often come across in this line of work. But it's by no means cut and dried. The man knows he's being watched, but appears unfazed. He finishes grooming the horse, without rushing, then leads him back into his stall. Daquin gets out of his car.

'Le Dem? I'm Superintendent Daquin.'

A young man of average height, square face, dark brown hair in a crew cut, light blue eyes, a slow gaze.

They go and sit in the bar, which is empty and sinister at this hour, in front of two cups of brown, lukewarm instant coffee.

Get him to open up so as not to have to grope around in the dark. Tell him what he knows already, and then come back to the question.

'With your superiors' consent, I've come to ask you if you would agree to transfer to my team, the Drugs Squad, for the duration of an investigation in racing circles. It probably won't be for long and you'll be in line for promotion.'

'Do I have the option of refusing?'

Daquin decides to smile.

'Straight off? You don't even want to know what it's about?'

'The thing is, I love my job here. I live with my horse, we patrol the park together. I protect the public, I help people when necessary, and my work is more about prevention than detection. I'm on very good terms with all the local kids, I give them a better image of the police. A public

27

service without violence you know, that's what suits me. The Drugs Squad is war. And I wouldn't know how to do that.'

A Martian in the housing projects. Just my luck to get landed with him.

'Would this transfer cause you problems shall we say of a domestic nature?'

'No, it's not that, I'm single.' Without showing any emotion.

Daquin stares at the cup he's toying with.

'I'm not going to tell you that we're non-violent. And I am aware that your concept of public service is different from ours. But if you agree to come on board, when this investigation's over, I'll have you transferred to Brittany, near your home town.' A glance out of the window. At the door of the loose box, the bay horse, his head reared, ears pointed, listens to the roar of the motorway. 'And I'll ensure you can take the horse you're working with at the moment with you.'

Blink. *Touché.*

'Could you do that?'

'Superintendent's word.'

Grin. 'Count me in.'

Monday 11 September 1989

'Gentlemen, I'd like to introduce our new colleague. He's a true horseman. He'll be our expert. He's from a highway patrol unit in La Courneuve…' glances at Lavorel and Romero. As expected, they immediately warm to him, '…and will be part of the team.' Then turns to Le Dem. 'Two things: nobody smokes in my office. And nobody comes in armed with their service revolver. You can leave it in the office next door or in the cupboard and collect it when you leave. Now, a coffee for everyone and let's get to work.'

Romero heads for the machine.

'You'd better like your coffee strong, without sugar, if you want to impress the chief.'

Le Dem smiles.

'I like it weak with lots of sugar. Tough.'

They all sit down and Romero opens with his report on the team's progress to date. Daquin, at his desk, takes notes.

'We easily found Meirens, identified Senanche, and found out about his customer network. He sells the stuff to kids who come in the mornings and ride the training horses, Olivier Deluc's mates most likely. We haven't seen him again, he's been keeping a low profile. The procedure: they arrive by car, park in front of the stables and hand the keys to Senanche. While they're riding, Senanche puts the stuff in the glove compartment and collects the cash. It's very neat. The cars are registered in the parents' names. We've got Jambet and Wilson, the fathers are high-flying executives, one at Parillaud and the other at Électricité de France, and Duran's father's a Venezuelan diplomat. We've also got the list of owners whose horses are trained by Meirens, it's in the file.

The second customer network is the local café, where Senanche goes several times a day and from where he makes all his phone calls. We've been tapping it for the last three days. I've made you a tape of the most interesting conversations, also in the file. You'll see that Senanche receives and sends a lot of messages which are obviously related to his dealing activities. The customers are men, only one woman's voice. The quantities being sold seem much bigger than those in the morning. The dealing seems to take place at racecourses. But Senanche hasn't once left Meirens' stables. As for his supplier…'

'Not so fast. Let's go back to the customers. Sounds as though they're mainly from racing circles?'

'Yes.'

'Amelot and Berry, dig further. Easy job. By checking the phone conversations against the horse racing schedules, you should be able to come up with a list of presumed customers.

Lavorel looks riled.

'Why are you going for the jockeys and grooms? That's not your style.'

'Don't act dumber than you are. We're going to keep the rich brats to ourselves, you never know, it might always come in useful. If we need the help of other departments to get to the big boys at the top, we'll need something to bargain with, and we'll chuck them the jockeys. I also want you to find out more about Jambet, Wilson, Duran and the owners, if you can. And, just in case, Amelot and Berry will also check whether there are any possible links with the Paola Jiménez case. Can we move on to the supplier? … Go on, Romero.'

'We don't have much. Senanche sells too much for an amateur just dabbling. He lives on site and never leaves the stables except to go to the café. At the café, we kept a close watch on him. There's no way he can be picking the stuff up there. That brings us back to the stables. That's where the drugs must be delivered.'

Daquin turns to Le Dem.

'Who can come into a stables regularly without arousing suspicion?'

'Apart from the stable-boys, the stable boss, the trainer, the jockeys in the morning, a few amateur riders, the owners, journalists from the racing press. During the day there are deliveries of horse feed or straw, and the guys who come to collect the manure. Then there are vets, farriers, and the drivers who transport the horses to the race-courses. I've probably left a few out.'

'That's a lot of people.' Daquin thinks for a moment, goes over to the coffee machine and switches it on. 'I'm going to see the chief to tell him we've made a start and that we're carrying on. It's much too early to start criminal proceedings. It makes no difference as far as you're concerned. Romero, Lavorel and Le Dem, find me Senanche's supplier. Who wants a coffee?'

Friday 15 September 1989

Concealed in the forest, Le Dem and Romero watch the farrier who has just pulled up in his white van. Le Dem follows him with binoculars, while Romero jots down notes on a little pad.

2 p.m. The van pulls up in front of the forge, in the right hand corner of the courtyard. The farrier gets out, accompanied by his assistant. Aged about thirty-five or so, dressed in a T-shirt and linen trousers, strong build, about six foot, very powerful shoulders and arms, and a gut. Beefy. Tanned complexion, black hair, moustache. His assistant is young, fourteen or fifteen years old, a kid. The stables manager comes out to greet the farrier. They chat, no contact, the manager goes off. The farrier opens the rear of the van, takes out his equipment – anvil, hammer, bag of tools. Puts on his leather apron. The van door remains open, the stock of horse shoes visible.

Nothing to report. The assistant goes off with some halters. Comes back with two horses, and ties them up inside the forge.

2.15 p.m. The two men are at work.

Le Dem, his eyes glued to the binoculars, describes the process step by step, Romero absently jots down a few notes. They carry on for a couple of hours uninterrupted. Le Dem remarks:

'Real pros, fast, efficient, good relationship with the horses. In my view, they can't be the suppliers.'

Romero chuckles.

4.15 p.m. Senanche walks towards the two men.

'Now concentrate.'

'He's carrying some cans of beer. Puts them on the anvil. And wanders off. No contact. The farrier and his assistant have a break, drink the beers. A groom comes over. Chats with the farrier. Goes away. Comes back with a horse. The farrier watches it walk, then trot, inspects its hooves. They talk. The groom leads the horse away. Le Dem turns to Romero: 'That's routine, the groom's asking the farrier's advice, that shows he's respected.'

4.30 p.m. The farrier picks up the beer cans, walks over to the van and opens the front door on the passenger side. Puts down the cans. Picks up a rag, a napkin? Mops his forehead and neck, and puts it back.

4.35 p.m. He goes back to work. His assistant also goes back to work.

4.45 p.m. Senanche comes back. He walks round the van. The front door is still open. He leans inside. I can't see what he's doing inside the vehicle. He straightens up and leaves. He's holding the empty beer cans, that's all. The farrier's still working.

'Right. The stuff's been delivered.' Le Dem is sceptical. 'Let's carry on, that's what we're here for. But I'm telling you, we've just witnessed the delivery being made. And it's not the first. The farrier's a real pro at this too.'

Le Dem continues to watch the horses coming and going, and Romero goes on making occasional notes, without much conviction.

5.20 p.m. An unidentified youth aged about twenty arrives at the forge.

Romero looks up from his notepad.

'Weird-looking kid. Pass me the binoculars. And take notes. The farrier carries on forging a shoe. They talk. Look, the farrier's on his feet. He's grabbing the kid by the shirt, he's lifting him off the ground with one hand. I don't believe it... he's grabbed his tongs... Shit!'

A howl in the stable yard.

'The farrier's just branded the kid's thigh with a red hot horse shoe. The kid's on the ground. The farrier gives him a kick to get him on his feet.'

'Come on Romero.'

'Don't panic. The kid crawls away, gets up, leaves. Are you still writing this down?' He glances at his watch. 'It's 5.24.' Picks up the binoculars again. 'Nobody's moving. This guy's scary.'

'Let's go and...'

'Wait a bit. The kid's limping off towards the road that goes to Chantilly. Now we can go. But not to the stables. Go and get the car, don't let anybody see you, and pick me up on the road.'

And Romero races into the trees to catch up with the kid. He walks on the opposite side of the road, waiting for Le Dem to arrive. When the car comes into view, he crosses over, goes up to the kid who's hobbling along sobbing and grabs his arm, opens the rear door of the car, shoves him inside and climbs in next to him.

'Drive, Le Dem, wherever you like, but drive. And wind your window up.'

'What do you want? Let me go, you've no right... Stop, I want to get out.' Interspersed with sobs.

Romero looks at him, and sniffs him. The kid, in shock, gives off the sour odour of needing a fix. Now's the time.

'Police. Tell me what you were talking to the farrier about.'

'That's my business. Let me go.'

Romero puts his hand on the boy's thigh which is streaked with a yellow and brown burn that's beginning to blister, shreds of burnt fabric clinging to his flesh. But seemingly not very deep. The farrier knew how to control his violence.

'I repeat. What were you talking to the farrier about?'

And he squeezes the thigh. The kid yells. Le Dem swerves. Romero glares at him in the mirror and goes back to the kid.

'I know you're a user, and I don't give a shit. It's the farrier I'm interested in.' He puts his hand back on the boy's thigh. 'Shall I do that again?'

'No!' he yelps.

'Come on,' hand still on the thigh, 'spit it out.'

'I wanted him to give me some stuff to deal.'

'And why did he refuse?'

'I owe him money.' The kid hiccups. 'I wanted to make some cash…'

'He burnt you when you told him you didn't have the dough.'

Almost inaudible. 'Yes'.

'You spent the money on smack, and now you're suffering cold turkey. You tell me who you wanted to sell to, and I'll give you your hit, right now, in the car.'

Slight pressure on the boy's thigh. Groan. The kid's in a sweat.

'There's a party here in Chantilly, tomorrow night, at Massillon the jockey's place, and you can always sell stuff at these parties.'

Romero takes out a square of paper from the breast pocket of his jacket.

'Slow down a bit,' he says to Le Dem, who's staring at the road.

The boy slips down between the seats and takes out his kit. He's trembling all over. Romero opens out the paper, holds the spoon. The kid prepares the stuff, heats it up, filters it, shoots it into his arm, inhales deeply, slowly, and lolls backwards, his eyes closed, onto the seat.

Romero taps Le Dem on the shoulder.

'Now head for the hospital, but not too fast. Give him time to digest. We have to get that burn taken care of.'

'I don't want to go to hospital.'

'What's your name?'

'I'm known as Blascos.'

Well you're going to hospital, Blascos. We've got to get that burn seen to, otherwise it can get infected. You won't have any trouble, I'll take care of it.'

When they reach A&E, Romero helps the boy out of the car. Holds him by the arm for a moment and whispers:

'I'll be at the party tomorrow night at ten. You'll be there too and you'll introduce me to your friends. And I'll make sure you've got something to sell. OK?'

He nods.

'I want to hear you say it.'

'All right.'

'If you let me down, you know what'll happen to you?'

'Yes.'

'Now get in there.'

Saturday 16 September 1989

Le Dem hadn't wanted to come. Romero didn't press him, so it's Lavorel who's waiting with him outside Massillon's villa. They're both wearing miniature tape recorders concealed under their belts. Romero's wearing a short-sleeved, floral summer shirt, and Lavorel a light blazer over a white shirt. A few cars crawl through the open iron gates and park in the garden. Two Porsches, a yellow Ferrari. And a lot of ordinary cars. Lavorel slips into the garden and makes a note of the registration numbers.

Blascos arrives on foot, at around 10 p.m., clean and neatly dressed. He's still limping but he looks in much better shape. Romero gives him an envelope, which he holds in a Kleenex.

'There's some coke in there. Top quality. You can sell it for a good price or cut it a little. Now get to work.'

Romero whistles. Lavorel comes over to join them and the three men enter the vast nineteenth-century villa surrounded by gardens. There's a flight of steps covered by an awning leading up to the front door which stands wide open. Entrance hall, to the left a drawing room which is empty for the time being, to the right the dining room where forty or so young men and women are gathered, chatting over drinks against a background of deafening house music. At the back of the room is a lavish buffet. Blascos greets everyone. Lavorel has his eye on six men, short, wiry, energetic, very well turned out, bespoke suits, luxury shoes, gold bracelets and chains. The jockeys, without a doubt. Very different from the others, young men of means, like Deluc, or others with more modest incomes, like Blascos. A dozen utterly beautiful girls. Romero feels a little tremor of excitement. And then a few others, nondescript.

Blascos steers Romero by the arm. Lavorel follows.

'Massillon, I've brought you two good friends of mine…'

'Pleased to meet you. We'll squeeze them in.'

He shakes their hands. Then everyone goes back to the bowl of punch on the buffet. Things are already hotting up, although it's still early. Lavorel wanders among the clusters of people, his ears pricked. The talk is of races, trainers, bonuses, bets or sex. Lavorel isn't able to follow it all, and fears he's wasting his time in this place which isn't his scene. From time to time he glances at Romero. He watches him down one drink, then another, and starts to worry. People are attacking the food. Romero, glass in hand, is sitting on a radiator, in front of a window, beside a bottle blonde with pneumatic breasts and lips. She slips her arm around his neck. When she moves off towards the buffet, Lavorel goes up to Romero and whispers:

'Be careful, please.'

'I can't resist blondes.'

'Your first wife was a redhead, the second very dark, and this one's not even a real blonde.'

'There aren't any real blondes left, didn't you know? What with pollution, nuclear power…'

The girl's on her way back, carrying two plates. With a flash of inspiration, Lavorel leans over to Romero, grabs his tape recorder and slips it into his own pocket. Damage limitation.

Just then, it's already approaching midnight, a new guest arrives, smiling. He's immediately the centre of attention. He kisses a few girls and then takes a pretty lacquered box from his trouser pocket. Hearty applause, and the box begins to circulate. Lavorel on the alert. As the box goes round, they all take a pinch of white powder and snort it from the base of their thumb. Things are hotting up even more. Lavorel helps himself and discreetly sprinkles the powder on the floor. Meanwhile Romero, with a big grin, stares at him and has a quick snort. By now, disaster is imminent.

Two girls jump up onto the buffet and start dancing among the dishes, high as kites, wild… They dance well. Everybody claps, the little box is still going around, faster and faster. The blonde has her hand between Romero's legs, and her fingers are moving up and down to the rhythm of the music. When she gets the expected response, she suddenly leaps onto the table and begins a striptease between the two dancers, who become even more frenzied. The guests shriek with delight. She's down to her bra… Romero rips off his shirt – Lavorel nervously pats the tape recorder in his pocket to reassure himself it's there – beats his chest, lets out a Tarzan cry and clambers onto the table.

Blascos, standing next to Lavorel, his eyes wide, says in an undertone 'Some cop, huh?'

Tarzan-Romero sweeps the blonde, now bra-less, into his arms, jumps down but misses his footing, crashes heavily onto the table, breaks a few plates, one or two bottles and gives himself a deep gash in his left buttock. Blood spurts everywhere.

Lavorel grabs Blascos by the shoulder.

'Help me.'

They each grab Romero under one armpit, drag him out to the car parked outside and lay him on his stomach on the back seat. Head for the hospital. Blascos laughs uncontrollably.

'I haven't laughed like this for years. Come back guys. Whenever you like.'

Once Romero's been taken care of and sent home in a taxi, Blascos and Lavorel return to the party, which is still in full swing.

'Tell me, who's the guy who's so generous with the coke?'

'A friend of Massillon's. He's called Nicolas Berger, and that's all I know about him.'

Blascos waits until the end of the party to sell to the guests who want to stock up before going home. And Lavorel waits for Nicolas Berger to find out a little more about him.

Sunday 17 September 1989

Nicolas Berger leaves Massillon's villa at around 7 a.m., seemingly on good form, with Lavorel trailing behind, rather the worse for wear. After about thirty kilometres, they approach a large farm, still in the Ile de France. It is an imposing stone-built, partially fortified construction. Some large trucks are parked in a field in front of the farm, their ramps lowered, and horses everywhere, tethered to the trucks, being led or ridden by young people wearing jeans, and competitors in white jodhpurs, black boots and tailored red or black jackets.

Nicolas cruises slowly around the thronging field, and Lavorel concentrates on tailing him without knocking anyone over. Then Nicolas pulls up beside a large green and white truck and Lavorel drives past and parks his car twenty metres further on, under a tree. Nicolas goes over to the truck driver. After changing his clothes, he leads a horse out of the truck, mounts it, rides around the farmhouse and disappears.

Lavorel picks his way across the field on foot. People are rushing busily all over the place, calling out; they all seem to know each other. The atmosphere is that of a cheerful gathering of old friends and there's a powerful smell of horses. Lavorel feels very out of place in his blue blazer, by now slightly grubby, and his smart shoes.

Behind the farm, a vast grassy field surrounded by white fences, with brightly coloured jumps and flower beds everywhere. Along one side of the field a bank has been made into a stand for the spectators and across the far end drinks are being served in a white canvas marquee. At first glance, it's tempting. Lavorel sits down and knocks back three disgusting cups of coffee. Behind him, a group of riders are talking about horses and business, thumping each other and joking, and drinking red wine. Lavorel consults his watch: 9 a.m. They're certainly not wasting any time. The first competitors arrive. Lavorel glances at them. His first impression is that horses and riders are all doing exactly the same thing, and that the bars fall at random. Then twice, a horse and its rider in fluid harmony jump with graceful ease, and the bars remain in place. But it soon becomes tedious to watch.

Snatches of conversation, behind Lavorel: 'Who's this gorgeous girl with you? Will you introduce me?' 'Come on, you're kidding, don't you recognise her? You slept with her last night...' 'I was pissed...' 'And you aren't now?' 'Of course I am! I'm riding in five minutes.' He raises his glass. 'To our horses and all who mount them!'

What the fuck am I doing here, in the middle of the field, surrounded by idiots? Lavorel stands up and wanders about aimlessly. He spots Nicolas Berger in a field on his own, cantering his horse, looking very focused on the task. Reserves of strength, this guy, after partying all night... Cop's hunch, nothing doing here. No whiff of coke. Wine for sure, but not coke. Keep an eye on the truck, rather. Lavorel goes back to the car park, settles inside his car in the shade, it's getting hotter and hotter, and falls asleep.

A resounding explosion. Lavorel wakes with a jump, and gazes horrified at Berger's blazing car, a single orange flame leaps several metres into the air. The car park's full of stampeding horses and screaming people. Just beside the inferno, hanging on to the green and white truck, in a sort of tragic bubble of motionless silence, a horse, its foreleg blown off, its head lowered, blood spurting everywhere. The animal crumples in slow motion. The emergency services arrive with an ambulance. Lavorel, in a state of shock, extricates himself from his car, walks over and watches two human silhouettes on fire.

Monday 18 September 1989

Nearly every morning, Daquin walks from Avenue Jean-Moulin to Quai des Orfèvres via Montparnasse and Boulevard Saint Michel, which takes him just under an hour at a brisk pace. But today, the weather's cool and fine, and Daquin is in no hurry. A detour to buy a kilo of Brazilian coffee from a coffee roasting shop in Rue Mouffetard, to try it out. Then he carries on via Place Maubert and a maze of back streets down to the Seine. He pauses and leans on the parapet. He always experiences the same thrill at the sight of the immense sky right in the heart of the city, today a very pale blue, and around him, every shade of grey. The Seine, grey-green, the stones of the embankment and the arched bridges yellowy-grey, and the grey-white bulk of Notre Dame standing out against the dark mass of a clump of trees. Daquin inhales deeply two or three times and goes up to his office, where his detectives are waiting for him.

Lavorel mechanically wipes his glasses and blinks. Romero is sitting awkwardly, one buttock resting on the edge of a chair. The other three are standing, trying to look inconspicuous. Daquin scrutinises them for a moment, sits down in his chair and prepares himself for the worst.

'Go on, I'm listening.'

Romero starts.

'We've identified the supplier. He's a certain Dimitri Rouma, farrier, a gypsy, residing in Vallangoujard in the Val-d'Oise.'

Surprised. 'Bravo.'

'Lavorel and I went to a cocaine-fuelled party in Chantilly on Saturday night, at the house of a jockey called Massillon. Several of Senanche's customers there, others unknown. We took a note of all the vehicle registration numbers, and there was a guy called Nicolas Berger dishing out coke to everyone.'

'Excellent. What next?'

Lavorel picked up:

'I tailed Berger from the party to a horse show he was competing in. And there, he was murdered. His car was booby-trapped and blew up twenty metres away from me. He was killed instantly, along with one of his friends who was sitting in the car next to him. Guy named Moulin. And I didn't see a thing, I was asleep.'

'Ah, now we're getting somewhere.' False innocence: 'Were you alone? Where were you, Romero?'

With as much dignity as he could muster. 'At the party, I accidentally sat on a plate and injured myself. I went home.'

'Don't feel bad Romero, it happens to all of us, more often than you'd imagine. Berry, your turn to make the coffee. We're going to try this one.' Hands him the packet of Brazilian coffee. ' Do a good job, it's an honour and a step up. And don't forget, a weak one for Le Dem. And then, to work.' Daquin smiles. 'Now we're finally getting to the heart of the matter.'

Audible sighs of relief.

After the break, everyone seated, pens and notebooks poised. Lavorel describes the explosion: two bodies in the car, the arrival of the gendarmes who took charge of the investigation, identification of the victims, clues, forensic reports, eye-witness accounts.

'I introduced myself to the captain and explained what I was doing there. He's expecting to hear from you.'

'Did you mention the party at Massillon's to him?'

'No, I decided to leave that to you.'

'You did the right thing.'

Daquin thinks for a moment, doodling on a blank sheet of paper.

'In two hours I want written accurate, detailed reports on the identification of Rouma, the party at Massillon's, and Senanche's customer network. Meanwhile, Le Dem, you come with me, I want to find Massillon before the gendarmes do. On my return, I'll edit your reports before passing them on to the chief, then I'll contact the gendarmerie and the public prosecutor. My line of action will be to try and cooperate with the gendarmes over Nicolas Berger's murder, and to give them the list of Senanche's customers in exchange. They'll be happy and it'll free us up to chase bigger fish. We'll have to be discreet about it, because the one thing the police department doesn't forgive is cooperating with the gendarmes.'

'Amelot and Berry will carry on with their job and finish it, cross-referencing all the lists, the new registration numbers, and the tapped phone conversations. Lavorel and Le Dem, you take Rouma. You can start by going to see the gendarmes in Vallangoujard. I'll let them know you're coming. I'm certain they already have files on him. A gypsy farrier in a godforsaken village in the Val-d'Oise is hardly inconspicuous. And Romero and I will handle Nicolas Berger's murder.'

Massillon's villa looks empty, door closed, windows open, but there's a Porsche parked in the garden and the gates are still open. Daquin climbs up to a wrought-iron balcony and clambers over it without any apparent effort. After a second's hesitation, Le Dem follows.

The ground floor is deserted, and is an indescribable mess. Daquin freezes, looks and listens for a moment. Nothing appears to have been touched since the end of the party, yesterday morning. There's disaster in the air. Daquin motions to Le Dem and rushes over to the staircase that leads up to the first floor. Doors open onto the landing. Only one room is occupied. Pale blue fabric on the walls, a pink and white en-suite bathroom, virtually no furniture, a big bed, a jumble of shot-silk sheets, and, lying across the bed, asleep on his stomach, a naked young man with a finely chiselled, slender muscular body. Daquin lingers for a moment, ill at ease. On the long-pile rug, a very young girl is asleep; she's naked too. The boy's hand is resting on her buttocks, and her hands are tied to the foot of the bed with a gold chain, secured with an elegant padlock inscribed with entwined initials which she probably wears as a necklace in other circumstances. A few red marks, dotted with dark spots on her lower back, buttocks and thighs. And beside the bed, next to an empty champagne magnum, a jockey's riding crop, a vicious weapon in itself. Judging by the marks, Massillon had used it with less enthusiasm than at the finishing line of the Prix de l'Arc de Triomphe, remaining within the bounds of decorum.

Daquin stifles an urge to laugh, you have to respect people's vocations, grabs the man under the armpits, hikes him up, carries him to the bathroom and dunks his head under the shower. The girl has woken up and is curled at the foot of the bed, her eyes dilated, trying to cover herself with a sheet, which isn't easy without hands. Daquin returns, dragging the soaking man at arm's length, and plonks him on the bed.

'Police. I want to ask you a few questions. Are you awake enough to understand what I'm saying?'

He nods, his teeth chattering. A damp patch slowly spreads on the silk around him.

'Your friend Berger was murdered when he left here yesterday morning. His car was booby-trapped, and it exploded. Killed outright.'

Massillon, stunned, gapes at him open-mouthed. Daquin turns to the girl.

'Is your master always as lively as this, miss?' She gives a little squeak. 'Le Dem, go downstairs and get me two glasses of something, the strongest drink you can find, I think it's the only way to wake them up.'

It takes a little while until it's finally possible to get some sense out of them. While Daquin ferrets around upstairs, Le Dem calmly explains the situation to Massillon, who's beginning to dry off.

'If you're nicked for cocaine trafficking and you cop more than three months inside, which is highly likely, you'll lose your jockey's licence, and there'll be no more parties, girls or the Porsche. Back to being a stable lad. It'll be tough.'

Everyone has forgotten the girl, still chained to the foot of the bed. Daquin comes back from his little stroll, having found nothing of interest.

'What do you want?' asks Massillon.

'The name of your dealer.'

'Senanche. He works at Meirens.'

A pushover. Le Dem had told him, jockeys are used to obeying. The owners, the trainers, why not the cops too?

'And Berger's?'

'Nicolas also bought from him, fairly often.'

'Yesterday, Berger came here with a large amount of cocaine.' Massillon looks panic-stricken. How do they know? Tries to recall who was at the party but his mind's a blank. 'Did Senanche supply it?'

'No, I don't think so. Actually, yesterday was a treat. Nicolas was celebrating an unexpected windfall. A company gave him a huge commission for getting them an advertising account. He brought coke the way anyone else would bring a bottle of champagne, you know?'

'Did he often do that?'

'No, it was the second time.'

'And where did he get his "treats" from?'

'I think it was probably at work. A big insurance company, Pama, where he was head of advertising.' Massillon looks up at Daquin. 'Will I be OK?'

'It's not up to me. I'm going to hand you over to the gendarmes, but I'm giving you a twenty-four hour headstart. You can finish off your girlfriend at your leisure, if you have the heart for it, and then it's up to you to find some way of protecting yourself because you're in for a rough ride.'

Tuesday 19 September 1989

Destination La Défense. Romero is at the wheel, as always. Daquin doesn't like driving. Leaning against the door, he maintains an aggressive silence.

'What's up, chief? Things not looking good?'

'I don't know. We'll see.' After a lengthy silence: 'I hate La Défense. It depresses me.' They turn onto the ring road. 'Look. The tower blocks have their backs to us in an untidy sprawl. The whole district is designed to look at Paris, and be seen by Paris. It's a theatre, not a city, and we have to enter from the wings.'

'I'm here, I won't abandon you in the concrete jungle.'

Romero misses the car park entrance and is off on another lap of the ring road.

'Great, take me on a tour of the area. We're in no hurry. It won't do any harm to keep Madame Renouard waiting.'

Sitting at her desk, her chair facing the bay window, Annick gazes at the blue sky, the glittering Arche, Paris in the distance. She chain smokes. What the hell does this cop want? Angst. A familiar chill, she finds it hard to breathe or move. She can hear them in the woods, she's fallen into the ditch, sprained ankle. They arrive, kick her to her feet, shove and drag her to the police van. She's shivering with fear. The police station stinks. A poky office, two chairs, a strapping inspector in his forties. Threats. Tied to the radiator, sit, stand, sit, stand. Slaps. The taste of blood in her mouth. Stripped, searched. Promises. How long does it go on… She gave the names of all her friends. He strokes her hair, offers a coffee, a handkerchief. And the inspector wrote everything down, smiling at her. Then, he came over to her. I'm going to fuck you then let you go. You were never here, you never told me anything. If you refuse, statement, court case and I'll tell everyone that you grassed on your friends. Understood? Say you want me to fuck you… She said it. The next day, she left Rennes for good. Twenty years later, all it takes is for a cop to come near her to rekindle the memory of her humiliation, and, worst of all, she can still hear the sound of her own voice… Hands trembling, a quick line, using the steel surface of the desk.

The secretary shows Daquin and Romero into the office. They take in the black and white décor, black carpet, white walls. More black above the bare matt grey steel desk, the Soulages triptych lit by a row of ceiling spotlights to show it off to advantage. Fascinated, Romero walks over to the vast bay window. The feeling of being suspended in a cradle at the fulcrum of La Défense. Daquin slowly walks around the Soulages to catch the play of light. Intense pleasure.

Annick, smiling, sophisticated, leads them over to the sofa in the lounge area. Elegant, beige suit over a green blouse, her thick hair in an impeccable chignon, softened by a few wisps framing her face, a hint of make-up, no jewellery, just a discreet gold Omega watch bracelet. A carefully contrived image, but static, it lacks a sense of mood. This woman has a real talent for setting the stage. Above all, be careful. And Daquin imperceptibly plays up his image of oafish, clumsy cop in jeans and trainers.

Annick stands facing them, leaning against the desk, mesmerised by Daquin. Similar build to the one who raped her, a fairly ordinary man, tall, square set, forty-something, but more muscular and no beer gut. The secretary brings in coffee. Daquin picks up his cup. Not the same hands either. The other guy's were thick and stubby, these are long, broad and bony. She must stop this stupid memory game, it's dangerous.

'What can I do for you, Superintendent?'

Daquin looks at her. That beautiful low, slightly husky voice…

'Did you know Nicolas Berger well?'

'Very well, yes, he was a childhood friend, and we work closely together.'

'He's dead.'

'What?' She straightens up. 'Is this a joke?'

'Not at all. He was murdered on Sunday morning.'

'Murdered…'

Daquin tells her about the car explosion, with precision and detachment.

Annick feels dazed. A deafening buzzing in her ears, again that cold clammy feeling of suffocation. She walks over to a cupboard, pours herself a double whisky, which she downs in one go, and comes back and leans against her desk, once again perfectly in control. Daquin continues in a neutral voice:

'Can you tell me what his work at Pama consisted of?'

'He was head of Pama communications department's image division, i.e. he selected the consultancies we work with and supervised production.' The past tense, so quickly, so naturally….

'You were his line manager?'

'Yes. He was a wonderful colleague, very knowledgeable about all the new technologies, with lots of ideas for applying them to corporate communications.'

Grotesque talking about Nicolas in this way. She goes over to the video and switches it on.

'His most recent project. It's still at draft stage.'

An airborne black horse jumps, turns, dances. The image continually morphs from the freely moving horse to the same animal with a rider on its back. Images, no sound. Slow motion, suspended movements stretching to infinity, fluid harmony, horse and rider as one, their movement pure ballet in space. Still on her feet, Annick watches.

'This is the visual for our new advertising campaign. As he loved horses and was a good rider, he was particularly committed to this video promo. More than usual.'

'Do you know if he had any enemies at work? Any ongoing conflicts?'

'Not that I'm aware of. He was really a likeable person, immensely charming.' A pause. 'And not ambitious. I've never seen him fall out with anyone.'

'Money worries?'

With a smile: 'He was on a good salary here.' Thinks for a moment. 'No, I think if he'd had any, he'd have talked to me about them.'

'Did you know he had a coke habit?'

A silence. Annick turns her back to them and walks over to the bay window, comes back and leans against the desk again.

'It's fairly common in advertising circles. Let's say I'm not entirely surprised.'

'Had be been having trouble with his dealers recently?'

Curtly: 'I know nothing about his dealers, Superintendent.'

'I find that hard to believe. Because on at least one occasion, you contacted his regular dealer, on his recommendation.' Turning to Romero: 'We have the tape.'

Romero is torn between admiration and irritation. How could I have missed that, I'm the one who made the tape…

Annick is caught completely off-guard. She quickly regains her composure. She leans forward, winning smile, the body of a Sèvres china doll and the voice of a blues singer:

'What have you come here for, Superintendent? To arrest me for using cocaine?'

'Not exactly Madame Renouard. Do you know if Nicolas Berger himself was dealing coke?'

'No.' Emphatic. 'I'm certain he wasn't.'

She stops. Over-reaction. Careful. Danger.

'The day before he died, he bought and re-sold around fifty grams of cocaine, which undeniably makes him a dealer. According to a witness, he allegedly acquired it here.'

'Superintendent, I know nothing about it and I don't want to answer any more questions on the subject.'

'As you wish.' Smile. 'You're not under any obligation. Could we have a look around his office? In your presence, of course.'

'Follow me.'

'Romero, in the meantime would you go and have a chat with Nicolas Berger's colleagues and ask a few questions? Discreetly, of course, as usual.'

In Nicolas Berger's office, much smaller and more ordinary that Annick's, a large framed photo: two horses led by a tanned, smiling young woman with fair hair.

'I think those are his horses,' says Annick. 'He rode a lot. The woman is Amélie Gramont, a friend of his. She's a breeder.'

'His mistress?'

'I have no idea. Nicolas had a lot of affairs, but no long-term relationship, as far as I know.'

On the desk, the video project. Daquin flicks through the folder. A lot of names and addresses. Notes, appointments. He opens the drawers. A diary.

'May I take the folder and the diary away? I'll have them brought back tomorrow. And I'll also take the photo.'

'As you wish.'

Lift, car park, gloomily lit. Guaranteed claustrophobia. Then back onto the ring road, hemmed in by tower blocks, and busy now, it's the lunch hour. Daquin relaxes once the car crosses the Seine.

'Are you mad at me for having identified the female voice on your tape?'

'A bit. You always make me feel I'm not a proper grown-up, it's exasperating.'

'What did you find out from Berger's colleagues?'

'Not a lot. The staff more or less confirmed what Annick Renouard told us. A charming guy, very professional, a bit of a dilettante. Everyone knows he did coke, and nobody seems to give a shit. It's a different story with the beautiful blonde. She's not really liked, too ambitious, but she's respected for her competence and capacity for work. She's rumoured to have been having an affair with Jubelin, the new CEO, for years. No other lovers on the scene. Apparently she's a woman who sleeps her way to the top. No conflict with Berger, he was her protégé. And she managed to pass on nearly all her weaknesses to him.'

'And what do you think of this woman?'

'None too emotional. It didn't take her long to get a grip on herself after the initial shock. Gorgeous looking. And she is a real blonde.'

Anxious look. 'Let me know if you're planning to fall in love with her.'

'No chance. She scares me.'

Daquin surprised. Flashback: in the main street of Perugia, suffocating heat, that cultured, voluble Italian friend, slightly grating accent: '*We should be afraid, Theo, women are so much stronger than we are*'. With a touch of humour and a great deal of sincerity. Daquin turns to Romero:

'But she's vulnerable too. She drinks, she snorts, never sits down, can't keep still. And she's trying to protect herself in every way she can, the way she dresses, the way her office is done up… If I can find her Achilles heel, I'll have her where I want her.'

Romero, downright sceptical, chooses to say nothing until they're back at Quai des Orfèvres.

Annick sits absolutely still, breathing slowly. I've got to get myself together. Nicolas… no point thinking about it now… Daquin's gaze, hazel eyes, ironic, dominant. *I find that hard to believe.* Shudder. Strongly tempted to have a little line. Not before I've pulled myself together, I'm not a junkie. I'm going to have to tell Jubelin the news.

Jubelin's secretary tells her that he's been shut in his office all day, having cancelled all his appointments and given orders that nobody is to disturb him.

'Is he shut up in there with some gorgeous female?'

'No, not this time. He's alone and he's working.'

'Well I'll take it upon myself to go in. It's an emergency.'

'It's up to you.'

When Annick pushes open the door, Jubelin looks up from his computer.

'I said I didn't want to be disturbed.'

'I know. Nicolas has been murdered.'

Jubelin stares at her, stunned.

'Here?'

'No, yesterday morning, at a horse show.'

She tells him about the visit from the two police officers, leaving out the references to cocaine.

'Who are these cops, which department are they from?'

'One is Superintendent Daquin. I don't know where they're from. I didn't ask them.'

'Do they think the murder has anything to do with Pama?'

'I got the impression that they think that's only one possibility.' A silence. 'They took away some of Nicolas's files.'

Jubelin reacts.

'And you let them? Without a warrant? Get those files back right away, Annick. Believe me, the less the police stick their noses in our business, the better. Do I have to spell it out?'

He gets up, plants a kiss on her forehead, and steers her towards the door.

Back in her vast office. Cigarette, inhales deeply. Persistent feeling of uneasiness. The memories surfacing, of course. But not only. Beware of the cops, Jubelin said. He's not wrong. Slush funds, backhanders, cash transfers and regular killings on the stock exchange… I know about all that. But that's not what it's about. Nicolas has been murdered, and Jubelin didn't even seem surprised, as if he were expecting it in a way. Flashback to the party on 14th July at Perrot's, Nicolas deep in conversation with Jubelin. They'd both stopped talking when she joined them: *We'll talk about it in my office.* What does he know that I don't?

A line… Not yet. Annick calls home. The familiar voice on the other end.

'Michel, is that you?'

Michel, who does everything, the shopping, the cleaning, who looks after her when she's ill and is her constant support. Michel, her entire family.

'I need you, right away. Can we have lunch together?'

Annick parks her little red Austin Mini outside her apartment building, Boulevard Maillot, in Neuilly, on the edge of the Bois de Boulogne. Michel is waiting for her. Tall, slim, fair-haired, around thirty-five, beige linen trousers and leather jacket. He leans over and opens her door, helps her out.

'I hadn't planned anything for lunch at home, so I booked a table at Sébillon's.'

'That's perfect by me.' She takes his arm. 'Let's go.'

A few paces in silence, in the opulent deserted streets of this little corner of Neuilly. Then:

'Nicolas was murdered on Sunday morning.'

Michel stares at her speechless. He's shocked.

At Sébillon's, a quiet table at the back. The head waiter comes over, and Michel orders a whisky for Madame.

'Which does Madame prefer, Chivas, Glenlivet…?'

Annick gives her most charming smile and, in a slightly slurred voice, says:

'Anything, as long as it's more than forty per cent proof.'

The head waiter looks disapproving. Michel continues:

'And I'll have a glass of champagne. Then we'll both have the leg of lamb, pink.'

The head waiter moves away. 'Now, what's going on?'

Annick tells him about the visit from the two cops, the booby-trapped car at the horse show yesterday. Her voice is slightly off key, as if she is surprised to hear what she is saying.

'Nicolas, a childhood friend. And up there,' she gestures in the direction of La Défense, 'entertaining, considerate… I scare myself sometimes. I should be in tears. Well I'm not. After the initial shock, nothing. I'm an emotional cripple.'

'No, it's not even that. You're no good at lying to yourself, that's all. You've always found Nicolas sweet but of no interest.'

'The cops think he was involved in cocaine trafficking.'

Michel's ears suddenly prick up.

'Was he?'

'How should I know? In any case, he supplied me. And the cops already know.'

'Shit.' A silence. 'Have you talked to Jubelin about it?'

'No. I don't like talking cocaine with Jubelin. My position's complicated enough as it is. He's the CEO, remember. And besides, this time, I can tell he's worried.' She hesitates, and then: 'I'm going to have to find a new dealer. At the moment, I can't cope without it. And with the cops on our backs, Jubelin cornered...'

'I'll deal with it, don't worry.'

She checks her watch.

'No time for dessert, I've got to get back. Can I leave you to pay?'

'No problem, I've got your cheque book.'

'I'll be back late this evening, and I'll be dining alone.'

'That's convenient. I've got a meeting with a publisher, a new comic strip album. It might go on into the evening. I'll leave you a cold dinner in the kitchen.'

I'm allowed a quick line now, and Annick works frenziedly all afternoon. Got to go through the proposal from the ad agency for the autumn promotional campaign which is based entirely on a sports metaphor. The Pama team, united, fights to win, to ensure its policyholders win. At Pama, as in sport, ready, steady, go and let the best player win, a democratic, egalitarian company. Flashback: Michel smiles at her, *you're no good at lying to yourself...* Even... But people keep disturbing her, no time to stop for breath. Phone calls. A departmental head wants to know... You have an appointment... A journalist on the line...

Annick isn't able to get back to work on her campaign until 7 p.m.

When she looks up, much later, it's dark outside. On her floor, there's total silence. Everyone must have left without her noticing. She walks over to the window. A luminous evening, the Arche illuminated and the lights of Paris in the distance, beyond the office blocks. Tired, an emptiness in her heart. She smokes a cigarette, has a whisky, thinks of Jubelin... Unease.

Think carefully about my relationship with him. We're a team, but there's never been equality. Those are the rules of the game, and I accepted them. It was that, or don't play at all. But until now, we've had no secrets from each other. And now, a rift. I'm losing ground, I don't know why. No way am I going to accept that. And if the investigation concentrates on coke trafficking, I'm in big trouble. Another whisky. I need some security. For example, find out what he was working on this afternoon, that was so top secret. Maybe something connected to Nicolas's murder?

There's a communicating door between the two offices, which they rarely use, and never in the other's absence. Annick rummages in her desk drawer and finds the key lying among the paper clips and pens. She sits at Jubelin's desk and turns on the computer. It says hello then asks for the password. Surprise. She hesitates. Unable to hack into the computer. But finding out Jubelin's password is an exciting challenge. Do I know him as well as I thought? What kind of password would he choose? A name? She tries her own, Jubelin's, that of his wife, his children. Rejected. The names of the companies he ran before the merger with Pama. Rejected. Outside the family and his business, who was important to him? The names of his horses. Rejected. She tries another ten words or so, unsuccessfully. This is getting really interesting. Tries to remember what might have been significant in the years she's known him. One outstanding memory, their trip to Granada. She tries Granada. Rejected. The night at the Parador hotel, the open windows overlooking the fragrant gardens of the Alhambra. Jubelin murmuring '*we're going to devour the whole world, you and I.*' Champagne. Drinking out of each other's glasses, laughing, in front of the window. Alhambra. The computer says welcome… Stop. Difficult to move on. The memory of their bodies perfectly attuned to each other. Well nearly… For a long time now, fucking Jubelin has been a tacit renewal of their alliance, without pleasure. I remember more clearly how he negotiated his way into Pama than the shape of his buttocks. An effort to visualise the said buttocks. Nothing doing. Men are hopeless romantics. Never mind the Alhambra. I'm going in.

Jubelin had been following share prices on the Frankfurt stock exchange. He had selected the company A. A. Bayern and had been monitoring the share prices in real time. Annick has never heard of this company. The shares had opened at a hundred and twenty marks, remained steady for a few hours and then fell heavily. At 4 p.m., they were at fifty marks. Then, Jubelin began instructing a Luxembourg-based financial consultancy that Annick had never heard of to purchase large numbers of shares. No way of knowing what he was up to exactly. But it didn't seem to be vital to Pama, nor to be connected to Nicolas's murder. Probably a tip-off Jubelin had acted on to make a fast buck. He's always loved money. Money and women. Any women, anywhere, as long as they're easy and it's quick. A half smile. You have to forgive him his little weaknesses. Reassuring feeling of superiority. For the time being, I haven't found any real reason to worry.

Just in case, she copies all the data onto a floppy disk, puts it in her pocket and switches off the computer, mentally muttering a few words of apology for the Alhambra. All she has to do now is lock the communicating door, put away the key and go home. Michel won't be there this evening.

Wednesday 20 September 1989

The sun is already up, but to the west, the sky is still tinged pink and pale blue. Le Dem is driving, calmly and skilfully. Daquin, beside him, is daydreaming. I don't like driving, I hate the countryside. Not a good start to the day.

'I paid a visit to Madame Moulin after the gendarmes had informed her of her husband's death.' Daquin suddenly perks up. 'She's landed with a riding stables to run, and has never worked in the place. She's a nurse at Saint Germain hospital. Naturally she feels out of her depth. We toured the stables together and discussed the options for selling some of the horses.'

'Interesting.'

Le Dem glances at Daquin, who remains impassive. He continues:

'Berger's two horses are in livery at Moulin's. He often used to bring them to the shows and meet Berger directly at the showground, like last Sunday.'

'What was Moulin doing in Berger's car?'

'Madame Moulin has no idea. It was around twelve noon. Perhaps they were going to have lunch together and then return to the show in the afternoon?'

'Did you talk to her about Madame Gramont?'

'Yes. Berger bought her horses and was a friend of hers. That's all she knows.'

Daquin glances distractedly at the countryside flying past.

'Romero told me how he got Blascos to squeal. Did that shock you?'

Le Dem thinks for a while, intense and earnest.

'I don't know. I think ultimately the kid was closer to Romero than he was to me.' He pauses. 'To be honest, I know this'll sound odd to you, what shocked me the most was that an extremely professional craftsman like the farrier is selling drugs. I find that really hard to swallow.'

Daquin gazes at him in silence. He's from another planet, but he's not stupid.

Madame Gramont's stud farm is in the middle of nowhere, at the end of a dirt track, in a dip deep in the Orne hills. Le Dem drove around in circles for a while before he found it. Three nondescript farm buildings, erected at random around a courtyard full of potholes, a huge truck parked in one corner, meadows marked off with grubby white ribbons, horses in the paddocks and, to one side, set slightly back, a vast corrugated iron hangar. Daquin pulls a face. It's ugly, and it looks deserted. They sound the horn and get out of the car. A man comes out of the stables, and a woman from the house. The woman in the photo. Late thirties, not tall, muscular, vivacious. Short, curly almost flaxen hair, very pretty grey-green eyes and a warm smile. They shake hands. Le Dem wanders off to talk to the groom. Daquin reserves Madame Gramont for himself.

'Call me Amélie.' Faintly mocking: 'Shall I show you around the place?'

Daquin, resigned: 'Fine, let's go.'

First of all she leads him towards the hangar. Once through the door, in the half-dark, books, magazines, newspapers, thousands of them, piled ceiling-high on the shelves. He doesn't attempt to disguise his surprise. She's delighted.

'It's my job, you know. I comb France buying odd magazines and newspapers. And I sell them to libraries all over the world seeking to complete their collections. I love horses, but I couldn't make a living out of them.'

Daquin starts seeing her differently. In such a godforsaken place. Who would have thought it?

'Shall I show you Nicolas's horses?'

'Lead the way.'

They walk over to one of the paddocks. She lifts the barrier and whistles. Two palomino horses canter towards them, heads high, and stop beside her, sniffing her pocket. She gives them sugar lumps.

'Are they race horses?'

'No, not at all. You really don't know anything about horses.'

She speaks to them softly, almost crooning, scratches their noses, stroking their breasts. They nudge her sides, playful flirtation. Amélie cocks her head to one side and looks at Daquin with a smile. One of the horses, his golden coat tinged with auburn, nuzzles Amélie's neck. His velvety lips are grey with white specks. He nibbles her blonde curls, breathes gently on her neck. She shivers. Incredulous, Daquin feels a surge of desire.

'I'm not interested in horses, but I am interested in you.'

She smiles again.

'Would you like a coffee?'

The ground floor of the house is all one room. In the centre, a square kitchen built around a vast range, very modern. To the left, the office area, two tables cluttered with computers, printers, telephones, Minitel terminal and fax machine.

'My best customers are Japanese universities,' she volunteers.

To the right, in front of a hearth, empty at this time of year, are three mismatched sofas covered with old blankets arranged around a makeshift coffee table. No television, but a hi-fi system and a collection of CDs. She sets the coffeepot and cups down on the table. They sit down.

'You know that Nicolas Berger has been murdered?'

'Yes, Moulin's wife phoned me after your detective went to visit her.'

'What was your relationship to him?'

'Superintendent, I didn't kill him. I can't even imagine who would want to.' Tears start in her eyes. 'I'm very upset by his death. So what's the point of talking about it?'

'To help me find his murderer would be the most conventional reply, but hardly convincing. You're going to talk to me because it will help you, it will help the grieving process. It's never easy, and here, alone like this, it must be even harder.'

She says nothing for a long time. Daquin drinks coffee, in silence, and waits.

'We'd known each other for a long time, since high school, in Rennes. Then we were involved in May '68 and afterwards we were in the same political group.' She smiles at him. 'Far left, "tomorrow belongs to us" and all that. We were sure of ourselves and had great hopes. That creates a bond.' She dwells on her memories for a moment. 'When it all fell apart, I'd had it, I went to pieces and for a few years I lived almost like a vagrant, ferreting around fairs and flea markets. And then, by chance, I began to buy and sell old books and magazines. I loved it and I realised there was an opening. I looked for a way of buying a place. I bumped into Nicolas, in Paris, almost by accident. He was working in an insurance company with Annick Renouard and had joined the fast set, living a life of luxury. He adored the whole thing, but at the same time he felt mildly regretful, as if he'd somehow betrayed his youthful ideals. He got me a very good mortgage deal so I could buy this place. He used to come and see me from time to time, and we started sleeping together again, as good friends, like before. We shared a love of horses, that made us close. They're very sensual animals, as I think you noticed.' She becomes pensive. 'Sometimes, I think he might have liked to live here, with me, but he couldn't stand the isolation of the countryside…'

Daquin smiles.

'I can understand that. Do you know if he had any enemies?'

'No, I don't. He was very well liked in show-jumping circles because he was always pleasant and didn't try and outshine others.'

'And at work?'

'He didn't talk to me about it much. He enjoyed his job, but he wasn't at all ambitious. If Annick hadn't been there to protect him, he'd have been trampled on a long time ago.'

'Do you know her?'

'Of course. Annick was at school with us, and then she was in the same political group.'

'What was their relationship?'

'I think Nicolas was always a little bit in love with her. But he wasn't ruthless enough to interest her.'

'Were there conflicts between them?'

'Not that I'm aware of. But you're asking too much. I hardly saw her again. To put it as tactfully as possible, we had chosen different paths in life.'

'I found Christian Deluc's name in Berger's diary. Do you know him too?'

She looks surprised.

'Of course. He was also in our group in Rennes. In a way he was even the ringleader.' She thinks for a moment. 'At one point I though Annick was in love with him, but no, she wasn't capable of it.' A silence. 'I didn't know Nicolas was still seeing him.'

'Also in his diary, "Le Chambellan". Does that ring any bells?'

'No, not at all.'

'Were there other women in his life?'

A winning smile.

'Of course, Superintendent. Probably quite a few, because he liked flirting. But he soon tired of his conquests. Perhaps too superficial, too vulnerable? I don't think he really had a mistress.'

'Did you know he was a regular cocaine user?'

'It's not a crime he deserved to die for.'

'Of course not, but it can sometimes bring people into contact with killers.'

'He never talked about that scene. He'd been using cocaine for a long time, since the aftermath of May '68. In our group, there was a lot of pressure. You had to conform to a strict code of communal living, with a quasi-permanent inquisition. Nicolas got into the habit of snorting then, in secret, to help him cope, and escape. He continued afterwards. But he managed his dependency very well. A bit like a social drinker.'

'You may see it like that, but the night before he died, he handed out between twenty and thirty grams of cocaine to his friends, a quantity that represents a considerable sum of money, and easily enough to get him convicted for pushing.'

She looks taken aback.

'I don't know anything about it.'

A faraway look, her hands clasped around her knee, she clams up. Daquin pours himself another cup of coffee and sips it.

'Thank you for confiding in me,' he smiles, 'and for the coffee.' He gets up, bends over and kisses her hand. 'Will you permit me to come and see you again, not as a policeman but as... a friend?' he asks hesitantly.

'If you like, Superintendent.'

She watches him leave. Le Dem is already by the car, waiting for him.

On the way back, Le Dem gives Daquin his report. The groom knows Berger well. He met him at Thirard's.

'The guy who owns the place where they shot the video with the black horse?'

'Yes. He's a former show-jumping champion, a trainer and a horse dealer, probably one of the best known in French show-jumping circles. According to the groom. So he worked for him and met Berger there on several occasions. One morning, he's fired by his boss, on the pretext that he'd been hanging around the stables one night when he had no business being there. He found himself out on his ear, furious and skint. Berger came out of the stables at the same time. The groom stopped him and asked for a lift to Paris. On the way, they talked, and Berger offered him a job here, he knew the owner was looking for a groom. One interesting detail: Berger had just had a row with Thirard, he was still very wound up, and kept saying that Thirard was a crook.'

'A serious row?'

'Apparently. No further details available.'

Daquin is pensive.

'Maybe we should check out this Thirard.' After a few moments' thought: 'By the way, Romero and I took from Berger's office the file he was working on, the famous video. Nothing of much interest – costings, materials, correspondence, work schedules, appointments, reports, everything you'd expect to find. Plus an undated sheet of plain paper, no heading, with notes in Berger's handwriting.'

Daquin takes a photocopy out of his pocket.

'Four columns. On the left, names that look like the names of horses.

Opposite each name, three dates. The interval between the dates is usually short, two weeks to three months. All the dates are within the last two years. I'm giving you this photocopy, see if you can make anything of it.'

The car heads towards Paris. The weather's clouded over, a fine drizzle begins to fall. For the last week, Lenglet has been so weak that he can no longer speak.

'Le Dem, drop me off at the hospital.'

Lenglet opens then closes his eyes when Daquin enters the room, or so it seems to him. They are alone in the room together. Occasionally, someone walks past in the corridor. Daquin listens to Lenglet breathing. He goes over to the window. In the courtyard, under the trees, children are playing dodgeball. Daquin watches them. He freezes. Behind him, he is aware of the silence. Absolute. Irrevocable. His hand pressing hard against the cool glass pane. Despairing, I'm going to feel this death as a release. Have the guts to turn around.

Thursday 21 September 1989

Lavorel is sitting in the back room of a café in Vallangoujard with two gendarmes. The owner has given him a choice between white or red wine. He's opted for the white, hoping it'll be more drinkable than the red, right on top of his morning café au lait. It's still quite acid. In front of them, a huge radio and a tape recorder. The wait grows longer. The owner comes over and sits down next to one of the two gendarmes.

'Well, has my wine order arrived?'

'Of course, yesterday evening, according to plan. I forgot to tell you, with all this trouble. Come and pick it up from the barracks, when you like, my wife will show you the cellar.'

The owner leans over towards Lavorel:

'One of the gendarmes, Sallois, has a vineyard, in the heart of Bordeaux, and he makes this wine… say no more. He supplies all the local bars, and nobody's complaining.'

A red light on the radio blinks, the owner discreetly leaves. A muffled, anxious female voice:

'I'm coming, I'm opening the door.' Louder. 'Come up.' A door closes. 'Sit down.' Chairs scraping. 'Have you brought the bedspread?'

The voice of another, very young, woman. The rustle of paper: 'Here it is. And have you got the money?'

'Yes. But tell me again nice and slowly. So that I remember everything. This bedspread...'

'Last year I took it on the pilgrimage to Saintes-Maries-de-la-Mer. Our gypsy pilgrimage. I touched the statue of the Black Sarah with it, while she was in the sea. You understand?'

'Yes. So far.'

'And I prayed to the saint, who has magic powers. She brings back unfaithful husbands. That's what you want, isn't it?'

'Yes. But I already bought a bedside rug that had touched Saint Sarah from you, and my husband didn't come back.'

'A bedside rug has less power than a bedspread, because you stay under the bedspread all night.'

'I do, for sure, but he doesn't, because he's not there.'

'The bedspread will make your wish come true. If you think about your husband very hard when you're under the bedspread, the first night, you'll dream of him, and he'll be back within the week.'

'Right. How much did we say?'

'Come off it? Have you got the money or not?'

'I've got it, I've got it. But I don't remember exactly how much we said.'

'Twenty thousand francs.'

Lavorel downs a second glass of white wine, in surprise. One of the two gendarmes leans towards him and murmurs:

'She works on the checkout at Mammouth, on the minimum wage, and she's already forked out ten thousand francs for the rug.'

'I want to see the money.' Sound of a drawer opening. They must be counting the notes. 'It's all there, take the bedspread.'

'I'll see you out.'

The gendarmes pack away their equipment, triumphant.

'There. We managed to convince this woman to press charges, and now, at last we've caught her red-handed. You'll see, once our devotee of Saint Sarah's banged up, complaints will pour in, that's what always happens.'

Gendarmes are waiting for the two girls in the street. They march them off to the gendarmerie, it's in the bag. And now they're in their stride, a search of the gypsies' farm.

Lavorel follows, resigned.

At the village exit, two blue cars are parked near an ancient fortified farmhouse, four stone buildings in a square without an exit between them, all facing inwards, a huge timber carriage entrance, closed. That's where the girl they've just arrested lives, with Rouma, the farrier, and a few other gypsy families.

First warnings.

'Open up.'

Voices on the other side of the door.

'There aren't any men here. Only women and children. We're not opening the door.'

After ten minutes of fruitless argument, the gendarmes break down the door and force their way in, brandishing their guns. Lavorel hangs back, his hands in his pockets, convinced that this is a sinister venture. Five caravans are drawn up in a circle in the beaten earth courtyard. In the centre, thirty or so women and children huddle together. The buildings looking onto the courtyard seem to be pretty much reduced to ruins. The gendarmes assemble the women and children in an empty room, place them under heavy guard, and the search begins.

While they gather up the bedspreads in their packaging, along with the cheap jewellery, two stolen cars, motorbike parts and other odds and ends, Lavorel goes through the caravans and all the buildings looking for a possible stash of drugs, without much conviction. The forge, the workshops, the garage, a large collective kitchen with all mod cons, there's even a cold store. Nothing. It's frustrating, all the same.

Lavorel leaves the gendarmes drawing up impressive reports. For them, the prospect of days and days of thankless graft. And I'm leaving empty handed.

Next day, the atmosphere in Daquin's office is tense. Lavorel gives an account of the storming of the farm, without embellishment or local colour. His reports never have Romero's panache, but he's not bothered.

'As far as we're concerned, in any case, it's a bad move, which is likely to prompt Rouma to stop his deliveries for a while. But the gendarmes had been planning it for nearly six months. They'd never have agreed to delay it. So I jumped on the bandwagon. They simply promised not to arrest the farrier, since he has a legal professional activity.'

'On the Berger front, it's not much better,' continues Daquin. 'Two women as different as you can imagine give an almost identical portrait of him. A nice boy, loaded, without passion, without ambition and with a degree of talent. A clean-cut, socially adept coke addict. At first sight, there is no obvious reason why anyone would want to kill him. Nor was he a dealer, and never had been. He generously shared his twenty measly grams of cocaine with his friends, that's all. At least, I hope so. Romero, you didn't pay for your dose, did you?'

'No, Superintendent. You know very well that it's against the rules.'

Lavorel grows impatient.

'But all the same, he was murdered.'

'The only little blip was an argument with a horse dealer by the name of Thirard.'

Le Dem interrupts him. The Martian's growing bolder.

'Actually, on the subject of Thirard, that list you gave me was indeed to do with horses. They all belonged to Thirard, or were in livery at his stables. And they all died on the date opposite each name in the first column. I haven't found out what the figures in the other two columns mean yet.'

'Right.' A long pause for thought. Then Daquin gets up. 'Today's Friday. Over the weekend, the gendarmes will be working. We're going to rest. And on Monday, we'll review the whole case with a fresh eye.'

Daquin makes himself a coffee then leans back in his chair with his feet up on the desk and allows his thoughts to wander. Lenglet. Don't want to let his death to get me down. I'm alive. Rudi, a certain weariness. The investigation's dragging its feet, but there's progress. Starting from almost nothing, two corpses already, possibly three, if we can link Paola Jiménez to our case. Daquin rises, straightens up, stretches, makes himself another coffee, and sits down again. A series of images. The farrier at his forge, the burning car, the gypsies' farm being stormed. And Amélie. Amélie living in the back of beyond among her books and horses. A persistent image of the golden horse with grey lips nibbling the blonde curls against the delicate nape of her neck. An urgent need to brush his lips against that neck, kiss that hair. He picks up the telephone.

'Madame Gramont, Superintendent Daquin. I'd like to invite you to dinner this evening, at a restaurant in your neck of the woods.'

'That's a good idea, Superintendent. It'll take my mind off my work. But let me invite you to dinner at my place. My groom's gone away for two days and I can't leave the horses.'

'I'll be there in around three hours.'

'I'll be expecting you.'

He hangs up. Hesitates for a moment. Shall I go home and get changed? Desire creates a certain sense of urgency, so no.

When Daquin arrives, it is still daylight. A flame sunset on the horizon, over the hills, but the farm is already in the shade. Amélie comes out of the house to greet him. Tight-fitting pale blue jeans and a green T-shirt. She exudes the warm smell of cooking. Even more attractive than he remembered.

'I've brought you a photo. It was on Berger's desk.'

Visible emotion.

They sit down side by side on a stone bench against the side of the house. Champagne, as they watch night spread from the bottom of the valley. Gentle sounds from the stables, the rustle of straw, the horses' breathing, a busy, cosy silence. It is Amélie who breaks it. She says, as if to herself:

'The grieving process has begun. Slowly.' A smile. 'And I don't know what to think about it.'

Grief. Daquin pictures Lenglet on his deathbed. Not now, above all, not now. He takes from his pocket a piece of paper folded into four and carefully opens it out.

'May I show you something?'

He hands her a photocopy of the list given to Le Dem. Amélie leans forward, her tanned neck exposed beneath the blonde curls, and reads.

'They're the names of horses. I know some of them. Famous show jumpers. And that one, Khulna du Viveret, the last one on the list, is the one Nicolas filmed for Pama.'

Night has completely enveloped the farm, and it's very chilly. Amélie rises. 'Let's sit down and eat.'

She has cleared one of the tables in the office area, white cloth, pastel crockery and a cluster of candles. On the table, a selection of cold meats, a local speciality, breads, a red Loire wine, well chilled. Then she brings a chicken in a salt crust, accompanied by creamed mushroom purée. She deftly breaks open the salt crust and carves the chicken. Daquin concentrates on savouring the firm, tender meat that has a tang of the sea. A little taste of happiness. Amélie watches him, her elbows on the table and her chin cupped in her hands. I like men who enjoy their food. Out loud:

'After your visit, my groom talked to me about Thirard and his row with Nicolas. I happened to mention Moulin's name.' Daquin stops eating. 'Moulin went to see Thirard two or three months ago. He was drunk and in a furious rage. He shouted abuse at Thirard in front of everyone, accused him of having sent the tax inspectors to ruin him and swore he'd get his revenge by destroying Thirard's filthy trade. Those were his words. Thirard didn't seem to think it was very funny.'

Daquin gets up, walk over to the window, gazes out at the dark courtyard. Is it possible that we have the wrong victim? His car, him at the wheel, the coke, under the nose of Lavorel who was tailing him to boot, no wonder we assumed it was Berger. It didn't even cross our minds that maybe the murderer might have been after Moulin. Or both of them? Even if it's unlikely. A beginner's mistake. In any case, the trail leads back to Thirard. Obviously.

Amélie comes over to him by the window.

'Finish your meal anyway. You'll have time to think about all that tomorrow.'

A creamy Livarot cheese. An apricot tart that sets his teeth on edge.

'I didn't have time to do anything more complicated,' says Amélie.

'Do you know this Thirard?'

'Everyone does. He's famous in show-jumping circles.'

Daquin gets up. Coffee is waiting on the low table. He sits down on one of the battered sofas.

'A joint, Superintendent?'

Smile. 'No, thank you, I don't smoke. I'd rather have a brandy.'

'No brandy, but I've got an old Martinican rum that's rather good.'

She brings him a bottle and a beautiful balloon glass that you warm between your palms, and pours him a generous amount.

Music. Monteverdi's *Madrigals of War and of Love*. Amélie opens the window, the horses love music. The chill night air blows in, nippy. She puts out the light, the night wafts into the room carrying the smell of the stables. Daquin, cautious, tastes the rum. Not much body but very fruity, in perfect harmony with the chicken and the apricot tart. Closes his eyes with pleasure. Amélie comes and leans against him, her head on his shoulder, and rolls herself a joint with great concentration. Daquin watches her.

'What were you doing in May '68, Superintendent?'

'I was abroad.'

'So you missed out on a whole chapter of French history.'

'It's very possible.'

'In a way our generation is slightly crazy.'

'Maybe.' He caresses the nape of her neck with his fingertips, then leans over, kisses her golden curls and nibbles them. 'Right now, I don't give a shit.'

Amélie shivers and laughs.

'It's said that a horse that submits to its rider "bends its neck".'

Monday 25 September 1989

After the fiasco of the search, they have to tail the farrier again, if that's still possible. But first of all, to find him. Lavorel and Le Dem have been driving around the Chantilly stables area for over an hour, looking for the white van. Suddenly, as they cruise past one of the stables, they see some of the lads shouting and waving their arms. People come out of the tack room, the office, and run over to a corner of the courtyard where the white van, in fact... Lavorel abandons the car by the roadside and races over to the van, followed by Le Dem. On the concrete floor of the forge, surrounded by a dozen horrified people, is a dead horse lying on its side, hanging by its halter from the forge's metal ring, its neck broken. And beneath the horse, the body of a man, three-quarters hidden from view, a corner of his leather apron and heavy shoes just visible. It could well be the farrier.

'Shit,' says Le Dem.

'Police. Make way.'

Lavorel breaks through the circle and leans over the body. Warm. They have to hoist the horse's body. After cutting the halter rope, several men set about moving it, tethers tied to its legs, bars slipped under its flank.

Avoid touching the man. A horse is incredibly heavy. The body slides a metre. And discloses the remains of what appears to have been the farrier. His face crushed, a few shards of bone in a bloody pink pulp. Not much blood. Horse hairs are stuck to the amorphous mess. The same colour as the few hairs that are still identifiable. A shattered hand. Very few injuries on the rest of the body, the leather apron seems to have protected him. The onlookers stand in horrified silence. He was dead all right.

'It's an appalling accident,' says the stables manager in hushed tones. The horse must have kicked the farrier, goodness knows why, perhaps because he drove a nail into its foot, he fell, the horse took fright, trampled him and broke its neck pulling on the tether. It's rare, but it happens.'

Lavorel straightens up, catches Le Dem's eye. He's not there any more. Unbelievable! The expert... He's probably gone off to throw up. Give me back Romero, I'm prepared to forget the blonde... Then he swings into the routine, call the gendarmes, tell them to bring a doctor to certify the death, take down the names of everyone present in the stable, start questioning the witnesses to establish the circumstances of the accident...

Le Dem had discreetly slipped away when everybody's attention was focused on the corpse. He walked down a line of stalls, carefully checking the bolts on all the doors, top and bottom. A precaution that ensured the door remains closed even if the horse manages to open the top one by playing with it. On stopping in front of the stall of an iron grey horse, Le Dem opens the door, goes in and closes it behind him. Against the wall, sitting in the straw, is the terrified farrier's assistant. Le Dem sits down beside him, without saying a word. He can hear the kid's heart pounding. A few long minutes go by. The horse munches straw, and comes over and gently sniffs them from time to time. Le Dem strokes its nostrils, its nose, and talks to it softly. He can sense that the boy is gradually calming down.

Le Dem still says nothing. It's the boy who speaks first.

'How did you know I was here?'

'I know that Rouma works with an assistant. I looked for you when I arrived at the forge, but you weren't there. Where could you hide? In a stall, of course. The bottom bolt on the outside of the door is open, so I could tell the stall had been closed from the inside and that it was highly likely that there was someone in here. And if you're hiding, it's because you saw something. And you're afraid.'

'Are you a... policeman?'

'Yes. Tell me what you saw.'

'My people don't talk to the cops. We don't talk to the others either. We sort things out among ourselves.'

Le Dem strokes one of the grey horse's legs, takes a sugar lump out of his pocket. The horse lowers its head, takes the sugar and creases its lips with contentment.

'Even when it comes to finding Rouma's murderer?'

'How do you know it's not an accident? They're all saying it's an accident.'

'The horse hanged itself on its halter. The knot tethering the halter to the ring on the wall of the forge couldn't have been tied by a farrier like Rouma.'

The kid stares at him. A certain respect. He repeats:

'My people don't talk to the cops.' His tone is less confident. 'Besides, what do you care who killed him?'

'I know that Rouma did some stupid things, but he was a very good farrier. We at least owe it to him to find his killer. So let's make a deal. You tell me. I won't take any notes. I won't ask your name. I won't tell anyone I met you. I'll even help you get out of here without anyone seeing you, and you can go home. But at least you'll give me a chance of finding the murderer.'

'You swear I'll be able to go? That no one will know?'

'I swear.' Le Dem smiles. 'I swear on the head of this grey horse.'

'There were two of them. I was putting a halter on the grey. Dimitri was working on a horse's rear left hoof. He was leaning over. They came up from behind.' The boy stops, looks at Le Dem, his eyes wide. 'The amazing thing is that Dimitri didn't hear them coming.' He continues. 'One of them hit him hard on the back of the neck, with a sort of short cosh. He fell immediately. I was frightened. I hid in the stall and peeped over the top of the door. Then, one of them pushed Dimitri under the horse while the other re-tied the knot, like you said. And he did something to the horse's neck too. I couldn't see very well. They went off through the woods, and almost at once, the horse went crazy, it trampled Dimitri before collapsing. Then the others began to arrive. I didn't dare come out.'

The boy sobs noiselessly.

'What did the two men look like?'

'Tall, dark hair and dark suits.'

'You didn't see anything else?'

'Yes. When everyone began yelling and running, I saw a black Mercedes driving past slowly on the road, past the stables. I'm sure they were inside it. The registration number ended in XY 75.'

Le Dem helps him to his feet.

'Come on, I'll get you out of here.'

The boy slips his hand under the grey's front and caresses the inside leg where the skin is softest, his head resting against the neck, and lets himself go for a moment.'

'Goodbye horses.'

Le Dem returns to the forge, where the doctor is examining the body.

'There you are,' says Lavorel. 'About time too.'

Le Dem draws him to one side.

'It's a murder. Have an autopsy done on the body. A blow on the back of the neck. And while you're about it, an autopsy on the horse. And a photo of the knot tethering the horse to the ring on the wall of the forge.'

Lavorel looks at him in amazement. Le Dem seems sure of himself, and calm.

'Fine. Will do.'

Amelot and Berry are sitting in the detectives' office, the list of horses found among Berger's papers in front of them, and are routinely phoning all the vets in the Chantilly area, and there are a lot of them. Fifth phone call.

'I'm a reporter for *Horse Magazine*, and I'm doing a piece on Khulna de Viveret, who's just died. I've been told you treated him, a couple of months or so ago...'

'Let me check... I didn't treat him, I simply certified the death. Heart attack.'

'Can you tell me what happened, for my article? Our readers like touching little details. The groom in tears, that sort of thing.'

'You can write what you like. The truth is that he died alone in the middle of the night. I was called the next morning to sign the insurance forms. The body was removed by the knacker, and I can guarantee that no one in the stables was crying.'

'He'd just been filmed for a promotional video for an insurance company, Pama.'

'What a coincidence, I do believe it was for Pama that I signed the death certificate.'

A few more phone calls and Amelot and Berry manage to establish that Java des Lauges, the last but one on the list, also died of a heart attack in the night, and was also insured by Pama.

The veterinary college of Maisons-Alfort:

'Yes, of course, horses can die of a heart attack, although it is a rare cause of death. Provoke a heart attack? Possible... No, the vet can't detect it, if he has no reason to suspect...'

After having identified the owner of Le Chambellan restaurant, a certain Perrot, Romero spends hours wandering from one Ministry of Defence department to another to find out whether the aforesaid Perrot had indeed served in the army in Beirut between 1972 and 1973. Daquin's orders, no explanation, do as I tell you. And he eventually obtains the answer: Perrot was enlisted in the marines and served in the security service of the French embassy from 1972 to 1975. Where does the chief get his tip-offs from? Annoying.

The tax office has been on strike for two months and all leave has been suspended. So Duroselle has not been able to get out of the meeting Daquin has requested. Since hearing of Moulin's death, he's been expecting this summons, and he feels vaguely guilty. A simple exchange of views on a case you dealt with, says the superintendent. Moulin, does that name ring any bells? What should he do? Answer the questions, after all, it's the police, and there's been a murder, or remind Daquin of his duty of confidentiality and refer him to his superiors? He discussed it with his wife who advised him not to say anything at all. It was the only way not to say too much. Treat him with disdain, a tax inspector was just as important as a police superintendent, and refer it to his chief. As it happened, it was absolutely impossible to get hold of his chief.

There's a knock at the door.

'Come in,' says Duroselle, entrenched behind his desk.

Daquin enters, a brawny one metre eighty-five, square jaw, thick neck as wide as his jaw, dark brown gimlet eyes, well-cut suede jacket, beige chino trousers, fauve leather English shoes. Duroselle feels ill at ease in his clothes. Daquin's cold gaze sweeps the room, then settles on him. Duroselle stands up to shake his hand across the desk. Countless stories of police brutality jostle inside his head.

Daquin sits down opposite him, without waiting to be asked. Duroselle finds himself standing up, his arms dangling by his sides. He hurriedly sits down, breaking into a sweat.

'You know that Moulin is dead, and that he was murdered?' Duroselle nods. 'To assist my investigation, I need to know who was behind the tax inspection you carried out.'

Duroselle feigns anger. Nobody had put them under any pressure. Suspecting the tax officials to be at the service of private or personal interests was unacceptable. As far as we're concerned, all tax-payers are equal...

Daquin lets him have his say, with an amused smile. Then:

'We're not going to go on playing cat and mouse. I'm not going to lean on you, whatever you thought when you saw me come in. As a matter of principle, I never hit a striking worker. But if you don't answer my question, your wife will find out who you left Moulin's riding school with on the evening of 13th June and what you did that same day between five and seven.'

Duroselle outraged: 'That's blackmail.'

'Quite.' Dazzling smile. 'Good detective work needs good informers, and how, in your opinion, do you find good informers?' Duroselle is sweating heavily. 'Of course, if you answer my question, I shan't mention my sources, your bosses won't know a thing. Nor will your wife.' Duroselle breathes more easily. 'I want an answer right away.'

Daquin ensconces himself in his chair, his hands crossed, and waits. Duroselle remains silent for a moment or two. Is already thinking what to tell his wife. Sober, icy, the honour of the tax office is intact.

'It came directly from the Minister's office. They called my chief, who passed it on to me.'

'How? Just a name and an address, or a bit more detail?'

'More detail. Moulin had sold a horse in Italy for two hundred and fifty thousand francs and had only declared fifty thousand. I was to find the remaining two hundred thousand.' Puffing with pride. 'And I did.'

'Well informed, the minister's office. That's reassuring. I feel as if we're in good hands.'

Tuesday 26 September 1989

'Gentlemen, now it's all hands on deck. No more leave, no weekends, until we've cracked this case. Let's begin with the easy bit: Rouma. The autopsy report confirms Le Dem's account. Rouma was indeed murdered. We even have a lead. We've identified the murderers' Mercedes. It belongs to the

Vincennes racecourse operating company. We checked it out and the company states that the Mercedes didn't leave the car park last Monday. But the new boys have established that the car park is unsupervised and that any smart employee of the racecourse could have taken the car. Conclusion: the first place to look for the killers is among the racecourse personnel. Any suggestions? Yes, Romero?'

'I know someone who's a regular at Vincennes who I could ask to be a grass. At least he'll be able to tell us how the racecourse operates.'

'Very good. Go ahead. Let's move on. Why was the farrier killed? We have no idea. But our theory is of course that the murder is linked to cocaine smuggling. Perhaps his supplier panicked after he heard about last Thursday's search. I shall put that in my report, and I'm going to ask for an investigation to be opened – investigating magistrate, search warrants, the usual routine, we're soon going to need them. There's still one little problem. I have to explain how we got onto the Mercedes. We can't mention Le Dem's ghost kid. I need someone who will state they saw the registration number. That'll be you, Lavorel. Any objections, Le Dem?'

'Yes, Superintendent. I'd rather it was me.'

'Why?'

'Lavorel was by the forge the whole time, and a lot of people can testify to that. From there, he couldn't have seen a car on the road. But I could.'

'Are you aware that would be giving false evidence?'

'That's not how I see it. I owe it to the boy.'

'As you wish. Let's move on to the next point: the murder of Berger and Moulin. Much more complicated.' A pause. 'Three deaths in ten days, right under your nose. Lavorel, you bring bad luck.'

'That's not funny.'

'No, all things considered, perhaps not. Let's recap. Berger and Moulin were murdered. Indisputable, according to the gendarmes' report. A powerful explosive... Detonator wired to the ignition. They had no chance of survival. Apart from that, nothing is certain. The car could have been sabotaged between eight o'clock, when it was left in the car park, and midday, the time of the explosion. A lot of comings and goings in the car park, people very busy with their horses. Or sleeping. Don't get mad,

Lavorel, I couldn't resist that one. Result: no description and no prints. Worse: we don't know who the target was or why.'

'Let's take Nicolas Berger. Two possibilities. One: he's eliminated because of some cocaine trafficking mix-up, which links his murder to that of Rouma who was involved in the same network. Two: he was blackmailing Thirard with that list of horses which seems to point to an insurance fiddle which Pama was the victim of, and Thirard gets rid of him.'

'That seems rather drastic by way of response.'

'Maybe Thirard is hot-tempered.'

Scepticism.

'Or else it's Moulin who was the target.' Daquin turns towards Le Dem. 'Who could have known that Moulin had sold a horse in Italy for two hundred and fifty thousand francs?'

'Thirard most definitely. Horses are often paid for in cash, on the basis of a simple verbal agreement between the parties. So, to find out the price, you have to ask the buyer or the seller. The buyer is Italian. Thirard virtually has a monopoly on the sale of French horses in Italy. So he has the contacts to find out how much Moulin had sold his horse for. And a good reason from wanting to stop him from competing with him in the Italian market.'

'Good enough to kill him?'

'Not necessarily. The tax inspection should have been sufficient.'

A silence.

'Odd character, this Thirard. He could pull enough strings to influence someone in the Ministry of Finance. That must be rather unusual for a horse dealer. Moving on: according to Madame Moulin, her husband had made several trips to Italy to drum up business and had come back more than a little intrigued by Thirard's activities there. He didn't tell her much, but he had talked at length to Berger. Then he'd let it drop, until this tax inspection business that had infuriated him. The most likely theory is that Berger and Moulin were both blackmailing Thirard who did away with the pair of them in one go.'

More scepticism.

'I'm obviously not getting anywhere today. Too bad. I shan't report on this aspect of our investigation at this stage. Too vague, too muddled. But my idea, Le Dem, is for you to go and get a job with Thirard, so you can tell us what goes on there.'

Le Dem turns pink with pleasure.

'I'd love to, but it's not easy to get taken on by a posh livery stables.'

'Leave Romero and me to take care of that side of things. There's still Pama. Berger and Annick Renouard who work there are both coke addicts. Thirard's swindling the company. I'll take that piece of action on myself.'

Thursday 28 September 1989

It's not yet dark when Fromentin stops for a drink at the café de Chantilly on his way home, as he does every evening. He lives alone and he's in no rush to get back. He leans his bicycle against the window, pushes open the door, greets everyone and goes up to the bar. The owner automatically serves him a glass of red. There's a guy standing next to him drinking white, a good-looking guy incidentally, looks like an Eyetie. Starts going on about horses in a very assured tone, he's talking a load of crap. Fromentin politely corrects him. He knows a thing or two about horses, he does. He was an apprentice jockey in his youth, and now he's been a groom for thirty years, ten at Thirard's stables. He's practically the only one who's lasted so long with such a difficult boss. The guy's OK. He admits he can be wrong, asks Fromentin's opinion, buys him a drink. Fromentin feels good. He starts talking, elated, it's so rare that anyone listens to him... Several hours and many drinks later, the café's about to close, the two men are the last customers. They shake hands, promise to meet up again, and leave.

Romero hurries to his car, parked a hundred metres or so from the café, drives off and hides a couple kilometres down the road along Fromentin's route home, in a spot that's deserted at this hour. Drunk as Fromentin is, Romero won't need to give him much of a push for him to end up in the ditch. Daquin said: Careful. One or two broken bones, no more.

Romero waits, the engine ticking over. Nobody. Looks at his watch. A quarter of an hour. Even if he's drunk, he should have come past by now. Does a U-turn and drives slowly back to the café. Closed. No trace of Fromentin. Romero wonders what went wrong. Maybe he got him too drunk and Fromentin's gone the wrong way and is heading in the other direction, towards Paris? Romero belts along in the direction of Paris. He soon spots the bicycle's rear light zigzagging madly along the road. Hurry up and shove him into the ditch before he gets mown down by a car. At night, cars tend to speed along this road. The remote forest spot is ideal. Romero drives up behind him, he's a few metres away. Just then, from his left, a flaming horse gallops wildly into view. A living torch. Thundering of hooves. Romero slams on the brake. A car coming the other way hits the animal full on, and immediately bursts into flames. Fromentin swerves violently and plunges into the ditch. Romero rubs his eyes and pinches himself two or three times. Then he gets out of his car and rushes towards the inferno. The horse was killed on impact and its body has smashed through the windscreen and is half inside the car, still burning. Inside, crushed beneath the horse, two bodies are also on fire. The smell of petrol and burning flesh is overwhelming. Romero tears off his jacket, wraps it around his hands and tries to open the door... Warped, stuck. The fire spreads to the back of the car, crackling. Intuition tells Romero that the whole thing's about to explode, get out quick, no way of knowing whether the occupants are dead or alive. The fire reaches the petrol tank. Romero flings himself into the ditch, puts out a few incipient flames on his clothes. The whole car is ablaze. He begins to feel the burns on his arms. Hears the wail of the fire engines. A little further, in the ditch, Fromentin is lying on his back with a knee at right angles. Fracture guaranteed, maybe more. He doesn't seem to be in pain, the alcohol probably, but he has a wild look and is mumbling: 'It's the wrath of God, the wrath of God.'

Romero gets into his car and drives in the direction of Paris. Absolutely pointless for me to be seen here. I'll try and find out what happened later.

Friday 29 September 1989

When Le Dem turns up at Thirard's looking for a job, at around 7 a.m., Thirard is already on horseback. Le Dem stops beside the outdoor riding school and watches, waiting for him to finish work. Not very tall, slim, expensive riding habit, beige jodhpurs, fauve leather jacket and matching boots, with a sharp profile, clearly defined lips, a ruddy complexion and stubby, rough hands. Hands that Le Dem knows well, a farmer's hands. A good seat, supple, sparing in his movements, Thirard exercises unquestionable, non-negotiable authority over his horse, an absolute power in a world of its own. Le Dem knows that feeling well. With a pang of nostalgia he remembers riding the bay horse early in the morning in La Courneuve, before the park opened. They would jump the picnic tables and pirouette on the lawns, at the foot of the seedy tower blocks. The horse submissive, the rider powerful, a harmonious couple. A sudden insight: that is real togetherness. Because even when I'm in bed with a woman, until now I've always felt somehow alone. Embarrassing. Le Dem feels his cheeks flushing and hastily switches his attention to Thirard.

They've finished. Long reins, walking back to the stables. Thirard stops his horse a few paces from Le Dem and murmurs, still in his own world: 'Lousy motion, pity...'

'Perhaps it's a pulled ligament on the left patella,' says Le Dem softly in an apologetic tone.

Thirard suddenly becomes aware of him, and eyes him suspiciously.

'Who are you and what are you doing here?'

Le Dem looks down.

'I'm looking for work as a groom...'

Before he can finish his sentence, two uniformed gendarmes appear, making their way over towards Thirard, who freezes, his eyes glazing over and his face inscrutable.

'Are you the owner of the Val-Fourré stables?'

'Yes. It's under management, but I am still the owner.'

'It burned down last night.' Thirard shows no emotion whatsoever. 'And my men suspect it was arson. The third case since July, all in the Chantilly region, and the second in a stables owned by you.'

'I'm not convinced it was arson this time. My manager installed an electrical system himself, which was unsafe in my view. I wrote to him about it a couple of weeks ago, and I sent a copy of my letter to my insurance company. Their assessor will of course contact you.'

'In the meantime, if you could accompany us to the scene...'

Thirard turns to Le Dem:

'What's your name?'

'Jean Le Dem.'

'Here, take the keys and go and fetch the four-wheel-drive over there in the courtyard. You can drive me and we'll talk in the car. I'll follow you, gentlemen.'

In the car:

'Where did you learn so much about horses?'

'My grandfather bred and trained Breton draught horses on the farms in north Finistère. I lived with him as a child and I helped him as much as I could.'

'And did your grandfather retrain as a tractor mechanic?'

'When the draught horses all disappeared, he more or less let himself die of boredom.'

A silence, then Thirard continues:

'Turn right, we're here. One of my grooms had an accident last night, he'll be off work for at least three months. The job's yours. After that, we'll see.'

Rounding a bend in the dirt track, a field of charred ruins. Two sides of the quadrangle are reduced to a mound of black ashes. On the other two sides, the roofs and sections of the wall have caved in. Set slightly back, a long, low stone house looks more or less intact. Not a horse in sight, they all bolted into the forest, not a man in sight, they're all out looking for the horses and will try and find them shelter in neighbouring stables. Only a few gendarmes and firemen sifting through the debris.

Thirard still seems unemotional. He gets out of the car, removes his fine leather boots, slips into a pair of Wellingtons lying in the back of the vehicle, and sets off to talk to the captain of the gendarmerie. Le Dem watches him wade through the black mud, upright and rigid in his beige jodhpurs, jacket and green Wellies gaping around the calves.

After dropping into A&E to get treatment for his few burns, which turn out to be only superficial, Romero is sprawled in an armchair in Daquin's office while the Superintendent makes him a coffee.

'I've never seen you in this state. Under the circumstances, a double coffee and a dash of brandy, for balance.' After a silence, while Romero sips the coffee. 'I've called Chantilly gendarmerie. A fire broke out at a riding centre this evening, not far from where the accident took place. The horses bolted, and some of them were burned to death.' A pause. 'Arson apparently. It wasn't you, at least?'

Romero groans, his eyes dark under his eyebrows.

'As Lavorel says, that's not funny.'

'By the way, Le Dem's got a job with Thirard.'

'Chief, don't you find life in the horse world a bit too hectic for us?'

As soon as Romero's left his office, Daquin immerses himself in the fat press file he's had compiled on Pama. Few cuttings before last June. But since the AGM when Jubelin took power, a positive avalanche.

Jubelin's personality gives scope for some lovely purple prose: the self-made man, the adventurer, hostile to the establishment and the educational elite. Daquin moves swiftly on.

More interesting is the presentation of the major strategic decisions that Jubelin has forced Pama to take. Refocusing on property, now that's a wise decision, according to the press, just when the price per square metre in Paris has doubled in two years and is forecast to continue rising. If the experts say so... On that point, they can perhaps be trusted... Daquin notes in passing, with a great deal of interest, that in July, Pama acquired a 20 per cent stake in Perrot's property development company. Well, well. Another reason to take an interest in Pama. And Perrot.

Jubelin is ensuring that Pama has a discreet presence in all the current major financial restructures. Discreet, but effective. The press make a great deal of Jubelin's past as a man of the right – some even suggest the far right – and now he has no qualms about being involved in operations that are remote-controlled by the socialist government. And his sole aim, claims the press, is to beat off international competition, in anticipation of the liberalisation of the insurance markets on 1st October. Which proves, they say, that in French society, now in its maturity, national economic interests transcend political divisions. Daquin rubs his thumb over his lips several times. I'm curious to know who he's working with in the government. That would surely be a lot more useful.

Pama's European ambitions are all the more evident from the strategic alliance between Jubelin and Mori's consortium, Italy's second biggest firm in terms of share value, and going from strength to strength. Italians. I note. You never know. I'm going to ask Lavorel to put together a dossier on Mori and his bunch.

Logical conclusion, Pama's shares are soaring. They've gone up 30 per cent in one month, and are part of the Paris Bourse's current boom. And the press, unanimously crowns Jubelin 1989 businessman of the year. Now I know.

On the subject of Annick, the press is more restrained. From a provincial family of pharmacists, law degree, worked her way up, recognised professional competence. Add to which subtle misogyny: rising in the shadow of the great man with whom she has a very special working relationship. In short, she's successful because he's screwing her. From what I've seen, that's rather a reductive point of view.

Finally, the last cutting is from the previous day. Pama has just made a takeover bid for A.A. Bayern, a medium-sized German insurance company, solidly established at regional level, a move that has to be seen in the context of its European strategy. For the moment, that doesn't mean anything to me. Put it aside.

Saturday 30 September 1989

Romero has a meeting at midday, at the entrance to the owners' enclosure at Vincennes racetrack. His friend is waiting for him, and greets him warmly. He is tall and slightly rotund with hunched shoulders and a pudgy face, dressed ostentatiously, cashmere jacket over a silk shirt, signet ring and chunky chain bracelet. Romero, in jeans, long-sleeved linen shirt to conceal his burns, sweatshirt slung around his shoulders and trainers, smiles at the thought that his friend's attire would have made him envious a few years ago. They go in. The security guards on the door greet Monsieur Béarn. They take a lift directly up into the panoramic restaurant at the top of the enclosure, reserved for regulars. Romero's stomach lurches. Before them, the restaurant is arranged like an amphitheatre, a series of steps leading down to the floor-to-ceiling bay window. The restaurant appears to be suspended above the track which stretches out seemingly within arm's reach. Beyond it is the green mass of the Bois de Vincennes, the white silhouette of Paris above the trees, and a vast sky. A discreet little lamp and telephone on every table, white linen and crockery, the place exudes luxury. By the exit to the lift, at the top end of the restaurant, they see a huge bar, carpeting, leather armchairs. Romero catches his breath.

A maître d'hôtel in black comes to greet them and shows them to Béarn's table. His table.

'Take a good look, Romero, this is the Temple.'

'Do you come here every day?'

'Not every day, but to nearly all the race meetings.'

They sit down. The room gradually fills up. All regulars, they exchange jokes and tips. The true believers, says Béarn.

The first race begins in two hours. Béarn orders two glasses of champagne, then two foie gras, two lobsters and a Pauillac. He puts *Paris Turf* down on the table, folded at the page showing today's racing schedule. Lots of notes scribbled in the margin. Picks up his binoculars and becomes absorbed in watching the sulkies, without numbers or blouses, doing little canters on the opposite side of the track, far from prying eyes. The waiter brings the foie gras.

Béarn loves trying to impress me. I'll give him some slack before cornering him.

'You've come a long way since our youth in Belle de Mai and pilfering from supermarkets.'

'Yes.' Smug. 'I've got a cab rental business that's doing well. What do you want of me, exactly, other than to swap childhood memories?'

'I'm working on a cocaine smuggling and murder case, and the trail leads here, to the racetrack.'

'What's it got to do with me?'

'Nothing, I think. But you know this place inside out, and you can help me find my way around.'

'I'm going to be straight with you: don't count on it. People in racing circles hate blabbermouths, and a gambler can't afford to get burned.'

'I'm going to be just as straight. You have no choice, Béarn. Your business may be going well, but the bulk of your income comes from somewhere else. You and a retired superintendent set up a charity for the families of police officers who've died in the course of duty. You collect funds from firms and you give them windscreen stickers so they are exempt from parking tickets. Much appreciated. And you give the charity ten per cent of what you collect, by doctoring the cheques. I have proof.' They attack the lobster in silence. 'You see,' Romero clenches his fist level with Béarn's neck, 'I've put a noose on you.' He squeezes his fist. 'I can tighten it. It depends what you give me.'

Cheese. Dessert. All the tables are now occupied.

'Ask away. I'll see what I can do.'

'Cocaine. Are people snorting the stuff here?'

'Not to my knowledge. The drivers run on red wine and Calvados. That's the tradition in French harness racing. Not like the steeplechasing scene.'

The horses for the first race come onto the track. Béarn becomes absorbed in *Paris Turf*. The sulkies ride backwards and forwards past the stand, at a slow pace, speeding up from time to time. The horses fly. Béarn picks up the telephone, presses a key marked 'Bets', gives his orders for the first race, in a language Romero doesn't really understand.

'The members' hotline,' explains Béarn. 'For regulars like me. I place my bets over the phone and settle my account once a fortnight, or once a month.' Still showing off, but his heart isn't in it any more.

The horses are at the starting line and they're off. The commentator's voice tirelessly drones the numbers of the leading horses. The tension in the room is palpable, but restrained. Romero remembers a previous visit to the racecourse, many years ago, when he was in the stands down below. The excitement was infectious, you couldn't help being caught up in it. Here, when the horses launch into the last lap, some of the punters jump to their feet, there's a bit of shouting, but most of them remain very calm. The numbers of the winning horses go up. Béarn sits down again.

'I've been jinxed for the last week. Haven't had a single winner.'

Romero continues his questioning.

'What about drugs in a wider sense?'

'The horses, of course, need a bit of "help" so to speak. You see the effort that's required of them... but that's got nothing to do with coke.'

'Who provides this "help"?'

'The owners, the trainers...'

'Keep that up and I tighten the noose a fraction.'

Béarn drinks the coffee the waiter has just brought. He lowers his voice.

'Look up there, next to the bar, in the armchair on the left. Pierre Aubert, a retired vet. He's reputed to be able to get an old nag to win. He was struck off after running into a spot of bother. But owners still consult him and he continues to supervise the condition of a number of horses. During race meetings, you find him in the stables or here, in the bar.'

Romero glances absent-mindedly at the horses coming onto the track for the second race. Tremor of excitement: there's a woman driver.

'Really? It's unusual, check in the bible.'

And Béarn proffers *Paris Turf*.

'Number 15. That's the one. An Englishwoman.'

'How can you recognise a woman under a helmet from such a distance?'

'The way she sits on the sulky, the way she holds her back, the set of her hips. There's no mistaking it. You recognise mares from the way they trot, don't you? I'm going to bet on number 15.'

'That's stupid. As far as I know, no woman has ever won at Vincennes.'

'All the more reason. You should do likewise. Things couldn't be any worse for you.'

Romero rises and goes over to buy his ticket from the window next to the bar. Two people ahead of him. Which gives him the time to check out Pierre Aubert. A ten-franc ticket, number 15 to win. It's 27 to 1.

The horses are ready, the starting signal is given... number 15 gets off to a good start... 15 is holding back, tucked into the main bunch... On the last bend, 15 pulls away and moves to the outside... It enters the last lap in third place. Once in the middle of the track, the driver goes hell for leather, releasing the horse's mufflers and the animal takes off, leaving the other competitors behind. As if they had stopped.

Romero laughs. Béarn, deep in gloom, not a single winner, once again, curses, with a tinge of respect for the winning gambler.

'Let's get back to business. There must be some heavies around on a racecourse like this!'

'Of course. Security guards at all the entrances, outside the stables, in the car parks.'

Romero gets to his feet. 'As you please...'

'Sit down. Here, with one phone call, vetted clients can bet huge sums on the races at Vincennes, but also up there.' He nods towards the telephone booths by the bar. 'At the bookies in London, you can imagine there are people who sometimes forget to pay. The client vetting department employs people whose job is recover the money. I'm asking you to be very discreet. I like this place, I couldn't live without it.'

'I have no reason to deprive you of it.'

'There are four of them. Two are always on duty. They're at the bar right now.' Romero flashes a look in their direction. Two tall, black-haired guys in dark suits. They're real thugs. That's what they're paid for. To scare people.

Romero gets up.

'Thank you Béarn. For the invitation, the meal, the company. I'm off, I don't want to jinx you any more.'

Romero goes up to the window to collect his winnings. Has a drink at the bar, next to the two thugs. They're deep in an argument with the vet about the chances of a horse in the next race. He's on familiar terms with them. As Romero picks up his change, he wonders if there's a way of chatting up the woman driver.

Sunday 1 October 1989

Daquin wakes slowly, there's no hurry, opens one eye, half asleep, then the other. Reaches over with one arm. Alone in the bed. Strains to listen, the sound of someone moving around downstairs. From the light filtering through the shutters, it must be a fine day. All the better, because this afternoon, the rugby season re-opens after the summer break. He stretches languorously. In a few hours, he'll be meeting up with his team-mates from last year, the locker-room banter, and put on shirt number 8. Then, first day of training, relaxed. Warming up on the pitch, a few passes, the first clashes. All his muscles beginning to work. The renewed pleasure of physical contact, the scrums, suddenly breaking away from the pack, violent dashes with the taste of blood in his mouth. And then, the locker room again, the warmth and intimacy of the showers, the dull aches and the sharp pains. The closeness above all. Enough to make him happy for a good while. Daquin rolls over in bed. This year, a new twinge of anxiety: and supposing, this afternoon, when the moment comes to dive into the scrum, supposing I'm afraid? Too old perhaps for this game? Don't want to have to give up, not now.

Daquin gets up, slips on a silk dressing gown and goes downstairs. Rudi, wearing a long, dark red Indian shirt, his immaculate blond lock over the corner of his right eye, is sitting on the sofa reading an Ismail Kadare novel that had been lying on the coffee table. I rather like him reading my books. Daquin goes behind the counter. Breakfast is all laid out on a tray: the coffee pot, two cups, a plate of bread drizzled with olive oil and tomatoes. Nice. He takes the tray, places it on the coffee table, kneels in front of Rudi, opens his shirt which is buttoned up to the neck, kisses his very pale pink left nipple, slowly draws the palm of his hand over his hairless, sculpted chest. Rudi distant, no reaction. He carefully does up the shirt again, sits down on the sofa, pours two cups of coffee and attacks the bread and tomatoes.

'Your friends from the security service came to see me the day before yesterday.' Daquin carries on eating. 'They know very well that I was in prison in the GDR, and that I still have contacts with the opposition there.'

Daquin smiles.

'It wasn't me who told them.'

'I'm sure it wasn't. They wanted to know why I'm living in France, and not in the GDR. I didn't tell them about you.' A silence. 'Your president's planning an official visit to the GDR in November and I've been told in no uncertain terms to behave myself until then.'

'That's not such a long time.'

'You have no idea what's going on back home. The mass exodus to West Germany is continuing, completely out of control. Every Monday evening, the Neues Forum organises a street demonstration in Leipzig, and the police turn a blind eye...'

'Yes, and Honecker's going to fall ill and a successor will be found.'

Rudi gets up, clearly annoyed. Beautiful legs under the Indian shirt. He goes behind the counter and makes some more coffee.

'Theo, I'm going to Berlin. I want to breathe the air of my own country, even if it is on the other side of the Wall. And in some way be part of...' he falters for a moment, '... the revolution that's happening there.'

Daquin stretches out on the sofa. An affair that began with the dizzying desire for a perfect body, that helped me cope with Lenglet's illness and to keep my head in the AIDS years. And now, the elegance of invoking the great tide of history to end a relationship entrenched in little daily pleasures and mutual respect, in other words, boredom. Like an *ex-voto*: Eternal gratitude.

'When are you leaving?'

'Tomorrow.'

'Come on then, quickly, let's get dressed. I'll take you for your last decent meal. I've got a meeting at three o'clock.'

Monday, Tuesday, Wednesday 2, 3, 4 October 1989

Check out the leads identified by Romero at the racetrack. Not difficult to track down the heavies from the debt recovery department who so terrified Béarn. Four Yugoslav cousins, the Dragoviches, who live together in a house in Nogent, run by a little old lady dressed in black, also Yugoslav, who acts as their cook, cleaner and nanny. Berry followed them on an intimidation and recovery operation. They don't seem inclined to metaphysical reflection and are confident that they are within their rights. So they don't take any special precautions, and don't watch their backs. They are sufficiently threatening not to have to resort to violence. On two occasions, they used the Mercedes belonging to the operating company without permission. They've probably had a set of keys copied. They bank at the Société Générale in Nogent. They have four individual accounts and a joint account, which they pay cash into fairly regularly. The last payment, of 50,000 francs, was made the day after the farrier's death.

'Leave them alone,' said Daquin. 'They're highly suspect, but there's no point going any further until we have some idea of who their boss is. And we know where to find them when we need them.

The vet is a trickier customer. First of all, he's hard to trail. He has a Golf GTI, drives fast and travels around a lot. Lavorel, Amelot and Berry, on duty round the clock with three cars linked by radio, managed to tail him for three days. Luxury apartment in Avenue Foch (in the car park, there's a Porsche, a Renault and a powerful motorbike, as well as the Golf GTI), a very pretty wife at least ten years younger than him, and two children, a girl and a boy, aged around five and seven.

He shuttles between a pharmaceuticals lab in Rouen, a stud farm near Lisieux, and a stables in Chantilly where he gives consultations. Breeders come from all over the region to show him their horses. He looks, examines, advises, hands out phials and various products (always unlabelled) and stuffs 500-franc notes folded in four into the breast pocket of his tartan lumberjack shirt, which he wears outside his jeans. He also visits the Vincennes racetrack stables, more folded notes, and finishes off the afternoon hanging out in the bar of the panoramic restaurant. Lavorel's team couldn't follow him there. And then at eight o'clock this morning, this hangar, in Rungis, not far from the big meat market. Sheet metal façade, locked. On one side, an office has been installed with a window and door to the outside. Across the whole width of the hangar, there's a sign: *Transitex, meat import and export*. Through the window, you can see a young woman bustling around, phoning, writing, filing. No sign of the vet. Around eleven thirty, a man parks his car outside the office, goes in and comes out half an hour later at the wheel of a refrigerated meat lorry. The vet comes out of the office shortly afterwards, gets back into his car and hares back to Paris. It is half past twelve.'

'Let's break off and see what the chief says,' decides Lavorel.

'What can a super-rich vet, who is on first-name terms with a bunch of hit men suspected of killing a drug trafficker, possibly be doing for a whole morning in a sleepy meat import-export company?'

'We'll tap Transitex's phones, no problem. As far as Aubert's personal residence is concerned, we'll have to wait until we've got a bit more to go on. As for the rest, Lavorel, you are just the man to answer your own question.'

Tuesday 3 October 1989

Eight horses to feed, muck out, groom and look after. Le Dem, in a check shirt, linen trousers and heavy shoes sets to work at six thirty in the morning. The best moment of the day. It's cool, the horses are calm, the work organised, methodical, no panics or arguments yet, and it's not too tiring.

At eight o'clock, Thirard comes to the outdoor school, a few metres away from Le Dem's loose boxes, with two breeders who show him some horses. Gimlet eyes, always on the alert, he watches a professional rider put the horses through their paces, at a walk, a trot and a canter, then taking the low jumps, without saying a word. Out of around a dozen horses, only one interests him, a slightly heavy iron grey, and he tries it on a higher jump. A fine performance. Thirard invites the breeders into the house to talk business over a bottle of wine.

At eleven o'clock, stable inspection. Thirard doesn't have a stables manager, he keeps an eye on everything himself, examines every stall and every horse with the groom in charge of it, runs a hand the wrong way over the croup to check it is clean, inspects the fetlocks and dispenses criticism and advice with the same authority he displays in the saddle. He is happy to listen to the groom's comments on the condition of this horse or that, and he is attentive to the reactions of his mounts, as long as they obey him. Nobody argues with Thirard's opinions or orders. Le Dem watches him at it. Ten years ago, if I could have really learned the profession properly, would I have ended up in the police? Almost certainly not. Better change the subject.

On reaching Le Dem's stalls, Thirard relaxes a little. After the inspection, the ghost of a smile, then:

'This afternoon, saddle up this horse for me and bring him to the small indoor school. I'll get him to jump.'

On the dot of three, Le Dem leads a big brown bay to the small school, concealed among the trees. Thirard is already there, waiting for him. It's the first time he's entered the school, which is completely closed off with no windows. Only one skylight in the roof lets in the daylight. In a box next to the jumps are bandages and a bottle of turpentine. He rubs the horse's legs. There's a strong smell. Le Dem coughs.

'Not used to the smell?' laughs Thirard.

Le Dem stammers, then carefully bandages the horse's legs.

'Get the whip and I'll set the bars.'

First of all the horse is allowed to canter freely around the ring a couple of times to loosen up. Then Le Dem drives it with the whip towards the hurdle, a few easy jumps. Thirard watches.

'He's a bit lazy with his forelegs. You have to make him pick them up.'

He constructs a much bigger jump with sharp black spikes on the top bar, then goes back to the centre of the school, holding a remote control. When the horse jumps, Thirard presses the button and the top bar is pushed up by two springs so that the spikes hit the horse's front legs. The turpentine heightens the pain. Several jumps, the whip is needed more and more frequently.

'Good, now the back legs twice, and that will be enough... Now, let's see the result.'

The bars are raised to the maximum height, without the spiked bar and without the remote control. A normal hurdle. Huge, thinks Le Dem.

'Keep up with the whip,' says Thirard. 'Don't miss him.'

The horse soars, legs folded to avoid the anticipated pain, its style impeccable. Perfect. They lower the bars, a couple of easy jumps without restraint. Thirard stops the horse which is coated in froth, its legs trembling.

'Hose his legs thoroughly and put cream on to soothe them.' Three or four little pats on the neck. 'A good horse. Groom him well, he's being put up for sale tomorrow and should do well.'

When Annick opens her front door, accompanied by Jubelin, Deluc is already there. He comes out of the kitchen, with his perpetual constipated half-smile.

'I got here a little early and I was chatting to your butler...'

He pauses ironically before the word 'butler', for emphasis. Annick, amused, (my relationship with Michel irritates him) walks over to the sofa and serves aperitifs. Deluc remains on his feet, leaning against the chimney breast.

'… we exchange a few thoughts on Nicolas's murder. Rather surprising, isn't it?' Silence. 'What are you going to do now, darling, who's going to feed your little habit?' Then, abruptly changing subject, he turns to Jubelin. 'Congratulations on the successful takeover bid for A.A. Bayern.' Annick glances briefly at Deluc. Was he in on it too? 'By the way, did Perrot talk to you about his luxury hotel project in Chantilly?'

'On Thirard's land?'

Annick jumps in surprise.

'Thirard, who owns the stables where we shot the ad? Do you know him?'

'Yes. A little. He's providing the land for the operation and Perrot the capital.'

'I'm in,' says Deluc. 'I'll reinvest my recent profits from the stock market.'

So he'd also been involved in the takeover bid.

'I'm not. The links between Pama and Perrot are too close, my personal involvement in the operation wouldn't go down well.'

Michel brings in a grapefruit and crab salad, served in the shells, places it on the plates and goes back to the kitchen.

Annick invites the two men to sit at the table.

'Suppose we move on to the serious business?'

Jubelin gets straight to the point.

'I and other company bosses are wondering about the effects of the measures taken at the Arche summit to clamp down on the laundering of drugs money.'

Deluc launches into a diatribe against the deathmongers and the danger they represent for civilisation…

'The new official line,' retorts Annick acerbically. 'Useful for reclaiming the moral high ground cheaply, in these times…'

'Don't act all virtuous, Annick, you're in no position to.'

Slight unease. During which Michel changes the plates and brings in a sauté of veal with leeks and raisins, Jubelin wonders why Annick is always so aggressive towards Deluc. Her childhood friend, she says, and so useful in his position…

A heated conversation about drugs money ensues. It touches on everything. True, these vast sums of cash risk causing international disruption and crisis. But the global economy also needs it, and besides, the Americans can make as much fuss as they like, but actually, when it comes down to it, they are the chief beneficiaries of the narcodollars. So, don't be naïve. And above all, above all don't interfere with banking secrecy on the pretext of fighting against dirty money, or the tax havens, which all businesses badly need. A section of the business community is worried about these two issues, seriously worried, and wants assurances. Message received, it'll be passed on to the necessary quarters who will act on it as they see fit.

When they rise to move on to coffee and liqueurs, the conversation switches to international politics.

Deluc embarks on a defence of Gorbachev, which amuses Annick. A few years ago, Deluc refused to shake a Communist's hand... Age, probably. And Jubelin is clearly sceptical.

'You know, we have associates in Munich who already have bridgeheads in the Communist countries...'

'The Munich correspondents of the Mori group who we met at Perrot's?'

'That's right. I guarantee that their contacts never go through official state channels, but through direct relations with very diverse and often rival interest groups. And our associates are banking on the implosion of the USSR and its satellites, not on the success of Gorbachev. I see it as a very tempting opportunity for Pama. The gambler and hunter in me, presumably.'

'But as for us, we have other concerns: European stability...'

They fix a date for an informal exchange of information between a few handpicked individuals.

Once they've left, Annick and Michel have one last drink, sitting side by side on the sofa.

'I'm getting old, Michel. Sometimes I feel as though I can't stand them any more, or perhaps I can't stand myself.'

'Stop feeling sorry for yourself. I like you indomitable.'

Wednesday 4 October 1989

Perrot is a man of punctilious habits. He lives in the penthouse apartment of the building he owns in Rue Balzac. A hundred square metres, Slavik-style interiors, done by Slavik, plus a fifty square-metre terrace with a view over the Arc de Triomphe, the Bois de Boulogne and La Défense, maintained by a landscape gardener. Every morning, at eight o'clock, his housekeeper brings him eggs, processed cheese, bread and his newspaper, *Le Figaro*. By this time, he is already up, she hears him showering in the bathroom. She brings him his breakfast in the living room or out on the terrace if the weather is warm enough. He has soft-boiled eggs with soldiers, the juice of two freshly squeezed oranges, and the cheese spread on the *baguette*. He drinks a lot of coffee. This is the only meal he eats at home, the routine never varies. There are no bookshelves in the apartment, he doesn't appear ever to read books, nor is there a desk, never any work documents. In the bedroom, a big radio, which he probably listens to before eight o'clock. A huge bathroom, with a round bath tub. And a living room dominated by television: two TV sets, several video players and a whole cupboard full of cassettes, which is kept carefully locked. He never invites anybody home.

Every weekday at nine o'clock, he goes down to the car park where his chauffeur is waiting for him.

After he has left, the housekeeper tidies up, does the washing (Perrot changes his clothes during the day), cleans the apartment and leaves at the end of the morning. For this work, six days a week, she is paid a full salary, which is why she says it's a good job, even though he generally tends to be rather rude: never so much as a good morning or a goodbye, as though she didn't exist. It's hard to take, day in and day out.

(Source: the housekeeper.)

At nine o'clock, Perrot gets into his car, a black BMW, the only car he owns, and is driven to his office in Rue de l'Université, a small private mansion set between a courtyard and garden, surrounded by high walls with a wide carriage entrance.

(Source: the chauffeur.)

His entire operation is in this building. He himself occupies a rather austere, medium-sized office on the top floor overlooking the garden. He never has any contact with the lawyers, architects, surveyors, designers and accountants who make up his staff. But he begins his day with a conversation with Dumas, his right-hand man, with whom he discusses everything, and who passes on his orders and ensures they are executed. The length of this conversation varies from one day to the next. For the rest of the day, Perrot works on his company's financial dossiers. It is always he, and he alone, who deals with the financial arrangements for his various business ventures. When he hands the dossiers over to the various departments, they are finalised. He receives a lot of telephone calls, vetted by his secretary, or on a personal direct line. Or on his car phone. He never holds meetings in his office, to which only Dumas and his secretary have access. His secretary believes he is the most powerful property developer in Paris. He specialises in renovating old houses and converting them into office buildings, mainly in Paris's 8th arrondissement. With residential space in this district worth about 20,000 francs per square metre, and office space around 80,000 francs per square metre, it's not hard to imagine the profits Perrot reaps from the dozen or so conversions he always has on the go. (*Given that my personal office space is five square metres, if I sold it at that price, I could contemplate retiring in two years.*) Furthermore, property prices in general have doubled in two years, which boosts his profits even further. At six o'clock, Perrot leaves his office.

There are only two exceptions to this strict schedule: from time to time, his chauffeur drives him to visit a building site with Dumas. And once a week, he has lunch in town. That is all. His secretary, a woman in her forties, rather unprepossessing, admits that her boss is authoritarian and rude, but he is also well-organised and not temperamental. She considers herself very well paid, and feels that all things considered, it's a very good job.

(Source: the secretary.)

Once a week, Perrot has lunch at Le Pactole, a classy restaurant on Boulevard St Germain.

(Source: the chauffeur.)

At Le Pactole, he has a table for two reserved. And there he meets a modest-looking woman, well into her fifties. He is attentive, pulls out her chair, chooses the menus himself (that day, fresh foie gras, a tureen of steamed scallops, cheese, pears cooked in wine). Their conversation is lively, he gives her the latest society gossip, she talks to him about the shows she's seen: lengthy account of the opening night of a concert at the Bastille Opera.

(Source: Inspector Romero, sitting at the next table, expenses attached.)

On leaving the restaurant, Perrot drives his companion back to her office. She works at the Paris City Hall planning applications department.

(Source: the chauffeur.)

This department deals with applications for change of use, for converting residential property to offices. In central Paris, developing office space at the expense of housing is prohibited. If you want to convert housing in one part of Paris, you have to obtain authorisation and compensate for it by converting office or industrial sites into housing elsewhere in the capital. And obtain permission from the Mayor of Paris for the entire operation. Mademoiselle Sainteny (Perrot's guest) is a lowly employee in this department: she registers applications, checks that they are in order, and passes them on to the appropriate department which makes the decisions. It normally takes six or seven months to obtain a reply. Which represents a major lost opportunity at a time when the price per square metre is doubling every two years. Thanks to Mademoiselle Sainteny, Perrot's applications are always on the top of the pile, and he receives a reply within two weeks. She is a sort of "application pusher", which has little risk attached, for there is no actual fraud involved, and which brings pleasant rewards: she, a low-down official on a paltry salary, a rather lonely spinster, has lunch once a week in an excellent restaurant, receives regular invitations to the opening nights of prestigious Paris shows, and, from time to time, little gifts – perfume, or leather gloves – which she shows off to her colleagues. Once, a rather smart suit. But never any money. Mademoiselle Sainteny therefore has a clear conscience and is perfectly happy.

(Source: Mademoiselle Sainteny's colleague.)

Every evening at six o'clock, the chauffeur drives Perrot from his office back home to Rue Balzac. There, the chauffeur parks the BMW in the car park, and awaits instructions. Perrot then goes up to the apartment on the first floor, where he has installed Madame Paulette who runs a call-girl network. There, for an hour or an hour and half, he has sex with one of the girls, the way other people go for a quick workout at the gym. And he always uses a condom. He asks them with whom and in what positions they had sex the night before, and gives them advice for the night to come. The girls, who often come down to chat with the chauffeur in the car park, don't complain about his ways because they are very well paid: a combination of a fixed wage and a fee for each trick. They often end the night in exclusive night clubs with Perrot's friends.

At eight o'clock, Perrot informs his chauffeur whether he's giving him the evening off or whether he wants to be driven into town for dinner. Dinners that are always in the expensive areas of Paris, and sometimes even at the Élysée. The chauffeur's job is therefore very demanding, but it will very likely enable him to open a bar-cum-tobacconists in his home town of Lyon within the next five years.

(Source: the chauffeur.)

After eight o'clock, if he's not dining in town, Perrot goes down to his restaurant, Le Chambellan, where a private dining room is reserved for him and his friends, sometimes one or two, often around twenty. He's a well-liked host, entertaining, elegant, excellent food and fine wines and spirits. He only invites men, and talks a lot of business. The guests shower the staff with tips. Aubert is a regular at these dinners, to which Jubelin is sometimes invited, along with many others whose names do not seem to have appeared in our files before.

(Source: the barman at Le Chambellan.)

Daquin closes the report on Perrot, signed by Romero who is sitting in the armchair facing him, waiting.

'Is this what's called a detective story?'

'I can copy out my notebooks if you prefer.'

'Don't get mad.' Smile. 'This report is perfectly satisfactory.' Glance at Romero's expenses form. 'I don't know Le Pactole. I'll check it out some time. Quite a character, this Perrot.'

Daquin falls silent and starts tinkering around on his computer. Romero gets up, goes and makes two coffees and sits down again. Daquin drinks his coffee, then:

'There are several points to be followed up.' Romero produces his notebook and takes notes. 'If I've understood correctly, Perrot's allowed to build new offices because he has previously converted industrial sites or offices into residential property. Is that right?'

'Right.'

'Where do these industrial sites come from? That's what you have to find out. And for that, it seems to me that it's essential to talk to either Mademoiselle Sainteny or her colleague. As for the office in Rue de l'Université, what goes on there is probably no more illegal than what goes on among all property developers. It's not within the remit of the Drugs Squad, and we won't nail him for that. What does interest us is of course Le Chambellan and its associated brothel, and the chauffeur is definitely a key person. Businessmen are always very talkative in their cars, they probably feel safe there. One of you must get as much gen on this chauffeur as possible. And I'd also like to know what he's up to with the girls who come down and see him in the car park.'

'Why? A man and one or several girls, doesn't that seem quite normal to you?'

'No.' Smile. 'Hopeless, you're a naïve guy, Romero. I want you to get inside that car park and see what goes one between six thirty and eight o'clock. Is that too much to ask?'

'Of course not.'

Thursday 5 October 1989

Lavorel sends the new boys to stake out Transitex, with instructions to establish an exact timetable of the company's operations, to be corroborated by tapped phone conversations, while he pays a visit to his former colleagues in the Fraud Squad to find out a bit more about Transitex.

A quick and easy task. A small family firm which belonged to a certain Jacques Montier until last year. It imported low-quality meats from South America, which were processed into dog food in an old factory. A year ago, the company was sold. Taken over by a property developer, a certain Perrot. Too good to be true.

'Stop. Why would a property developer want to get involved with a meat business?'

'Perrot split Transitex into two companies. He kept one of them, Transimmobilière, a real estate company, which took over the factory and the land it stood on, 10,000 square metres in the middle of Paris's 20th arrondissement. Then he demolished the factory and is building a housing development on the site. Let's do a quick calculation... the price Perrot paid for the whole of Transitex is lower than the sale price of 10,000 square metres of building land in the 20th. There are two possibilities: one, there was some restriction on developing the land which was removed after the sale, or the former owner is an idiot. In any case, Perrot's come off very well. We should talk to the lawyer.'

'Get me the details of this supposedly idiotic former owner. What about the other company?'

'It's kept the Transitex name and is continuing to import meat from South America. It's been bought by a certain Pierre Aubert.'

Lavorel listens to the new boys' report. Transitex's activities are perfectly legitimate and give little cause for concern. Around midnight, a meat lorry arrives from Rungis market. The driver parks the lorry in the hangar and leaves. The secretary arrives at nine o'clock in the morning. The tapped conversations reveal that she telephones customers – butchers' shops in the Paris area, no supermarkets or institutions apparently – to confirm or change their orders. Around midday, a driver collects the lorry, does the deliveries, then drives directly up to Le Havre where he reloads the next day. There is a rota of three lorries and four drivers. One lorry arrives at the company's premises each night. The secretary works every morning, six days a week. The company is closed in the afternoons. The vet only seems to pay rare visits. In short, a nice little business that seems perfectly uneventful.

'Import-export: I'm going to find out how customs clearance works at Rungis. And you, get in touch with a guy called Jacques Montier and ask him why and how he flogged Transitex to Perrot.'

At eight o'clock in the evening it's chaos in the customs house at Rungis. A constant stream of around fifty HGVs and a perpetual coming and going – drivers, vets in white coats and uniformed customs officers. The air is heavy with the cloying smell of meat. Lavorel eventually finds the man called Mariani with whom he has an appointment. Mariani starts off by looking through his files.

'Transitex, yes, I know them. Their lorry usually arrives around 11 p.m. Wait there. I'll come and fetch you as soon as it gets here.'

Lavorel, sitting in a corner, settles down to do a crossword.

An hour later, Mariani's back. He takes him to a lorry manoeuvring into the customs bay. Transitex. The driver switches off the engine and gets down from the cab. Holding a sheaf of papers, the customs official checks the door seals and watches the opening of the rear ramp. A vet in a white coat stands a little way back from the lorry. The doors open. The lorry is full of beef half-carcases hanging from hooks on a rail. On the floor of the lorry, under the carcases, are some large oblong cases.

The customs official and Lavorel enter the lorry.

'You see, all the documents seem to be in order: shipper Irexport, Dublin. Approved slaughterhouse in Killary, Ireland. I'll check a few carcases. Here, no problem, here's the Killary stamp.' He opens one of the cases, full of offal. 'You see, you can barely make out the stamps, but it's always the same with offal, the ink runs.'

'Is this what always happens? Nobody else comes near the lorry?'

'No, you can't load or unload stuff here. Now let's go down and see what the vet thinks.'

He is young and fairly disenchanted. He says OK. Mariani stamps a few documents, the driver locks up the lorry and moves off.

Lavorel turns to the vet.

'Can you tell me what your health check consists of?'

'You really want to know? I stand near the rear door when it's opened, but not too close, question of habit, to get a good whiff of the first wave of smells. I can tell whether it's fresh and clean or if the meat is warm. That's it. Otherwise, I have a very small budget for having samples analysed, and anyway, by the time you get the results, the meat has long since been eaten. There are two vets here for more than a thousand tonnes of meat. Have I answered your question?'

Lavorel backs away from this outpouring and takes Mariani aside.

'You can't rely on a health inspection to detect the presence of drugs, fair enough. But could you get your Irish friends to check the slaughter and shipping side of things in Ireland?'

Monday 9 October 1989

The two replies arrive on Daquin's desk more or less at the same time.

Jacques Montier left Paris with his entire family and set up as the manager of a seed merchant's in Annecy. Berry immediately buys his train ticket.

And there's no slaughterhouse in Killary. Irexport is merely the Dublin PO box of a company whose registered address is in Antigua.

'Right,' says Daquin, summing up. 'Transitex had commercial connections with Latin America. It is sold in vague conditions to a vet who traffics drugs and hangs out with hit men implicated in the murder of a coke dealer. Transitex is a front. We must be getting close to the guys at the top. And we have to be ready to swoop. I'm writing a report, but I'm not handing it over yet. I want to have some room for manoeuvre. And Lavorel, Amelot and Berry are investigating the entire Transitex operation. Now to Perrot. Property developer, mixed up in Transitex, partner in Pama, probably implicated, but we have nothing concrete. I'm slipping his name into the Transitex report, to see, that's all. And Romero will see if he can dig anything up on Perrot. Now, Le Dem, what have you got for us?'

Le Dem looks happy.

'I make a very decent groom, according to Thirard.'

'Is that all?'

'Not exactly.'

Le Dem launches into on a detailed account of his day-to-day work, including the bay horse's 'training' session. Irritated, Daquin wonders whether Le Dem's taking the piss or not.

'We aren't members of the animal welfare society yet, Le Dem.'

'Nor am I, Superintendent. You asked me for a report, I'm giving you one. Shall I go on?'

'Go on then.'

'Almost every week, Thirard sends a truckload of horses to Italy. He boasts to all and sundry that he sells them for several million. Now of the ones I saw leave, two are first-class racing horses, and the others are old nags, worth no more than the price of dead horsemeat.'

'What do the other grooms have to say about it?'

'That their boss is a crafty guy.'

'Does that sound convincing to you?'

'No. There's some sort of scam, but I don't know what.'

'First of all, let's perhaps try and find out where he sends his horses. If I get you a bug, can you fix it underneath Thirard's lorry before it leaves for Italy?'

'Of course.'

'We'll get to the bottom of this, sooner or later.'

Taxi, roads less congested than expected, Daquin arrives in Saint-Ouen early for his lunch with his friend Chamoux, editor of a major sports daily. He enters the Auberge du Coq on Chamoux's estate and is given a warm welcome. Downstairs, a medium-sized dining room, bay windows, vast mirror, yellow lighting with an orange glow, the overall effect luminous, white linen, small red hexagonal floor tiles, lots of plants. And countless cockerels, in all kinds of materials and colours. In a corner, a log fire burning in a hearth, slightly unexpected at the beginning of October, but actually rather pleasant from a distance. He'd been dining with Chamoux beside this same fireplace in the middle of winter, it must be about five years ago, when Samuel had come in. Chamoux knew him and introduced them. Samuel sat down at their table. He and Daquin left together. He's been living in the USA for nearly three years now.

'It's always a pleasure to come back here.'

The owner says thank you. There aren't any customers yet. Daquin chooses a table near the bay window. Chamoux arrives a little later, accompanied by a short, wiry man with a wrinkled face.

'Jean-Claude Hubert, France's top racing journalist. A brilliant writer... they call him the David Goodis of horse racing.'

Aperitif while they study the menu. One glass of champagne and two whiskies, accompanied by cubes of home-cured ham and parsley in aspic. Daquin is staunchly traditional, leek in a pie crust and coq au vin. The other two also go for classics, veal blanquette and pig's trotter. The conversation touches on recent scandals in the sporting world, Ben Johnson... Goodis junior remains silent, slightly vacant.

'Let's get to the point. What do you want, Theo?'

'I happen to find myself stumbling around the horse racing milieu, about which I know nothing...'

Goodis junior emerges from his silence.

'Are you from the Drugs Squad?'

'Yes.'

Aggressively: 'Those jockeys who were arrested two days ago, was that you?'

They seem to have got off on the wrong foot. 'No, nothing to do with me. That was the Chantilly gendarmerie. No connection with what we're doing. We operate on a completely different level. Wholesale trade only. With a few murders thrown in.'

'That's more like it. Because I find it unacceptable to lay into the jockeys, who have a very tough job and get stick from all sides, while the Paris rich set snort away to their hearts' content amid general indifference.'

Chamoux turns to Daquin.

'Precisely what is it you want to know?'

Start off as neutral as possible. 'I find it hard to tell the difference between what is usual practice and what isn't in these circles. For example, how is the price of a race horse determined?'

Goodis junior relaxes a little.

'There are no rules. The price of a horse is however much a buyer is prepared to pay. A horse can be sold for 50,000 francs by an unknown breeder, and a month later, the same horse can be sold for 200,000 francs by a fashionable dealer. Or a million by a famous rider. Besides which the market is fairly hard to pin down because most deals are verbal and transactions are paid in cash, like in the old days. Generally, there's no way of confirming rumours about the price a particular horse supposedly fetched.'

'Are there dealers who are in fashion?'

'Of course.'

Goodis junior mentions three names, including Thirard.

'Thirard? Near Chantilly?'

Goodis winks. The Superintendent's better informed than he's letting on. Watch your step. Don't get on the wrong side of Chamoux, he's useful, but don't grass on your friends.

'That's right, yes, near Chantilly.'

'I read in the papers recently that there's been a spate of stable fires in the area...'

Chamoux interrupts: 'That's not a matter for the Drugs Squad. It's more to do with insurance fiddles. A horse of no value, insured for a large sum, dies in a fire. Plus the insurance on the buildings. It's possible. Or property speculation. A good way of sweeping the board clean to build from scratch.'

'Charming.'

'No worse than anywhere else.'

Aggressive as ever, Goodis junior. It's beginning to annoy Daquin who asks: 'And is soring a horse usual practice?'

Now he's completely relaxed, to the point where he's almost smiling.

'All the professionals do it, but none of them will admit it. Fear of losing their customers. When you sore a horse, you inflict pain, and it jumps higher to avoid the pain. It doesn't go down well with horse-lovers, who find it barbaric. But it saves time, and therefore there's money to be made.'

'If a well-known trainer were to be shown on television soring a horse, would he be finished?'

'Probably not, but it would spark off a campaign in the racing press and among the animal welfare associations. That means he'd be in for a rough time.'

'Could that possibly be a motive for murder?'

Goodis junior looks taken aback.

'Quite frankly, I don't think so.'

'Do you know Pierre Aubert?'

'Hard not to. He published a book five years ago which I reviewed at the time. He believes that top-level competition has become so demanding for the horses that doping, which he calls "rebalancing the hormones", is a necessity. He went so far as to advocate that rather than a policy of prohibition which results in cheating, it would be better to have doping under veterinary control instead of allowing the breeders, trainers and riders to dabble unsupervised. Naturally it triggered a massive controversy. And a few months later, he was struck off on some pretext or other.'

'And what does Aubert do now?'

Curtly: 'I don't know, I've lost touch with him since. He's probably moving in different circles. I have to go now, I have a meeting. Thank you for lunch.'

Goodis junior rises and leaves.

'Didn't I mention that he doesn't like cops?'

'So I gather.'

'By the way, I heard from Samuel recently. He's still in the USA. At the moment he's doing a documentary on Carl Lewis and the Santa Monica Track Club's training methods.' Chamoux pauses, smiles. 'A nice way of mixing business and pleasure. After which he's coming back to France...'

Daquin looks up from his plate, suddenly interested, no point disguising the fact.

'... He asked me if you're still alive.'

'Good question. I think so.'

Coffee, brandy, the bill.

'Well, did you get what you wanted?'

'Yes, and even a bit more.'

Tuesday 10 October 1989

Superintendent Daquin is due to arrive in fifteen minutes. Annick paces up and down her office smoking. You've got to put on a good performance my girl. This Daquin, his expression, his tone of voice… she can still hear: "*Hard to believe, Madame*". As if he had undressed her. Like the other guy. Don't think about him. Cigarettes aren't going to be enough.

Intercom: 'Superintendent Daquin and Inspector Romero are here.'

'Ask them to wait a minute.'

She opens her desk drawer, cuts a line of coke directly on the polished steel surface, with a firm hand, snorts it, then retouches her make-up. Today, I'm staying in control.

'Show them in and bring some coffee.'

As they enter, she waves them over to the sofa.

'You know your way around. Make yourselves at home.'

Then she gets up, perches on the corner of her desk swinging one leg, facing Daquin who stares at her with his penetrating dark brown eyes, his elbows on his knees, hands clasped. A slight tightening of the chest. He knows I've just done a line.

'What can I do for you this time, Superintendent?'

'We're still investigating Berger's death and cocaine isn't the only thing we've found in his past. We have a few more questions we'd like to ask you.'

'Go ahead.'

Daquin moves towards the video, without asking her permission, and inserts a cassette. Annick reacts sharply.

'You seem to think that my office and video are at your disposal, fine, but my time is very limited.'

The video images flash past. A horse running free, goaded by the whip, jumps over bars covered in spikes which lacerate its legs. Pretty brutal stuff.

'The camerawork isn't brilliant,' says Daquin, giving Romero a big grin.

Not so bad, thinks Romero, recalling how he climbed onto the roof of the indoor school, waited two hours lying flat on his stomach next to the skylight, then the acrobatics to keep the horse continually within the frame. During which Daquin waited for him quietly just inside the forest.

Annick doesn't seem particularly interested.

'What are you driving at?'

'On this video, it's Thirard we see whipping the horse.'

Thirard again. Annick registers the name and watches more closely.

'The journalist who shot it, under cover of course, wants to sell it to television. Which would be very damaging to Thirard. And, incidentally, to the image of Pama because of its association with him.'

Annick leans towards Daquin, dazzling smile, husky voice:

'What exactly do you want, Superintendent? For me to buy this video from you for its weight in gold?'

Daquin carries on, unperturbed:

'No, not quite. The journalist showed this video to Berger, who probably told Thirard about it. Worse, Berger had made a list of around twenty horses that conveniently died a few days before the expiry of their insurance policy, and they were all insured by Pama. Here, I'll leave you a photocopy of the list we found in Berger's file. So he and Thirard certainly had several reasons for their violent argument, in front of witnesses, shortly before the murder. Had Berger mentioned this scam to you?'

'Never.'

'Had he told anyone else in Pama about it?'

Annick pictures Jubelin and Nicolas deep in conversation during the 14th July celebrations at Perrot's, then clamming up as she approached.

'Not to my knowledge.'

'Let me make myself clear. Berger's dealing cocaine, and according to witnesses, he sells the stuff to his work colleagues, in other words, at Pama. He is mixed up in shady dealings and scams, again in connection with Pama. We haven't managed to put our finger on anything yet, but we're moving forward. Logically, we think that his murder is linked to Pama's internal affairs, and as you were his direct boss and his friend...'

Annick stands up, frosty. And one of his customers, say it you bastard, seeing as you know.

'I know nothing about any of this and I'm sorry I can't help you at all. If you wish to see me again, Superintendent, you will need a warrant in future.'

In the lift down to the car park, Daquin turns to Romero.

'I'll be surprised if she doesn't react, but we'll have a job keeping tabs on her.'

Annick sinks down onto the sofa and thinks. First precaution, check the contents of that list. Of course I recognise Nicolas's handwriting, but that's not enough. A phone call to the appropriate department. A few moments to check. Thirard did indeed have an account with Pama. But it has been closed. There is no longer anything in it.

'Closed when?'

'During this current year, that's all I can tell you.'

Annick starts pacing up and down in front of the bay window. Something really did happen here, and someone knew about it. Nicolas? He wouldn't have closed the account. Someone else. Jubelin? Highly unlikely. I can't see why he'd be interested. A moment's reflection. And he'd have talked to me about it... Perhaps... Probably an accomplice of Thirard's in the department. What should I do? If I tell the police about it, I can kiss my career here goodbye. Talk to Jubelin? I can't bring myself to, and I don't know why. An instinctive wariness? Stop for a moment. She pours herself a whisky. Smiles. The sincerity of an alcoholic. Am I ready to put my career on the line in order to find out who killed Nicolas? Answer: no. There's only one thing to do, get back to work and forget about all this.

She attacks the file sitting on her desk. Draw up a provisional corporate communications budget for 1990 – advertising, advertorials, sponsorship and veiled incentive gifts to journalists. It has to be a bigger spend than last year because now the stakes are higher. And the income figures have got to be recalculated now that Jubelin has been made CEO. He can finance his personal publicity from the company purse, whereas in 1988–89, he had to do it from a slush fund. And now she has to evaluate and reattribute the amount spent from this secret fund and produce a proposal for Jubelin.

Annick bashes away at her computer, goes straight into the accounts of Sotopa, a financial company registered in Guernsey managed by one of Jubelin's former chartered accountants, Anglerot, whose sole job is to manage the secret funds which Jubelin devotes to promoting his own career. Anglerot, Annick and he are the only people who know of its existence.

Annick works for a while, takes notes, then stops, intrigued. She hunts for the list Daquin left her. Third column, the dates of payments. She checks Sotopa's accounts. The day after each payment to Thirard, a cheque equivalent to exactly 90 per cent of the sum is paid into the slush fund. Origin: a financial company in Luxembourg.

She sinks back in her chair. She needs to think about this. It seems as if Jubelin has been running an insurance scam with Thirard for two years, and is using it to sustain his secret fund. What difference does this make? Probably not a lot. A secret fund is always financed from rather dubious sources. And yet... in agreeing to this kind of a swindle, Jubelin is putting himself at the mercy of this Thirard. A horse dealer. Another world. It's dangerous. Why has he never told me about it? A memory, the other evening: *do you know Thirard?...* A bit... He's wary of me. If he's keeping Thirard from me, what else is he hiding? Come on, wake up, it's looking more and more as if Jubelin is connected to Nicolas's murder in some way. Hard to swallow, even so.

Back at her apartment, Annick crosses the vast living room decorated in subtle browns, leather, lots of plants. Gazes at the right wall which is covered from floor to ceiling in drawings in every different style, ranging from French eighteenth-century red-chalk sketches to contemporary works, all tastefully framed. Deliberate disorder. Michel's wonderful way of choosing, sure of himself: I like this, I don't like that, this must go here. Whereas I haven't a clue what I like, I have no taste. But what Michel does is perfect, and I feel good in this room. In the bottom left-hand corner is an Indian ink drawing: a full frontal picture of Annick, walking, relaxed, her hair streaming in the wind, a long duster coat, tight trousers, cowboy boots, and two big colts hanging from her belt. Michel did it a couple of years ago, when Jubelin and she had just decided to team up with the Italians to take Pama by storm. A wink at her image. 'Onwards and upwards!'

For the moment, Michel is on the patio, weeding and dead-heading the flowers. The French window is wide open.

'Come back in, Michel, I'm cold.'

Annick pours two whiskies. They sit side by side on the sofa. After a while, Annick says, in a neutral voice:

'Unfortunately, there's a possibility that Jubelin might be mixed up in Nicolas's murder.'

'Indeed.' Michel takes two slow slugs of whisky. 'Don't you feel like taking a holiday? I'll finish off my commission and we'll go to New York. There's a wonderful photo exhibition at MoMA, and we'll mooch around the art galleries and second-hand shops. It's just the place for you, you know.'

'I can't go away.'

'Actually, nor can I.' A silence. 'What are you going to do?'

'First of all, I'm going to tell Jubelin how I booted the cops out of my office. That'll reassure him, and it'll give me time to think how to handle this. And then I'll discreetly start looking for a potential successor. The cops already know a lot about him, in my opinion, and he's got himself mixed up in some nasty business. It won't be long before he jumps. I don't want to jump with him.'

'Remind me who that crazy fool was who claimed that women were fragile creatures?'

Annick smiles, sprawled on the sofa, her head on Michel's shoulder, her eyes half closed, letting herself drift as she finishes her whisky. A delicious moment of floating.

'Go and have your bath. When you come out, dinner will be ready.'

Wednesday 11 October 1989

Thirard's lorry left in the night for Italy with eight horses on board and a bug under the chassis. It's Le Dem's day off, and he and Daquin are waiting in the office for news.

'Any trouble fitting the bug?'

'Not really.' A broad grin. 'I hid and had to fumble around in the dark. It was like playing hide and seek when I was a kid. Back in Brittany. It wasn't at all what I imagined a police officer's job to be. I'd anticipated something more… dignified.'

Daquin leans back in his chair, his feet resting on the edge of the desk.

'You are very dignified, Le Dem, I assure you.'

Then he becomes absorbed in a fat dossier he's had compiled on Pierre Aubert. Press cuttings, the book on horse doping, a few articles in the racing press when he was struck off. The thrill of the chase.

Le Dem is ensconced in an armchair, snoozing.

Telephone. Daquin picks it up. The lorry has entered Italy via the Mont Blanc tunnel. Now it's over to the Italian police.

'Let's have lunch.'

Mariani arrives at Transitex's office at 9 a.m. and shows the secretary his ID: under Article 65 of the Customs Regulations, I have come to inspect your company's accounts.

The secretary panics slightly:

'Have I made a mistake?'

'Not at all, Mademoiselle. It's just a routine check. Customs are carrying out a concerted operation on all the meat import-export companies in the Rungis area. As I'm sure you'll understand, at present, with the new EU regulations, hormones in meat... just let us use a quiet little office and my colleague and I won't disturb you at all.'

'There's only one office here, and that's mine.'

'What about that one?' Mariani points to a door at the back of the room.

'That's a little laboratory where our manager, who's a vet, regularly comes to do quality controls.'

'I see. Well, my assistant and I will work at this little table and we'll be as discreet as possible.'

Mariani and Lavorel sit down opposite each other.

'First of all, give me your correspondence with Irexport, your supplier. I already have the customs clearance certificates. I'd also like your drivers' delivery permit books and bills of loading. And your customer orders. We'll look at the accounts another time.'

They work quietly, passing the documents back and forth. In the same room, the secretary carries on with her day-to-day work without showing any visible anxiety.

Lavorel works in silence. He soon becomes excited when he comes across deliveries made in Vallangoujard, to a certain Amedeo. The name doesn't matter. Roughly once a week. Suddenly, an image. The cold store in the ruined farm. A glance inside, two half carcases of beef hanging... Not very efficient on that occasion. I'm not necessarily going to tell the chief about it.

'You wouldn't happen to have any reports of checks carried out by your vet, would you?'

'No. Should I?'

'It's not compulsory. Does the vet come often?'

'Around once a week.'

I'll make do with hypotheses for the time being. To sum up: it's not always the same driver who delivers to Vallangoujard. The drivers' rotas seem regular, and unconnected to the delivery destinations, which would seem to exonerate them if there is some sort of trafficking going on. Vallangoujard disappeared from delivery records three weeks ago. That figures. Check all the deliveries made by the same lorry on the same day as Vallangoujard, over the last year. Eliminate the regular customers, those who receive other deliveries. Appearance of a destination that only receives one delivery a week, at the same time as Vallangoujard: a certain Roland, at Chantilly, same address as Thirard. Moments like this make a cop's life worth living. The next delivery should take place next week. A note to Mariani: I've got what I need.

'Right,' says Mariani, 'it's time for a drink.' The secretary glances at her watch: eleven o'clock. I don't know, public employees... 'Thank you again for your cooperation. Everything is in order for the moment. I'm not able to say when we'll be back to go through the accounts.'

'It doesn't matter.' Smile of relief. 'I'm here every morning.'

Outside, Mariani taps Lavorel on the shoulder:

'Let's go and have that drink, and you can tell me all.'

A glass of white wine for Mariani. A tomato juice for Lavorel, under Mariani's reproachful eye.

'Well?'

'I've found evidence of regular deliveries to the middle man we've already identified. I'll have to talk to the chief, but I think we're onto them.'

'I've stuck my neck out, Lavorel.'

'I owe you one. I'll return the favour whenever you want.'

In Annecy, Berry's having a drink in the garden of a canalside bar with Montier, a short, rather tubby man with a round, open face.

'Yes, I sold Transitex, and believe me, I have no regrets. My life in Paris had become a nightmare. The business wasn't going too well. I was working myself into the ground to keep it afloat and living in a perpetual state of anxiety. On top of that, some friends took me to the races and I had the odd flutter, out of jitteriness perhaps. I met Aubert at Vincennes. And then one thing led to another and I began to gamble larger sums. Aubert lent me money several times. To thank him, I gave him a bit of space at Transitex. A classic story, one day I had a dead-cert tip, I borrowed quite a large sum of money from Aubert, among others, and of course the horse didn't win. Total disaster. I received threats, I didn't dare go home, I was on the verge of killing myself, I'll spare you the details. In the end, I told my wife everything, and she took charge of things. We sold Transitex, Aubert found us a buyer within a few days, a man called Perrot – an estate agent I think –, who was interested in the factory land. I was able to pay off my debts and we moved here. A very pleasant lifestyle, fishing, hunting, a bit of swimming and skiing in winter. And my wife won't let me out of her sight. Bliss, you see. I wouldn't dream of pressing charges or anything like that.'

Romero arrives quite early in the Paris city hall canteen where the planning permissions personnel eat. He sweet-talks the waitresses and is allowed to wait by the cash desk. One of them promises to point out Mademoiselle Sainteny, who is well-known for her affability. Lavorel has lent him a blue blazer that's a bit too tight for him, a white shirt and a tie that makes him look very rigid but allows him to avoid suspicion skulking behind the cash desk with his sensibly laden tray (a little luxury, a half-bottle of Bordeaux, just in case).

Mademoiselle Sainteny arrives with three of her friends. She helps herself – a simple meal, mixed salad, yoghurt and fruit – pays and heads towards the tables. Romero follows and speaks to her softly before she sits down:

'I'd like to have a quiet word with you, can we eat together?'

She stares at him, apologises to her colleagues, and they go and sit in a far corner. Mademoiselle Sainteny is a little tense and anxious. She is in her own little happy bubble, and has the vague feeling that anything out of the ordinary could be a threat. Romero immediately sets about putting her at ease. He smiles at her, flings his tie over his shoulder so as not to get food on it, and says in a confidential tone:

'I am a journalist...'

He waits a moment. As Mademoiselle Sainteny shows no interests, he goes on:

'I'm doing a big feature on Monsieur Perrot. He doesn't like talking about himself very much, out of modesty no doubt. But he told me to come and talk to you. According to him, you've helped his career enormously. He's very fond of you, too.'

Mademoiselle Sainteny blushes with pleasure, her head bent over her plate. Romero pours her a drop of Bordeaux and she does not protest.

'You see, with this article on Perrot, I'd like to show how in a liberal society, it is always possible to grow rich through hard graft and thrift.'

Mademoiselle Sainteny looks up at Romero. The touching gaze of the short-sighted. No glasses. Vanity?

'That's exactly what I think.' Romero inwardly berates himself with 'you bastard'. 'What do you want to know?'

'I know about Perrot's childhood, father a farm labourer, he was one of ten children. Sent out to work at the age of thirteen, enlisted in the army at eighteen.'

He pauses for breath, a little worried all the same.

'I had no idea.' Full of admiration.

Relieved. 'He's a man of great reticence. Now he's one of the biggest property developers in Paris. He's known as the Emperor of the Golden Triangle...'

'That suits him very well, the Emperor of the Golden Triangle...'

'Doesn't it?' A knowing smile. 'What I don't know, is how he obtains the authorisations for the major conversion schemes that have enabled him to own so many office buildings in the 8th arrondissement. When I asked him, he told me to come and talk to you.' Another drop of Bordeaux.

'Well it's quite simple. A real stroke of luck. In 1981, the Bastille district was not much in demand. And the furniture makers of the Faubourg

Saint-Antoine were having a very tough time. They sold off their workshops cheaply, and not many people were interested. He bought up a lot of those workshops during the summer of '81, to renovate them. And then, in the autumn, President Mitterrand launched the Bastille Opera scheme. The price per square metre more than quadrupled within a few months. So Monsieur Perrot converted his workshops into apartments, sold them and transferred his planning authorisations to the 8th arrondissement.

'And it's still going on, eight years later?'

'You know, with a good architect and a good lawyer, you can multiply an area almost infinitely.'

Romero looks at her, suddenly baffled. Is the old dear naïve? Not to that extent... As Daquin says, never underestimate women... Even spinsters.

She blushes again.

'Everybody knows that. By the way, you didn't tell me what paper you work for?

'*Le Pèlerin Magazine.*'

At five o'clock in the afternoon, almost every member of Daquin's team is there to report back on the day's activities when the Italian police telephone. The horses have been delivered to a stud farm outside Milan. One of the best race horse breeding centres in Italy. Which belongs to Ballestrino, a wealthy Milanese owner and breeder.

'Known and respected, this Ballestrino?'

'Of course. Financial advisor to some of our biggest companies...'

'Like the Mori group?'

'Yes, among others. And we have nothing in our files about him.'

There is a clear note of reprimand in his voice. Daquin thanks the Italians, promises to stay in touch and hangs up. He turns to Le Dem:

'You swear that Thirard's horses aren't highly valuable star horses?'

'Listen, Superintendent, I know something about horses. These are mediocre. Besides, I had a look at their documentation when they were being loaded onto the lorry. More than humble origins. Of no interest to a breeder of thoroughbred racehorses.'

Amelot clears his throat. Daquin looks at him, amused.

'Be brave, you can speak, nobody's going to bite your head off.'

'While I was cross-checking all the names in the files... Ballestrino had two horses running at Longchamp on 9ᵗʰ July when Paola Jiménez was murdered.'

A thrill. It takes a moment for the information to sink in.

'We're going to have to bust a gut.'

Thursday 12 October 1989

'The dates of Transitex deliveries to Chantilly tally with the departure dates of Thirard's lorry for Italy. We're going to bring Transitex down, taking a few precautions in case things go wrong, of course.'

'If we act now, we'll never incriminate Perrot and Pama.'

'I don't see it that way. Listen carefully. Ballestrino, Perrot and Thirard are part of Jubelin and Pama's entourage, where we also find Nicolas Berger and Annick Renouard. The detective's ABC tells us that such coincidences are no accident. Right. But we don't know how these different pieces fit together. For the time being we have hardly any evidence to implicate all these good people, and, as they are cautious, we won't easily find anything. Our only chance is to take the initiative and force them to react. Which we will do in bringing down Transitex. Convinced, Lavorel?'

'Not really.'

'Too bad, I'm sorry, but I've made up my mind. We'll review the situation afterwards. The delivery should take place during the coming week, but we can't be sure of the date. So we'll keep Transitex under surveillance. And if the vet puts in an appearance within the expected time frame, we'll pounce. Now, open your notepads, we're going to organise this down to the last detail.'

Thursday 19 October 1989

Amelot and Berry have been taking turns to watch Transitex round the clock for a week. This morning, the vet arrives at eight o'clock, parks his Golf and vanishes into the office. Amelot calls Daquin: 'He's here.'

'OK, let's go.'

When the refrigerated lorry emerges from the hangar, around midday, Romero and Amelot set off in pursuit, following it on its delivery round in the Val-d'Oise, then on the road to Chantilly. Shortly after Beaumont, Romero overtakes and cuts in front.

'Police.' Climbs in next to the driver. 'Follow that car.'

The driver, stunned, anxious: 'What have I done, what's going on?'

Romero, aloof, no explanations: 'You'll find out.'

The car and the lorry move off and pull into the yard of the nearest gendarmerie. There, Daquin, Lavorel and Berry are sitting on the bonnets of their cars waiting for them. Arms folded and grim faced. Uniformed gendarmes everywhere. The driver's stomach lurches. Romero and Amelot stand either side of him.

'Stay there and keep quiet.'

Lavorel slips a long white coat over his clothes, puts on a pair of rubber gloves and opens the rear door of the lorry. There are only five cases of offal left, to be delivered to Chantilly. Romero helps Lavorel lift them and carry them into a small room off the yard, followed by the whole group surrounding the driver. Heavy, very heavy these cases. They put them down on a long table where a whole set of nickel-plated instruments has been carefully laid out. It's important to set the scene, Daquin always insists. The driver is torn between panic and curiosity. Lavorel opens a case, pushes aside the hearts and other offal, and pulls out a strong plastic sachet full of compressed white powder, wrapped in bloody intestines. Around twenty kilos in weight. Relief. After all, it might not have been there. Don't give anything away. The driver thinks he's going to pass out. Each case in turn delivers up its packet of cocaine. Around a hundred kilos in total.

'Weigh them exactly,' says Daquin. 'You never know. Thirard might be helping himself to some of it on the way.'

Romero grabs the driver by the arm and drags him into an adjoining room, and Lavorel sets to work. After carefully washing a packet of cocaine, he makes a little incision in the sealed edge of the bag. With surgical tweezers, he inserts a bug deep inside the packet, while removing an equivalent volume of powder. He puts it carefully aside, it might always come in useful. Quick flashback to Romero-Tarzan and his mate Blascos. Come back whenever you like, guys. Repeats the operation on the other packets. Then he seals them again, as neatly as possible with the bag sealing machine brought along specifically for that purpose.

In the neighbouring room, Romero taps the driver amiably on the shoulder.

'Doesn't look good, my friend.'

'It's nothing to do with me. I had no idea there were drugs on board. I'm just the driver, that's all.'

'That's what they all say. And you're going to have plenty of time to prove it. If it's true, of course. Meanwhile, you'll be banged up. Unless...'

'Unless what?'

'You cooperate with the police.'

'Hold on, I keep my nose clean and I have a family. With all they say about drug dealers...'

'There's no risk attached to the offer I'm making you. You're simply going to make your delivery as though nothing had happened.'

'And then?'

'And then you'll drive the lorry to a police garage at an address we give you, and you'll stay there until tomorrow morning. That's all.'

'Looks like I don't have any choice.'

'I'm fixing a microphone to the inside of your overalls. While you're making your delivery, we'll be listening to everything, and we won't be far away. So no funny business. Don't try and switch it off, either. If there's the slightest break in communications, you're going straight to jail, and for several years. If everything goes smoothly, tomorrow you go home and you'll never hear from us again.'

Half an hour later, the carefully reconstituted cases of offal are delivered to Thirard by a nervous, mumbling driver, to whom nobody pays the slightest attention. Daquin and his inspectors concealed in the forest a few hundred metres away check the presence of the bugs on their control monitors. Phone call to the Drugs Squad. Phase one accomplished. Embark on phase two.

Night of Thursday 19 October 1989

At 10 p.m., the bugged horse lorry leaves Thirard's stable. Romero, Daquin and Le Dem, who has come to join them after work, follow it at a distance as it heads for Paris. Lavorel stays in the vicinity of Thirard's place, and the new boys return to HQ.

The lorry turns onto the Paris ring road at Porte de la Chapelle. Takes the exit for the motorway to the south. Two Drugs Squad cars join the one being driven by Romero. They drive in convoy, keeping a good distance. Speed between ninety and a hundred kilometres an hour, two men in the lorry, nothing to report.

At thirty-five minutes past midnight, the lorry turns into a service station, heading for the petrol pumps. Now's the moment. Bullet-proof vests, guns at the ready. This is it, thinks Le Dem, it's war. I can't do this. I'm scared, but it's exciting, for sure. One of the Drugs Squad cars drives past the service station and positions itself so as to block off the exit onto the motorway. The other two cars drive slowly onto the forecourt. The lorry pulls up by a diesel pump, a man gets down and starts filling up. Romero draws up alongside the lorry on the other side of the pump. The third car screeches to a halt under the nose of the lorry, blocking its path. It's the signal. All the inspectors leap out brandishing their guns. Romero points his gun at the man standing by the pump, Daquin just has time to open the passenger door and fling the man to the ground, when a third man whom nobody had spotted – he'd probably been sleeping in the back – begins spraying the cops' cars with a submachine gun in one hand, while with the other he wrenches the gears into reverse and the lorry roars off with a screech of tyres. The cops shoot at the lorry, causing it to sway. The horses are whinnying and kicking against the sides, the lorry accelerates, leaving behind it rivulets of blood on the road. Diesel gushes from the blasted pump, spreads on the asphalt, stinking, slippery. And flammable. Total bedlam. Vehicles damaged, two cops wounded, one of the crooks lying on the ground, the other takes to his heels. The lorry gathers speed and – instinct or quick thinking – reverses back up the slip road instead of heading for the exit. Daquin lets out a yell and rushes after the fugitive. A shadow running, too far away. He pulls out his gun from deep in his jacket pocket. Just the time to think one day this thing's going to go off in my face, and he shoots. The shadow vaults the fence and disappears. Daquin spots a dark stain on the asphalt, feels it with his fingertips, it's wet and sticky, sniffs. Fresh blood. A piece of luck, he's wounded, definitely not by me. Walks up to the fence, which is sagging a little. On the other side, a ploughed field. He goes back to the service station. Le Dem drags the wounded men out of range of the diesel jet. The third team pursues the lorry on the motorway, shooting at the tyres and bursting two. The lorry swerves and crashes into the central reservation. Barely slowing down, the cars and HGVs weave around them to avoid the shooting and the accident. In the service station, the drivers who've stopped to refuel see the bullet-riddled cars, two injured men and another in handcuffs lying on the ground, stare round-eyed and drive off without pausing. The service station manager has switched off all the lights.

'Romero, take someone with you and bring me back the third man, dead or alive. I'd rather have him alive, but dead will do. That way, the field over there.'

A lengthy and thorough search of the ploughed field. Hard work advancing over the furrows, and it is a very dark night, far from the lights of the capital. Cautious approach towards a dark mass slumped in a hollow. The man has lost consciousness.

When the two cops return carrying the injured man like a sack, they find the service station looking like the aftermath of an urban war. Police cars and fire engines everywhere, blue lights revolving ominously. The damaged lorry has been towed back to the service station forecourt by a breakdown truck. The fire-fighters have stemmed the diesel leak and are pouring mountains of sand around the pumps. The fumes are suffocating. The two injured cops and Romero's prisoner are driven off in an ambulance and the two other prisoners locked in an armoured van with barred windows. Four horses have been herded together on a square patch of grass a little way away, and two dead horses are lying in a pool of blood a little to one side.

'They were very badly injured, one had the jugular severed and the other, two broken legs. I put them out of their misery,' says Le Dem.

'Don't apologise,' says Daquin. 'As long as you haven't finished off our colleagues...' Romero gives a nervous laugh. And now, we have to find the cocaine. By 5 a.m. at the latest. We've got three hours left.'

The remaining Drugs Squad cops start pulling the lorry apart. Engine, wheels, petrol tank, seats, chassis, the lining of the bodywork. Nothing. They become increasingly edgy. The receiving device has been destroyed by bullets, but when the lorry turned into the service station, the cocaine was still on board. Or at least the bugs were. A shudder of anxiety.

Le Dem, standing aloof, gazes at the bodies of the horses.

'Get up off your ass Le Dem and come and help us.'

He appears not to hear but leans over the croup of one of the dead horses and lifts its tail.

'This is where the coke is.' Daquin and Romero come over. 'Look, it's a mare. Her vulva's been sewn up.'

Le Dem crouches down, takes his Opinel knife out of his pocket, cuts the thread, thrusts his arm into the mare's vagina up to his shoulder and brings out a blood-streaked plastic sachet full of compressed powder. There is a huge sense of relief. Daquin sits down on a kerb. Romero gives the bloodstained Le Dem a hug.

'What do you feel like, a butcher or a midwife?'

Then he goes over to a car phone, forcing himself to speak calmly. It is twenty past four. Lavorel's on the other end.

'It's over. We've got the goods and the delivery men.'

'Can we launch phase three?'

'We can.'

At 6 a.m., a team from the Drugs Squad picks the lock of the empty Transitex office and swarms in. Another arrests the Dragovich cousins and carries out a search of the racecourse, and a third quietly picks up the vet from his home.

At the same time, a young investigating magistrate accompanied by Lavorel and ten men as backup rings the bell of Thirard's house, a traditional-style stone farmhouse, away from the stables. After a while, Thirard comes down.

'Open up. Police.'

Thirard opens the door. He must have been in the middle of getting dressed. He's wearing jodhpurs, T-shirt and a smoking jacket. Lavorel stares at him intrigued. Calm, unperturbed, a totally expressionless face. The man Le Dem admires. Thirard checks their search warrant, then politely stands aside to allow the magistrate and police officers inside.

The search progresses without incident and without yielding anything of interest. Thirard lives alone in a comfortable house whose rustic style has been fairly well preserved, but without much personality. Nothing to report. Lavorel's bored.

Up to the office, which is in the converted attic. A huge bay dormer window has been put in the roof, and in front of it, stretching the entire length of the room, is a table. When he works there, Thirard has an unrestricted view of his stables. On the table is a computer, diskette boxes, and underneath, columns of drawers. Obsessive tidiness, not a scrap of paper or a pen lying around, not a speck of dust. While Lavorel opens drawers, Thirard sits down in a fauve leather armchair in a corner, and doesn't say a word. He waits, without impatience, and seems barely interested. Lavorel soon finds the records of his horse dealings. Kept with extraordinary meticulousness. Names of the horses, identification numbers, amounts, names of buyers consortia and vendors. Bank statements showing commissions paid and transfers, most of them to banks in Luxembourg. Same for the administration of his stables. Salaries, social security contributions, the horses' upkeep, VAT calculations. Everything seems to be accounted for down to the last cent. There are also the insurance policies for the horses, with Pama, and the payments of the premiums. They all died one or two months before their insurance policy expired, what organisation... and the compensation paid out by Pama. Watertight in the event of a tax inspection, and Thirard above suspicion. As long as one is unaware that part of his horse dealing is quite purely and simply fictitious. A glance at Thirard. Touching, in a way, this obsessive neatness and his determination to be above board. What would Le Dem say? Trying to convince himself that Thirard is truly, and solely, a major horse dealer? The magistrate orders some of the files to be taken away in boxes.

Lavorel carries on searching. Standing against the back wall is a big, heavy iron cupboard with a sophisticated lock system.

'It's open,' says Thirard.

So it is. At the back are five empty post sacks. And a sixth, tied up with a simple piece of string, which Lavorel undoes: stuffed with banknotes, small denominations of lire and dollars. On the outward journey, cocaine, on the return, money to launder. Put it through the bureaux de change leaving no evidence, then the half-laundered cash is paid into the various bank accounts without any difficulty. In this business, aren't the majority of payments in cash? It will be harder to establish whether some of the cash has stayed in France, and what it has been used for, or whether everything has gone back to the Italian partners. Need to dig further. Thirard hasn't moved a muscle. The sack of notes and the empty bags join the accounts files in the boxes to be taken away.

Friday 20 October 1989

There's a buzz of excitement at the Drugs Squad headquarters. The vet, Thirard and the Dragovich cousins have been taken into different offices. Daquin, Romero and Le Dem, reeking of diesel, mud and blood have gone to get changed. On their return, council of war in Daquin's office.

'Let's try to separate out the problems and define our objectives. First of all, the Italian ramifications. The three men stopped driving the horse lorry are known to the Milan police: some departments are keeping them under surveillance while others are protecting them. For the time being, we'll hold them. But without any hope of getting them to talk. We have nothing to bargain with. And it's a waste of energy and time trying to beat anything out of them. I'm absolutely convinced that Ballestrino is in this up to his ears. But I don't know what our Italian friends are going to decide.' A pause. 'Milan, capital of the north. The reputations of a fair sprinkling of Italy's financial elite are likely to be tarnished. Fancy a trip to Italy, Lavorel?'

'If you don't mind, chief, I think I've got plenty to keep me busy here.'

'Here. In Paris.' Groan. 'Too true. It's a bit soon to start crowing, we've still got a long way to go. At least we now have a proper motive for the

Moulin and Berger's murders. They must have got wind of the Italian trafficking connection. And it's very likely that the hit men who murdered them came from abroad and have probably already gone back. Almost impossible to prove.' A pause. 'Barring a miracle, we can hardly expect Aubert or Thirard to grass on their bosses. Too dangerous for them. Depressed?'

'Not yet.' Romero smiles. 'Go on chief, you're on great form.'

'So initially, we're going not going to aim too high. We'll see about Perrot and Pama later. Lavorel and Le Dem, you handle Thirard. Do what you can. The new boys can take care of the Dragoviches. Question them separately, make up any old excuse to justify their arrest, and whatever you do, don't mention Rouma's murder. I only want to know how they operate, how they organise their teams, and about their movements over the last month. With a bit of luck, one of them will be in the clear the day of the murder, and that will help us focus. Romero and I will deal with the vet.'

Thirard is sitting in a chair, his elbows on a table, in a tiny, windowless office, impeccably elegant as always and apparently unruffled. When Le Dem enters the room, slightly ill-at-ease, and comes and sits down opposite him, Thirard's eyes flicker.

'How did the cops manage to recruit such an excellent groom?

Le Dem smiles. 'I still do have a grandfather who bred draught horses.' A silence. 'But in my neck of the woods, it's hard to find work.' Another silence. 'My chief wants you to take the rap.'

'I think he'll succeed.'

'Sure. Unless I can help you.'

'Listen, Le Dem. My father was a jockey. The first time a trainer asked him to restrain his horse, he refused, and the next day he had a broken leg. After that, he did as he was told. Three years later, he lost his licence, because he'd taken part in a race that had been rigged. And he ended up broke, as stables manager for the trainer who'd fixed the race. I made the decision to get out of the racing world, to get away from the thugs. I easily found people to lend me money to get started, and I found out a little later, when one of my horses had all four legs broken in transit, that they were friends of friends of my father's. The day you turned up at my place, one of my stables had just burned down. Very delicate things, stables.' (Le Dem had a flashback of Thirard's grim face and heavy green Wellington boots pacing among the charred ruins. *I so wish I could believe him...*) 'Your chief can do what he likes, but don't expect me to cooperate, whatever happens.'

Romero takes down Aubert's particulars...

'Profession?'

'Veterinary surgeon.'

'Add "struck off",' says Daquin. 'A veterinary surgeon who's been struck off. Which is a pity. I've read your book on horse doping, it's a clever approach.'

Embittered smile, silence. A bit cack-handed, this superintendent. Not exactly subtle. So much the better for me.

Aubert's too sure of himself. He's within my grasp. End of the observation phase. Now, the chase is really on.

Aubert has a ready-made story. He went to Medellín two years ago on behalf of a French owner who wanted to import Colombian horses to set up a breeding operation in France. He was entertained by Don Fabio Ochoa himself, at his splendid stud farm. They signed a deal, and he came back with two mares and a stallion... and some contacts with the sons who invited him to set up a business, through one of their right-hand men, a certain Martínez, who's now gone back to Colombia...

A well-honed story, perhaps even partially true. Let it go.

'I thought the Ochoa family never worked with cocaine addicts.'

He raises an eyebrow.

'I'm not.'

Daquin gives him a sharp look. 'I thought the issue came up when you were struck off.'

'What if it did.' Smile. 'OK, I do occasionally snort. Do you think that makes my case worse?'

'Probably not. We'll come back to that later. Go on.'

Transitex, a detailed description of the operations, exoneration of the secretary and drivers... Daquin doesn't learn anything new.

'What about Thirard?'

'I don't know him. Martínez gave me the address I was to deliver to, and I didn't attempt to break the confidentiality.'

'But Thirard knows you. Let's go back to Transitex. What did you do in the lab?'

'I identified the boxes of offal and the carcases in which the powder was hidden, sometimes the mark had been obliterated. Then I supervised the loading into the lorry, and the documents. To make sure nothing went astray.'

'Of course. So you didn't touch the goods?' Silence. 'How come we found traces of powder in your lab this morning?'

'When the packaging's damaged, it has to be re-done.'

'And then for a coke user there's a strong temptation to dip into the goods.'

'I'm not suicidal.'

'Probably not, but perhaps you're too sure of yourself. As long as you shield your partners, as you're doing right now, everything's fine. They'll hire you a lawyer, look after your family, put your money in a safe place. Four or five years inside, and then you're free. But if they find out you've siphoned off some of the goods for your own use, how do you think they'll react?'

'Nobody will believe a word of what is obviously a police fabrication.'

Berry knocks at the door, enters and places a sheet of paper in front of Romero. The Dragoviches always work in pairs. Georges with Milon, and Boromir with Pierre. On the Monday of the murder, Boromir went to the dentist's in the morning.

'The Dragoviches have talked,' announces Romero, pushing the paper under Daquin's nose. 'They've confessed to Rouma's murder.'

'A farrier called Rouma.' Silence. 'Unluckily for them, there were witnesses. And Daquin gives a detailed account of the murder.

'When Georges and Milon realised they were in a tight spot, they admitted you had ordered the killing, for a contract of 50,000 francs,' adds Romero. 'What do you have to say about that?'

'I categorically deny it. Never heard of this Rouma, nor of his murder.'

'Think hard.'

Romero nudges a file towards Aubert, the new boys surveillance report, with all identifying features and signatures removed.

'Open it.'

Aubert opens it. A shock. Photos of his wife, in the street, in the doorway of their building, the children at school, in the park. Detailed schedules... times, journeys.

'I confiscated this report last night from Thirard's,' Romero continues. 'You can see where this is leading?'

'Not exactly, no.'

'The Mafia never works with anyone without taking precautions. Do I need to refresh your memory with a few recent stories?'

'No need.'

'So, make your mind up, Monsieur Aubert,' says Daquin. 'Either you admit to paying the Dragoviches 50,000 to kill Rouma and we accept your version of the motives behind it – your sentence will be a bit longer, but you'll still have your support, your money and your family – or you deny it. In which case, we will try and prove that you had Rouma killed because you were supplying him with cocaine stolen from the Colombians, and it had become dangerous. You know that we have solid evidence to back this up. And you and your family will be wiped out.'

There's a lengthy silence. Daquin rocks slowly in his armchair and Romero doodles on a blank sheet of paper. Then Aubert says in a low voice: 'I had Rouma killed.'

Not really that tough, but entertaining all the same.

'You know, Aubert, if it hadn't been for the murder, we'd never have been able to trace you.'

The Dragovich cousins' case is soon resolved. Aubert confesses, bank transfer, coshes and duplicate keys to the Mercedes found at their home, all that remains is for Le Dem formally to identify Georges and Milon without any qualms, and the case is closed.

When Daquin walks out onto the embankment, it's dark. He hadn't seen night fall, it is nearly 10 p.m.. On the go for thirty-eight hours, and a few very tense moments. And some very enjoyable ones. Exhausted, and a feeling of being profoundly alive. Walk home to Avenue Jean-Moulin via Montparnasse to experience the city at night, and sleep for at least twelve hours without a break.

Friday 20 October 1989

Deluc walks into Le Chambellan at around 10 p.m. and makes his way over to a small, secluded table at the back of the restaurant where Perrot is calmly waiting for him drinking whisky and smoking a cigar. In a foul mood, Deluc sits down stiffly. Perrot signals to the head waiter to serve him.

'I've left my wife to go on her own to a dinner hosted by the President of the Assembly, at the Hôtel de Lassay, one of the best tables in Paris.' Little smile. 'I hope you haven't ruined my evening for nothing.' The full gamut of condescending nuances to betray slight annoyance.

'You won't be disappointed.'

Perrot, grave, meticulously fills the glasses with red wine from a carafe.

'What's this about?'

'You know Pierre Aubert, the vet?'

'Of course. I've had dinner with him a couple of times here.'

They start eating.

'He was arrested this morning for cocaine trafficking.'

Deluc raises his eyebrows. Cocaine. Nicolas, Annick, and then a recollection, the phone call from the superintendent of the 16th arrondissement, your son... Nothing had come of it. A little thrill of pride. There's one law for the rich and powerful and another for everyone else. Not accountable to anyone, impunity guaranteed, you get used to it. Back to Perrot.

'What have Aubert's filthy habits got to do with me?'

'You weren't listening to me. Aubert isn't a cocaine user. At least, not only. He's a dealer.' He adds, seeing Deluc's puzzled expression. 'A serious dealer. His network stretches from Colombia to Italy, via Paris.'

A dealer, that highly respectable man whose company is rather enjoyable... Deluc has a feeling there's more to come. He snaps:

'The police are doing their job.'

'Absolutely, and I've nothing to say about that. Aubert's going to spend a few years inside. I'll take care of his family, and his lawyers.'

'A loyal friend.' Ironic half smile. 'Admirable. But aren't you afraid of being compromised?'

'Not really, at this point. Aubert organised his trafficking through a company, Transitex, which I used to carry out a major property deal.'

Deluc pales slightly and the half-smile is wiped off his face, along with the irony.

'Stop. I don't want to hear any more. Our collaboration concerns property dealings. I helped out a brilliant developer, a bit of an entrepreneur. The sort of man we need to shake up officialdom, reshape Paris and make it a European-class business capital. Occasionally bending the rules slightly, perhaps. The end justifies the means, as we used to say when I was young. But I'm not in any way involved with this drug trafficking business. And I don't even want to hear about it.'

'Cut out the fine talk about France's best interests, Christian. This isn't a party conference. I would put things a bit more simply. You've done me some huge favours, for which I've paid a very high price. But that's not all. Aubert didn't go down alone. Thirard was the number two in the ring, and he's also been arrested, caught red-handed.'

An abrupt silence. Deluc shudders. Thirard, the property investments in Chantilly, extremely compromising. Play for time. He takes a metal cigarette case out of his pocket. Slowly lights a cigarette. An Indian cigarette. He stares obstinately at the glowing tip.

'There's never been any question of drug trafficking between us.'

He looks up, meets Perrot's insistent, steely gaze. Feels an unpleasant tightening around his heart.

'Oh really? We met in Beirut, remember?' A nod. 'I wasn't exactly rolling in it at the time. A warrant officer's salary, no family, no inheritance. Seven years later, in Paris, I buy up half the Bastille district, mostly paid for in cash. Didn't you wonder where the money came from?' Silence. 'And the suitcases I got you to carry for me? Cash again. Still no questions?'

Another silence. I knew it. I've always known that this had to happen one day, disaster... The waiters bring the desserts. Don't lose your grip. Take this blow on the chin and do away with Perrot at the first opportunity.

'What do you want from me?'

'That's better, now you're being reasonable.' The tone he uses to talk to the girls. Deluc doesn't react. 'Besides, I'm not asking much of you. I've taken my precautions, obviously. I sold off Transitex ages ago, legally too, there's no way I can be implicated in the company's activities. But my name is likely to come up in the Thirard case, and so is yours. And I want to avoid a zealous cop using it as an excuse to come and poke his nose in our business. You know as well as I do that it's very complex and not always completely above board. In other words, delicate. This is what I want from you. The cop who arrested Aubert and Thirard is Superintendent Daquin, from the Paris Drugs Squad. He's reputed to be really tenacious. I'm asking you to have him taken off the case. They've got Aubert and Thirard, very clever, that's enough. I'm not asking for the moon.'

Daquin. The same Superintendent who'd nabbed Olivier, and who dropped the case when he found out he was my son. A cop who has respect.

'It can be done.'

'I didn't doubt it for a moment.' Half-smile. His brown eyes cold and staring. 'They're waiting for you upstairs.'

In the bedroom, always the same one, Evita, sitting on a stool at a low table covered in beauty products, is applying her make-up with precise little dabs. Behind the table is a huge mirror. As soon as she sees him enter, she smiles and rises to greet him. In her high heels, she's almost a head taller than him. Shoulder-length dark hair, heavily made-up chestnut eyes, blood-red bee-sting lips. Wearing a very short, clinging lamé dress with a plunging neckline and long sleeves that shows off her lovely shoulders, high breasts, slim hips and long legs sheathed in black, she has a beauty that turns heads. Standing in the doorway, Deluc lights one of his cigarettes.

Evita walks over to him and leads him over to the mirror, then undresses him as gently as if he were a baby. He surrenders, already thrilling to her touch. Once he's naked, she hands him a white towelling bath robe. Welcome to the realm of love. He sits down on the stool and she kneels beside him. And starts applying make up to his face. Backcombs his hair, a squirt of hair spray. Rubs cream into his hands, massages his face, fingers light on his eyelids, his temples, cheeks and neck. He feels the muscles around his eyes and mouth relax one by one. Bliss. In front of her, a palette of fifteen or so colours, tubes, an arsenal of brushes. She begins with his eyes. Darkens the lashes, paints his eyelids. Uses white to distance the eyes from the nose, a line to make them look bigger, blue to make his gaze more intense. She stops to contemplate her work. Deluc takes on a different persona.

Evita dabs foundation over his whole face with a sponge. Then she applies her brushes to smooth away the wrinkles, fill out his cheeks, soften the wings of his nose and his jaw. She redraws the shape of his eyebrows, thinner, lighter. Deluc likes this calm face. There's still the mouth. With a brush she thickens his almost non-existent upper lip, gets rid of his twisted smile, paints his mouth a screaming, triumphant red. A shoulder-length chestnut wig, the same colour as her own hair, fringe. Then she adds the finishing touches, softening the effect with a powder puff. Fondles, caresses, whispered promises.

She takes his hand and leads him over to the big square bed covered in a huge white duvet. He lies on his back, his bath robe open. Above the bed is a mirror; he contemplates the reflection of his naked body for a moment and begins to float. Evita, standing before him, undresses. With a gesture she unzips her dress which crumples at her feet, a pair of pneumatic breasts, with small, hard, dark nipples. She steps out of her shoes, removes her black tights and G-string. A penis, pubic hair meticulously plucked.

She comes and lies down beside Deluc. More sighs and whispers. He buries his face in her voluminous breasts, which loll from side to side, frenziedly grabbing her penis. She caresses him much more gently. Kisses, caresses all over. A magic moment, fulfilment, two bodies become one, with four arms and legs, passionately caressing itself. Evita slips a condom on him and he eventually takes her. She always hurries him a little at this point, he can't hold out any longer. His real pleasure is before, and he would like to draw it out longer.

Then, lying on his back, his arms folded, Deluc contemplates, between the white of the bed and his reflection in the mirror on the ceiling, his elongated slender body, like that of an adolescent, his slightly hazy, slightly careworn vamp's face. The image spins, revolves, no more inner tension, no more space, no more time, a slow, nebulous drifting sensation, his body feels liberated.

He rises, and returns to the vertical, a little unsteady. Evita is in the bathroom, washing and dressing. He comes and sits in front of the big mirror, and begins to remove his make-up. The ritual of the descent, before landing, bringing with it regrets, a fleeting shame, the tensions and anxiety come flooding back. Much worse this time than usual. Perrot's caught up with me. When he closes his eyes, he distinctly hears Perrot say: '*That's better, now you're being reasonable*'. As if talking to a girl. He opens his eyes. There, in the mirror, staring back at him, is Perrot's face, his cold, staring brown eyes. And a contemptuous smile. A surge of adrenalin and fury. Grabs a big pot of cream and hurls it at the face in the mirror, which cracks and shatters in a shower of dazzling stars. Deluc will never remember the noise it made. On the bare wall facing him is the lens of a camera.

Saturday 21 October 1989

A pleasant awakening. It's already late morning. A grey light, drizzle, body aching slightly. Today, he can take his time. A long, hot bath, images from last night floating around his head. Fascinating, the packets of cocaine that Le Dem delivered, one by one, from the mares' wombs. Then a cold power shower. And the shaving ritual, the whole works, since he's in no hurry. A long, supple shaving brush, English soap, and the best razor in the collection, a Swedish-made open razor. The silky caress of the steel on his skin, the precision and tension of the gesture, no room for error. This face and this body suit him.

And then, a carefully prepared breakfast. Frothy eggs scrambled over a bain-marie, and a very fresh goat's cheese with bread, washed down with steaming coffee, a whole pot. Daquin eats lounging on the sofa, his feet on the coffee table, flicking through yesterday's papers. Fancies a fuck. A few precise images of certain lovers' bodies, an especially tender gesture or caress. Need to go cruising. But for the time being, he's got to go down to the Drugs Squad headquarters. A whole day of work ahead of him, in the office, in the utmost calm. Go through the files, read the statements carefully. Don't overlook a thing, think, plan the next stage. A fresh pot of coffee. Good.

By evening, the rain has stopped, the whole city plunges from greyness into night. Leaning on the parapet of the embankment, he watches the Seine flowing past, dark and peaceful. Once again, like this morning, desire. For life, for sex.

The Marais district isn't far. Barely more than five minutes on foot. He turns into a narrow little street between ancient buildings, full of memories like a familiar garment. The tarmac is drying out. Young men and women, mainly men, amble around amid the lit-up shops, shady bars and cafés spilling onto the pavements. The occasional burst of music. Dreadful music, but it's part of the scene. Gorgeous boys walk in the middle of the road, tantalising arses and bright eyes, all attainable, all anonymous. Daquin walks behind a tall, slender fair-haired guy, tight sweater, hip-hugging jeans, with a slit below the buttocks. Couldn't be more explicit. The outline of a pack of condoms discernible in his back pocket. His shoulders sway as he walks, exchanging greetings, smiles and banter with various people. A regular. Daquin slowly draws closer.

Ten minutes later they are together, leaning on the bar of a dark, overcrowded café, having a drink: Daquin a margarita, and the fair-haired Adonis – 'My name's Michel' – fine features, huge eyes, delightfully calm and available, a rum.

Daquin slips his hand inside the slit jeans, feels his way to the inner thigh. A burning in his belly. Kisses the velvety base of his neck. Discovers the taste of his skin, a faint citrusy tang, or is it the margarita? His lips move very slowly round to the corner of Michel's mouth. Not yet. Take his time, prolong the ache of desire until it becomes almost unbearable. And then, the cool lips under his tongue, the warm mouth. The ever new thrill of chance and discovery.

A few drinks later, Michel: 'A friend has lent me a studio flat just around the corner. Shall we go there?'

A small apartment on the top floor of a seventeenth-century building, exposed beams, white walls. Daquin slides his hands inside the tight sweater, smooth, narrow chest, nipples tautening at his touch. Removes the sweater, then pulls Michel by his jeans belt, has him kneel on the big bed in a dark wood frame with a white crotchet cotton bedspread. Undoes the buttons, one by one, very slowly, to reveal the paler skin on his stomach, feels a pang, the curly tuft rough to the touch, the pubes of a fair-haired man, sparser than usual. Slips the jeans down over his hips, then down his long, slightly too slender legs, which feel hard under the curly down that electrifies the palms of his hands.

Michel now completely naked on the bed, golden as warm bread. So happy to be gazed at, admired, caressed and licked. Your pleasure kindles mine. You are the one I've dreamed of.

Monday 23 October 1989

On arriving at his office on Monday morning, Daquin finds a note: *Urgent. The director wants to see you.* Immediately on the defensive.

And in fact the atmosphere is decidedly frosty. Daquin sits down, ensconces himself in the armchair and waits. The director opens fire.

'A remarkable investigation. Bravo.'

Daquin, slightly taken aback.

'You haven't had my report yet.'

'But I expect to receive it later today. Don't forget we have a press conference on Transitex this evening.'

'I'll be ready.'

'I wanted to see you before you finished writing this report of yours, to ask you to be discreet concerning Perrot. He's the biggest property developer in the Paris marketplace, and it would be better if his name didn't appear. Especially of course in front of the press.'

Daquin is flabbergasted. He thinks I'm mentally incompetent.

'Perrot has already been mentioned in my earlier reports.'

'What's done is done. I'm talking about the report you're about to write.'

So the intervention from on-high is recent, probably today. Say something.

'Is that your opinion sir, or that of the Minister?'

'It's not an opinion, Daquin, it's an order. That should be enough.'

'It's enough, Sir.'

Daquin rises and takes his leave.

Daquin goes back up to his office, where his entire team is waiting in a mood of elation.

'The director of the Drugs Squad congratulates you all on the Transitex case...' A pause. '...which he now considers closed.'

What an anticlimax. Daquin silences Lavorel with a gesture.

'I don't want to hear you, Lavorel, I know what you're going to say. As our activities are going to slow down considerably, I suggest that Amelot, Berry and Le Dem make up for their lost days off. Lavorel and Romero will stay with me today to help me write our final report. And we'll meet back here in one week.'

Le Dem and the new boys move into the neighbouring office to gather their belongings. Daquin remains silent, listening to the noises from next door. The door closes. Footsteps in the corridor. Then a knock on the communicating door.

'Come in.'

Le Dem, beetroot. Daquin smiles at him.

'What do you want?'

'I'm not bothered about taking days off...'

'What next?'

'I consider myself as part of your team, on a par with Lavorel and Romero.'

'You may find yourself involved in something that's going to get very messy.'

'I'm sure.'

'Well, sit down. Here's the truth. Our investigation has been halted by the director, on orders that come from higher up, but I don't know where, because someone's protecting Perrot.'

Lavorel interrupts, aggressive:

'What do you intend to do?'

'We don't have a lot to go on. Deluc junior: no longer a part of this. Nothing specific on Pama, or on Perrot. So, I'm going to do as I'm told. There's absolutely no other option.' Lavorel silently fumes. 'At least officially'. A sudden revival of interest. 'The director has asked me not to implicate Perrot in my report. I'm not going to implicate him. I shall spend my day writing, and listening to the magistrate, the director and the journalists. But there's nothing to prevent you from wandering around in the meantime, since you're more or less unemployed. May I remind you, Romero, that we know virtually nothing about Perrot's chauffeur.'

The atmosphere is suddenly relaxed.

Romero gets up.

'Well, since we are agreed, I'll make the coffee.'

It's not exactly difficult for Le Dem to follow Perrot's chauffeur when he leaves Le Chambellan at eight o'clock. He walks to Étoile métro station. Takes direction Nation via Barbès. He alights at Colonel-Fabien, walks up towards Buttes-Chaumont, turns off into the side streets that are all dead ends and enters an elongated, three-storey apartment block in Rue Edgar Poe. He goes into the concierge's lodge on the ground floor, and does not come out again. Le Dem goes home to bed, in his two-roomed flat in La Courneuve. He'll be back tomorrow morning at seven.

Tuesday 24 October 1989

Le Dem wanders down Rue Edgar Poe which is deserted at this hour. At 7.10 a.m. the chauffeur sets off in the direction of the métro. Nothing to be gleaned here, we know where he's going. At eight o'clock, the concierge, pinafore, slippers, mops the lobby, distributes the mail and goes down to the basement. During this time, Le Dem hangs around outside. A hundred metres away, the little grocer's shop raises its iron shutter. Le Dem drops in. Buys some biscuits and half a litre of milk. Chats about this and that. The concierge is married to the chauffeur.

At nine o'clock, the concierge comes out of the building. She has changed. A nylon raincoat with a leopardskin pattern, kitten-heels, she's put on lipstick and is carrying a large shopping bag in her right hand. The perfect fifty-something housewife. Le Dem follows her, with no illusions as to the usefulness of the exercise.

Bus 75. She alights at La Samaritaine. Buys a few bits and pieces from the DIY department. The shopping bag fills up, insulating tape, adaptors, light sockets, bulbs, a very nice Phillips screwdriver. Then she walks back up towards Hôtel de Ville and Rue du Renard. Stops at the corner of Rue du Renard and Rue des Lombards and waits, clutching her shopping bag.

Her first customer arrives straight away, and now they're going upstairs inside one of the first houses in Rue des Lombards. Le Dem can't believe his eyes. Between ten o'clock and midday she goes up three times. At midday she has a simple lunch at the café on the corner, a toasted ham and cheese sandwich with a fried egg on top and a bottle of sparkling water. At one o'clock, she goes back to her post, still clutching her shopping bag. Le Dem takes advantage of the first trick of the afternoon to go into the café himself, eat a sandwich and have a drink at the bar.

'Strange get-up for a tart, that old girl on the corner.'

The owner laughs.

'It works, believe me. The best clientele in the street. Only regulars.' In answer to Le Dem's puzzled look: 'She's reassuring.'

At five o'clock on the dot, the woman in the nylon leopardskin-patterned raincoat gets back on the 75 bus. She does her shopping at the market on the way and walks back to her lodge. And probably starts doing her housework and cooking dinner for when her husband gets home.

Lavorel has got hold of a little scanner and an unmarked car with tinted windows. Now he's parked in Rue Balzac, Romero beside him, in front of the driveway entrance to Le Chambellan. It is half past three, a good time to find the street almost empty. Pretending to read a newspaper, Romero fiddles with the scanner, switches frequencies. The pleasure is no longer physical as it used to be, when they used to force locks and feel the catch give way in their hand. You can't stop progress. After several attempts, the automatic gate to the car park opens. Romero grabs his bag and dives inside. Lavorel starts the engine and goes and parks a little further away.

Pitch dark. Torch. The car park isn't big, only one level, spaces for twenty or so cars, only half of them occupied. On the other hand, no obvious hiding places. The air vents are much too small. No recesses. Two fat pipes running along the ceiling, not boxed in, insulated with fibreglass. Romero jumps, grabs a pipe, steadies himself and pulls himself up athletically. Lies down in the space between the pipes and the ceiling. The ideal place. If he lies still in this ill-lit car park, it should be all right. In any case, difficult to find anything else. Takes off his shoulder bag and puts it in front of him. Fishes out a walkie-talkie.

'Lavorel, can you hear me? I'm in position. Don't abandon me, will you?'

At 6.30 p.m., Perrot arrives at Le Chambellan. Lavorel alerts Romero. The chauffeur drops him off on the pavement, then takes the car down to the car park. And parks not far from Romero, who crawls along the pipe to get a glimpse inside the car. He is dirty, stiff with cramps, but suddenly alert. Barely ten minutes after the arrival of the car, a pretty female figure, short black skirt, turquoise silk camisole, black hair, comes out of the lift and heads straight for Perrot's car, opens the passenger door, sits down, and starts unzipping the chauffeur's fly, apparently without saying a word. Romero is torn between the triumph of being right over Daquin, and huge disappointment. Let's see, three hours lying still, wedged between pipe and ceiling amid flakes of fibreglass to peep at a girl giving a blow-job to a faceless groin. It's over fast. A quickie. The girl raises her head and spits on the car park floor, while the chauffeur does up his fly. Romero still can't see his face.

The girl gets out of the car.

'I haven't got time to chat today. Perrot won't be long.'

Then she leans through the lowered window and holds out her hand. The chauffeur gives her ten little plastic sachets. She counts them, takes out a few banknotes stuffed in her belt, drops them on the passenger seat and sashays back to the lift.

Romero feels less tired.

'In two days, the balance of power has considerably swung in our favour. We still don't know how the conglomeration around Pama and Perrot is organised. But we have something to blow Perrot out of the water. The chauffeur. That's a small miracle.' Romero remembers the hours he spent hiding, sandwiched between the pipes and the car park ceiling. A miracle that cost some effort, all the same. Pimp and pusher. He can legitimately be arrested. He has a lot to lose, so he'll talk. A chauffeur always knows everything. Need to fine tune him. Take the time to find out who his dealer is. Concentrate on the wife. The chauffeur is too close to Perrot, it's hard for him to take risks. When we feel the time's right, we'll move in on the dealer and that will lead us by chance to Perrot's chauffeur. Once things are in motion, it'll be very hard to stop them.

Doorbell. Michel opens the door, and Jubelin enters stiffly. He can't bring himself to feel at ease with him.

'Annick's waiting for you on the balcony.'

The table is set, and Michel has prepared some food and left it on the sideboard: a platter of cold meats, cheeses and fruit. Annick comes to greet Jubelin.

'There's not much for dinner. You hardly gave me any warning...'

'It's perfect. Most importantly, I want to talk to you undisturbed.'

From the living room, Michel indicates that he's leaving. Annick smiles at him.

'See you tomorrow, Michel.'

Annick pours aperitifs. Jubelin wastes no time.

'Thirard was arrested four or five days ago, in a sting on a cocaine trafficking network that he was at the centre of...'

Now, it's a certainty. The slush fund is definitely drugs money... So Nicolas's murder... of course Jubelin knew. And I'm becoming a nuisance to him. This is no time to lose my grip.

'... and I wanted to talk to you about it.'

'How does it affect us, Xavier?'

'We have a promotional campaign coming up, don't forget. Some of it was shot at Thirard's place, and we sponsor him too. Doesn't look good.'

'True. I think I can sort that out before the launch of the campaign. Thirard's name won't get out.'

'That's not all. From what I've heard about the investigation, Nicolas is thought to have been involved in the drugs trafficking.' Annick raises an incredulous eyebrow.

'Do you think that's possible?'

'Actually, I do. He knew Thirard, and that would explain why he was killed.'

'I don't believe it.'

'Whether you believe it or not, is irrelevant.' Stifled anger. 'What matters is what our clients think. One of our executives murdered over a drugs trafficking matter is pretty disastrous for our corporate image.'

Annick remains silent. I see what you're driving at. Don't count on me to make this easier for you.

'Not to mention that the investigation won't stop there.' Jubelin's expression becomes serious. 'To be absolutely honest, Annick, the police know that you snort coke too.'

'I'm not the first person to do so in the circles we move in. Nobody gives a damn. Including the police.'

Jubelin leans across the table and gently grabs her wrist.

'You must look after yourself, Annick.' In a caring, gentle voice: 'Your name may be cited in an investigation into drugs trafficking and a murder. We need to protect you.'

'And protect Pama.'

'Of course. You are the company's public face, you alone. But that's not what I'm worried about. You must take a holiday. A long rest. In an establishment where they'll help you get over your addiction. I'll find you the best there is. If you take care of yourself, I have assurances that the police will leave you out of any proceedings.'

Annick looks at him. Nice try. An acute instinct for opportunity, speedy action, long-term strategy, and a hell of a nerve. No wonder you're CEO, and I'll have a job finding someone of your calibre. But you don't know what cards I'm holding.

'Do you want my resignation? Right away?'

'There's no question of you resigning. I was talking about a holiday. Think about it, and we'll talk again at the end of the week, before the police come to see you for the third time.'

'Coffee? Or a liqueur?'

Wednesday 25 October 1989

Daquin arrives at the scene of the crime, Boulevard Maillot, accompanied by Romero. They go up to the seventh floor where Inspector Bourdier is waiting for them.

'A gruesome murder, Superintendent, discovered by Madame Renouard when she returned home less than an hour ago. On questioning her, I gather, amid a number of inconsistencies – as you'll see, she's pretty shaken up – that she's implicated in some way in your investigation into cocaine trafficking...'

'That's correct, she is mixed up in it. As a witness for the moment.'

'I thought it best to inform you.'

'You did the right thing, thank you. Is she a suspect in this murder?'

'It's highly unlikely. At the estimated time of the crime, she was at her office, several people have confirmed it. The victim, a man called Nolant, was an illustrator, something arty. And had a strange relationship with Madame Renouard according to the concierge. Separate apartments on the same landing but constantly together. He did the shopping, the cooking, the housework. Joint bank account. They got on wonderfully, again according to the concierge, but didn't sleep together because he was as queer as a coot. Come and see the carnage.'

The inspector pushes open the front door. Small hallway. To the right, a huge room used as a studio. Two large drawing boards in the corners, professional lighting, shelves for storing rolls and sheets of paper. Two big armchairs in the centre of the room. A kitchenette behind a counter. Everything is immaculately clean and neat. Daquin goes over to one of the drawing boards. A sheet covered in pencil-drawings of silhouettes, a lot of movement but no faces. Rather good.

'This way,' says Bourdier.

Daquin and Romero follow him. Door to the left of the hall. Two men are already at work in the bedroom which has been ransacked. Television, hi-fi, lights, telephone and Minitel smashed, books and records strewn over the floor, the bed bare, the sheets pulled off, and, at the foot of the bed, on the carpet, face down, surrounded by a dark stain, the naked body of a man.

That long, slim, fair-haired body. The light, curly down on the legs. Daquin walks over to him. His skull has been smashed. Kneels down. A painful wrench in the gut. With his thumb, he traces the line of the nose, the half open lips (memory of fresh lips), cold, stiff. Michel that night, blond, sensual, tender, attentive, smiling... What a waste to destroy that life. Daquin stands up, a shattered expression on his face.

Bourdier shows him a cast-iron lampstand with dried bloodstains on it.

'The crime weapon, most likely. Forensics haven't confirmed yet. Looks like a gay pick-up that turned nasty. What do you think?'

'Looks like it.' Terse. 'Unless it's been made to look like that. Can I talk to Madame Renouard?'

'Of course. She's in her bedroom. I asked a woman police officer to stay with her, as a precaution.'

'Come on, Romero.' Then, turning to Bourdier. 'Inspector, don't leave here before I've had a word with you.'

On entering the vast main room of Annick's apartment, Daquin stops, amazed. On the walls, a pale tobacco-coloured Japanese wallpaper, white oak parquet floors, to the left, a huge sofa in front of a stone and timber fireplace with a fire laid in the grate. In one corner, facing the door, a forest of bamboo and plants, and sitting in a wicker armchair amid the plant containers, a golliwog in a red bowler hat and suit stares at the visitor. Several Eames chairs, two Regency wing chairs covered in duck-egg blue velvet. And on the right-hand wall, a mosaic of tastefully framed drawings. Daquin walks over to it. Works from very different periods, of varying quality and techniques, but the overall effect has tremendous charm, Michel's charm, his desire to seduce. And in the bottom left-hand corner, an Indian-ink silhouette of Annick portrayed as a heroine of a spaghetti western, advancing towards him. Not hard to recognise Michel's style, and, beneath the irony, tremendous affection. Beyond the room, a vast flower-filled balcony overlooking Paris. But who is this woman? I'd never have pictured her in an apartment like this, nor living with a man like Michel.

He heads for the bedroom door. Just before entering, he turns to Romero:

'Here we are on the threshold of the dark continent. Not too scared?'

Baffled, Romero gazes at the golliwog.

Daquin signals to the woman police officer to leave. Annick is sitting on the bed, whey-faced, puffy-eyed, staring vacantly, her nose pinched, shivering. She stares at them blankly. Then she gets up, her body tense to breaking point, her hands clenched, knuckles white, and with explosive energy grabs a crystal ash tray from the bedside table and hurls it with all her strength at Daquin's head. He manages to duck just in time, and the ash tray shatters against the wall sounding like an explosion.

'Filthy rapist, I've been waiting for this for years, bastard, I'm going to cut your balls off.' Laughs. 'At last it'll be over. No more nightmares.'

She moves towards Daquin, who frankly feels more intrigued than afraid.

Romero, who always tends to take this kind of threat very seriously, edges towards her and tries to seize her bodily. She breaks away with surprising strength, gives him a resounding slap on the left ear, pain in the eardrum, and screeches shrilly:

'Don't you touch me, you filthy Eyetie, you're all the same, garbage...'

Daquin encircles her waist from behind, and sits her on the bed. Her body rigid, arched, resisting all the way, she tries to free herself, twists, kicks out, smashes the bedside light.

'Did Jubelin send you? I hate Jubelin, he killed Michel.'

Her voice is already less shrill. Then, suddenly, she sinks into apathy, her eyes vacant. Daquin lays her on the bed, without relaxing his hold, and talks to her very softly, almost in a whisper:

'What's this got to do with Jubelin?'

'I don't want to talk to you. Leave me alone.'

Daquin gradually loosens his grip. Lying on the bed, she begins to sob tearlessly, in fitful spasms.

'Romero, get me a damp towel from the bathroom, a glass of water, and some tranquillisers – there are bound to be some.'

While Romero coaxes her to drink, Daquin inspects the room, opens the drawers and cupboards. Inside the bedside table drawer is a diskette. He picks it up. You never know.

Ten minutes or so later, Annick, still lying on the bed, is breathing more calmly, her eyes closed.

'We're not going to get any sense out of her. Get the car and take Madame Renouard to Doctor Senik's clinic at Le Vésinet. Tell him I sent you and explain the situation. Cocaine, terrible shock, no way can she get out of this by cutting out and telling us to go to Hell. He's used to dealing with this type of case. Tell him to register her under a false name, and take some precautions. After all, she may be in danger. We'll meet up tomorrow. I'm staying here. I've got to have a word with Bourdier.'

Thursday 26 October 1989

On Daquin's desk is a big brown envelope which must have been delivered by hand. No address, no stamp, just his name in block letters.

He makes himself a coffee, sits down and opens the envelope. Four glossy photos, large format. Michel and him in the bar, Daquin's hand inside Michel's sweater. Daquin's lips on Michel's face. The first kiss. It was just before they left together. Both clearly identifiable. At first they stir the acute memory of the pleasure of that evening. Daquin feels a pang of gratitude towards Michel, who was so alive. With his finger, he traces Michel's features. Flashback, his cool lips, his warm mouth. The photos are very slightly fuzzy, as if they had captured the heat of their touch. And then Daquin's anger at the memory of the naked corpse at the foot of the bed, the battered skull, came flooding back. Finally he tells himself it's about time he reacted as a cop.

Picks up the four photos and pins them to the cork board on the back wall of his office. A phone call to Inspector Bourdier.

'Come and see me in my office as soon as you can, I've got something to show you.'

Who? It could be an intimidation tactic linked to the busting of Transitex, to discourage us from going any further, either Perrot or Jubelin could be behind it. But it could also be someone from within the police. A cop from the Horseracing and Gaming division out to protect the debt recovery boys from further snooping. Daquin thinks long and hard. Or it has nothing whatsoever to do with our investigation. An opportunity seized by a clandestine intelligence and blackmailing outfit within the police, the Ministry or elsewhere. There are all sorts of possibilities.

Phone rings. Daquin picks it up. The switchboard.

'Please hold for Monsieur Deluc who's calling from the Élysée.'

'Let me introduce myself. Christian Deluc, presidential advisor. I have just met your director and I'd very much like to make your acquaintance.' Silence. 'Would you be free to have dinner with me, tonight, at the Élysée, I'm on duty, I can't leave the building.'

'Certainly, Monsieur Deluc.'

'Perfect. See you this evening. Eight thirty?'

'Fine.'

Perrot, Deluc, Beirut, this is it. The photos too?

A few minutes later, the phone rings again, his direct line. It's the director of the Drugs Squad.

'Come and see me in my office.' Curt.

I'm certainly not going to sit twiddling my thumbs today.

When Daquin enters the director's office, he finds his superior ashen-faced. With rage? The photos are spread out on his desk.

'Sit down, Daquin. I received these this morning.'

'So did I.'

'Is it a set-up?'

'No. I spent an evening in that bar, with that man.' A smile. 'And it was a great evening.'

'What else do you have to say about this?'

'That it concerns my private life, Sir. When these photos were taken I was off duty. It's a chance meeting in a bar where there are many chance meetings. With a consenting adult.'

'I find these compromising for my department. That's not all. There was an anonymous note with these photos.' Silence. Daquin doesn't bat an eyelid. 'Apparently the second man is a certain Michel Nolant, murdered a few days later.' Still no reaction. 'In all likelihood in the course of a homosexual pick-up that turned nasty. And you were apparently seen in the vicinity.'

Daquin laughs.

'Do you suspect me, Sir?'

'Not yet. But I'd like you to take the situation more seriously. The director of the Crime Squad is hopping mad.'

'I'm taking it very seriously. Maybe you're aware that I was called to the scene of the murder by Inspector Bourdier of the Crime Squad, who's in charge of the investigation, because this murder ties in with my own investigation into the Transitex case. The minute I recognised Michel Nolant, I informed Inspector Bourdier of the encounter which these photos so touchingly record. I also informed him this morning, before coming to see you, that I had received some souvenir photos. He's coming to have a look at them this afternoon, in my office.'

'I'm going to talk to the Crime Squad and see if they can order an internal investigation. Meanwhile, I'd like you to consider yourself on leave.' An ironic smile. 'Well deserved too, now that the Transitex case is closed.'

'May I inform my inspectors of your decision myself?'

Terse. 'Of course'.

'Have you asked yourself, Sir, who might be trying to intimidate me, or even remove me, and why?'

'Daquin, you don't need to teach me my job.'

Daquin is leaning against the parapet of the embankment once more. Grey sky, an intense, mellow light, like in a film. In the same spot as the other evening. Go back to that evening, relive it moment by moment. He left from here, on foot, heading for the Marais. He walked past the cathedral, crossed the bridges, inhaled the cool air of the Seine deeply then turned into the narrow back streets with their stone buildings and their promise of pleasure. At no point had he worried about whether he was being followed. So it is possible that he was. He'd walked up Rue Vieille-du-Temple. A little further on, in front of him, he had spotted Michel and begun to follow, not approaching him immediately, watching him wiggle his arse. When he'd turned into Rue du Bourg-Tibourg, Daquin had followed him, moving closer all the time. It was definitely he, Daquin, who had gone up to Michel, a few metres from that bar. No chance, therefore, that Michel had been involved in setting him up. Which one of them had suggested that bar rather than another? Neither. It was chance. It was the closest one to the spot where he had spoken to Michel. None of this is getting me anywhere.

Standing outside the bar, which is closed at this hour of the morning, Daquin replays their movements one by one, the movements captured in the photos. Of course, it's obvious. Those photos were taken from behind the bar, some way from where he and Michel were. The barman. Goes over the entire early part of the evening in his mind. And only the barman. A glance around: the street is almost empty. No iron shutters, a simple wooden door and yellow and brown tiles. Not very sturdy. Walks up to it, touches it with his fingertips. It's locked. Behind the door, there's the sound of someone moving around, probably the cleaner. Visualise the place. The bar on your left as you go in. The big, dark room with tables, curtained off booths. And to the right, the toilets, three separate little rooms, spacious, all tiled in red and white, decorated with magnificent posters of naked men. A smile as he recalls the big mirror in a wooden frame next to the toilet bowl. And in each one, a huge washbasin. Daquin gives the door a sharp, powerful shove, the bolt pulls away from the frame and the door opens. Daquin goes in and closes it behind him. The barman from the other evening is there in jeans and shirt sleeves, a black apron around his waist, mopping the floor between the tables. He straightens up. Backache, Daquin notes automatically.

'What do you want? Can't you see we're closed?'

A step forward. With one hand, Daquin grabs his arm and raises him, clamping his other hand over the barman's mouth. He catches him completely off guard. Drags him into the toilets. Muffled protests. He's probably recognised me. Flings him into one of the toilets and locks the door. Grabs his hair, jams him up against the washbasin with all his weight, turns the tap full on and shoves his head under it. Holds him there for two long minutes. The best way to stop him from yelling once the conversation gets under way. Pulls his head up out of the basin. The man's knees are wobbly, he's dripping wet, and half choking. Not really in a position of strength. Daquin vigorously shakes his head.

'To wake you up a bit. Do you remember the photos you took on Saturday night?'

Dunks him again. Someone's moving around in the bar. Daquin, ears pricked, goes into the next toilet. Another long minute. The barman's racked with spasms. A couple more minutes. Then Daquin returns. The hardest thing in these circumstances is to be patient. He lets the barman breathe. The man retches violently and vomits water and the remains of his last meal into the washbasin. Daquin barks:

'Next time will be even worse. Who were you working for the other evening? Quick or you go under again.'

'A cop, Rostang.' A barely audible croak.

'Has he got a hold on you?'

'Yes.'

Daquin lets him go. The barman slumps onto the floor, glancing at his reflection as he slides down and ends up wedged between the toilet bowl and the big mirror.

'Fancy yourself, do you?' He grabs him by the hair and twists his face round towards the mirror. 'Take a good look at yourself.' Without letting go, a kick, not too hard, in the lower back, as a warning. 'Tell me about this Rostang.'

'He's a cop in Intelligence.'

He tries to look away. Daquin forces him to face the mirror.

'Go on.'

'He knows a lot of people around here.'

'What about Saturday evening?'

'He followed you. He asked me to photograph you. I couldn't say no.'

'You know what you're doing, it's not the first time you've done this for him.' The barman says nothing. 'This time, you'd better take a few days' holiday until all this blows over.'

And he lets him go.

'Martinot? Hello, Daquin here. Do me a favour. You know everyone. A colleague of yours in Intelligence, a guy called Rostang, does the name mean anything to you?'

'Not much. There's always been something odd about him, though there have never been any specific complaints about him. Ex Crime Squad apparently. In 1986, he was attached directly to the Ministry of the Interior.'

'Didn't he return in '88?'

'No.' Laughs. 'He must have worked miracles, he was moved to the Élysée.'

'Martinot, I owe you one. Any time.'

An Élysée usher leads Daquin through a maze of corridors to a small apartment located on the corner of Avenue Matignon for the use of the advisor on duty. Deluc, informed of his arrival by security, is waiting for him on the threshold. Daquin sums him up at a glance. Tall, slim, rigid, very rigid, glasses with delicate frames, thin almost non-existent lips, and on his face, a permanent sort of ironic smile. Remember, an uptight pervert. He stares lengthily at Daquin. Is he trying to find a resemblance to the photos? Not just that... An unhealthy curiosity. So here he is, the cop who goes cruising in gay bars... Daquin puts on a suave, solid and impassive front.

'Thank you for agreeing to come here. I didn't want to delay meeting you.'

More than friendly, almost charming. Why? He doesn't need to be.

Deluc takes his elbow and stands aside to let him into the apartment. Small, antique furniture, low ceilings, comfortable, intimate. A drawing room, dining room, the table is laid for two. A manservant, white jacket, black bow tie, perfectly trained without being unctuous, serves aperitifs. Champagne for Daquin, whisky for Deluc.

'I waited until you'd finished your investigation. Brilliantly, so your director tells me. You have completely smashed a cocaine trafficking ring...'

Completely... Is that his sense of humour?

The phone rings. Deluc replies, takes notes, makes a phone call, returns. Busy, important. He's showing off.

'Let us eat. A simple meal, I hope you won't hold it against me.'

The manservant again. Attentive, discreet service. Warm oysters washed down with a Coulée de Serrant.

'I waited for this case to be closed so that my contacting you would not be misinterpreted. I wanted to thank you personally for the way you acted concerning my son.' Daquin raises his eyebrows. 'The Superintendent of the 16th arrondissement informed me what happened on that unfortunate occasion. I'm grateful to you for sparing him the whole judicial process. You can now count on my support if you need it.'

So this is what it's about. Not very subtle. Does he think I'm finished and not capable of tracing things back to him? More likely, he simply doesn't give a damn. He thinks he's in a position of strength. Too sure of his power, this guy. Another phone call, fax, it's Georges, for François. Deluc casually leaves the fax lying on the table, next to Daquin's plate, while he calls the general secretary of the Élysée. He comes back to the table, puffed up, happy. Throughout this dinner at the Élysée, Deluc was putting on a performance, it was rather pathetic. This guy, take away his office and his chauffeur-driven car, and he's lost.

After the oysters, rack of lamb, baby vegetables, accompanied by a Château-Carbonnieux 1983. That at least, absolutely perfect. The meat, impeccably cooked, a masterpiece. In all, with Deluc's play-acting, a memorable meal.

Deluc in a confidential tone:

'The situation could have been even more embarrassing for me as I'm part of a working party to crack down on drugs that has just been set up here at the Élysée and which reports directly to the President. You know that the battle against drug trafficking is one of the President's priorities?' Daquin nods. 'A battle for civilisation that must be won...'

Overwhelmed by a flood of violent images and feelings, Daquin closes his eyes for a second. A battle for civilisation... Opens his eyes again. Careful, don't lose track.

'In short, our team is tasked with drawing up a coherent policy and taking action without getting bogged down in red tape like the interministerial mission, or getting caught up in interdepartmental squabbles either. The people are sick and tired of drug-related crime, and we need to come up with some effective solutions. This team includes some of the President's inner circle, and a few men on the ground. At our last meeting, yesterday afternoon,' a pause, 'yes, that's right, Wednesday afternoon, I mentioned your name. The door is open to you, Superintendent Daquin.'

Daquin smiles. So this is the carrot.

'You do me a great honour.' A hint of irony. 'If we're talking about territory, I'm afraid that I might not be suited to that of the Élysée.'

Deluc's expression suddenly becomes grim. End of the charm offensive?

Cheese. No, thank you, I'll keep to this wine. And a baked Alaska. Haven't had one of these for years. Memories, memories. At the Grill Bar of the Ritz, with Lenglet, and a few others. With champagne. And a strong coffee.

'Let's have coffee in the drawing room. Brandy?'

Two brandies. He's not certain that Deluc is used to drinking so much, or, more likely, the part he's playing has gone to his head. He's just slightly losing control.

'The chief of the Drugs Squad told me that your investigation took you to Pama's doors. A member of Jubelin's staff was apparently somewhat involved in drug trafficking before being murdered.'

'Correct.'

'Is it news to you if I tell you that Madame Renouard, whom I know well in another context, is a regular cocaine user?'

'No, you're not telling me anything I didn't know.'

In a confidential tone. 'I myself am a Pama shareholder.' Laugh. 'A small shareholder, of course. I don't have the means... I bought some shares because I believe in the reconciliation between the socialists and private enterprise and the free market, after years of a mutual lack of understanding. It was a political gesture...' Deluc seeks a sign of understanding, which is not forthcoming. Daquin sips his brandy, staring at his glass.

'Jubelin has succeeded in creating an active and profitable private company in a field dominated by huge, nationalised state-run machines, and suddenly he has revived the entire sector and paved the way for the whole industry to break into new international markets. He has enterprise in spades. And enterprise is what we need nowadays. I consider him as a hero of the '80s. It would be a pity if this firm's reputation were to be damaged by the behaviour of a couple of its senior managers...'

'On that point, you may rest assured. I don't think that's likely to happen.'

Daquin has finished his brandy. Stretches his legs with a sigh of satisfaction. Perrot must be extremely important for Deluc not to say a word about him.

'You're very quiet, Superintendent.'

'Because I don't have very much to say. But I'm listening to every word you say.'

Friday 27 October 1989

Daquin has come in to work very early on the diskette found at Annick's place. Frankfurt stock exchange, Tuesday 19 September 1989, fluctuations in A.A. Bayern's share values. Interesting, the company for which Pama has just made a takeover bid. Pass this on to Lavorel, if... But first of all, carefully plan how he's going to tell his inspectors that he's been told to go on leave. Romero and Lavorel. A slice of his life. At this precise moment, the most important. He's playing for high stakes.

The inspectors arrive. Daquin points to the board.

'I received these yesterday morning, sent anonymously.' Le Dem turns pink and stares at the floor. Daquin annoyed. 'I did chat up this guy in a bar in the Marais a few days ago. These photos aren't rigged. You can look at them, Le Dem. Of course, I didn't know who he was until I found myself staring at his corpse, last Wednesday. This guy is Michel Nolant.' Romero recalls Daquin's shattered look in the ransacked bedroom. 'Naturally, the same evening I informed Inspector Bourdier who's in charge of the investigation.' A pause. 'Just as well. And I think I'm impervious to this kind of blackmail because I've always been open about my taste for boys. But that's not all. First of all, the director of the Drugs Squad received the same photos at the same time. And he's decided to send me off on leave, pending the results of an internal inquiry. I'm only here today because he gave me permission to inform you myself of his decision.'

Romero and Lavorel exchange glances.

'We resign.'

'Don't get carried away. I'm not sure what to do myself.'

'You know very well that you can't go off on holiday. Not after all this.' Romero points to the photos. No need to spell it out.

'It's true that if I agree, I'm finished. But the enemy is a big fish. I think that a certain Deluc is behind this intimidation effort...'

'The kid's father?'

'Yes, the kid's father. Presidential advisor. In all likelihood, he's the person who had me followed and photographed – by one of our chaps, incidentally – and who had someone tell the chief to sideline me. With one major question mark: did he go so far as to have Nolant killed simply to give his blackmail attempt more weight? And yesterday evening, he invited me to work directly with him, at the Élysée. Don't worry, Lavorel, I said no.'

'What does he want?'

'It's obvious. To protect Perrot and Pama. Especially Perrot, I'd say.'

'Chief, if you drop this now, I'm going back to being a delinquent. And with the experience I've gained thanks to you, I think I still have time to make a brilliant career at it.'

'What about you, Le Dem, what do you think?'

'I've been thinking about it for a while. A farrier is murdered. We nab a horse trader and a vet. All in the trade. Everybody's delighted. Although I was shocked, I believe it was right. But when we get to the fat-cat financiers and politicians, they stop us. I don't know how to explain this but I take it as an affront to men like me.'

'How far have you got with the chauffeur's supplier?'

'We've found him. It's the grocer on the corner. A hundred metres from the concierge's lodge. A Moroccan. He received some heroin in orange juice cartons from Holland. We nicked one from him. It's in the cupboard in our office.'

Daquin remains silent for a while. Efficient, they really are efficient.

'Romero, make us a coffee. We'll carry on the conversation afterwards.'

The all get up. A fifteen-minute break, then Daquin goes on:

'I'm going to try and sum up. You'll see, it's not straightforward. One thing is certain: we've smashed an international cocaine ring that goes from Colombia to Italy via France, and arrested those directly running the operation, which isn't bad going compared with some of our colleagues' recent operations... A hunch: Transitex is only one link in a much wider network, as is suggested by the involvement of Ballestrino, a major player, as is suggested by the murder of Paola Jiménez, and which explains the pressure to have us pulled off the investigation. Remember, Romero, Aubert told us a whole story about meetings with Colombians to do with horses. A good lie always includes an element of truth. Like Ballestrino, the Ochoas breed horses. Imagine that the Colombians and the Italians, at high level, used the cover of a race meeting to arrange a summit meeting, on 9th July at Longchamp, in the owners' enclosure, which Jiménez chanced to witness. We've seen the bosses meet in the luxury hotels and casinos of the Riviera.'

'In that case, why would Paola call me, and not her CIA contact?'

'Good question. Le Dem, you should block your ears to protect your innocence. Suppose that Paola Jiménez did happen upon a meeting between the Colombians, the Italians and her CIA contact... She must have realised her life was in danger.'

Romero shudders. He hears the breathless voice on the phone. He sees the sun, the naked girl on the carpet. Daquin smiles at him.

'It's probably because you were late that you're still alive. As far as this aspect of the case is concerned, you can see we're completely in the dark, so we'll ignore it, at least for the time being. And we'll concentrate on the French ramifications of Transitex. Now, we have a clearer idea of the Pama conglomeration's internal organisation. Perrot controls Deluc whom he's known for a long time.' Quizzical looks from Romero and Lavorel. 'They met in 1972-73, in Beirut. He uses him for his property deals, like those in the Bastille district, but above all, he's used him at least twice to protect Transitex: to get the tax inspectors to come down on Moulin, and to put a stop to our investigation. So Transitex is him. He must have an equally important role within Pama. He goes in as a shareholder, two years ago, at the point when Jubelin decides to ally himself with the Italians to take control. It figures that he acted as intermediary between Jubelin and Ballestrino, who's an associate of his in Transitex. He could also have introduced Thirard to Jubelin. And he's the prime mover behind Pama's new focus on the property sector, which I imagine serves as a front for money laundering operations. I'm leaving out Nolant's murder. I don't know how that fits in with the rest.

'If I'm more or less on the right track, our situation isn't hopeless. We have three lines of attack. First of all, definitely, the chauffeur. Romero and Le Dem, you contact Dubanchet and his team. We have similar working methods, and he knows that I've been put on leave. Tell him about the grocer, and catch him red-handed. In other words, from now on, don't let the chauffeur's wife out of your sight and nab them when she comes in for supplies.

'But we're not dropping Pama. Lavorel, I'm giving you this diskette. I found it at Annick Renouard's place the day Nolant was murdered. It's a listing over one day, the 19th September last year, of the share prices of A.A. Bayern, a company for which Pama has just made a takeover bid. See if you can make any sense of it.

'And lastly, I'll go off on leave as soon as this meeting is over, I have no choice, and I'll make use of the time to dig up more on Deluc and try and grasp the nature of his links with Perrot.

'We won't meet here again. You can reach me at home, it's up to you to stay in touch. If anyone asks, you don't know where I am. And if the chief gives you a job, you do it.' A smile. 'I'd be surprised. He'll try and avoid pissing you off, at least for a few days. And as the saying goes: May God watch over and protect us all. We need that at least.'

Daquin rises and takes down the photos of Michel from the cork board. He'll keep them. As a souvenir.

Duroselle tells himself it's a nightmare when, on leaving his office, he sees Daquin walking towards him, elegant as ever, with a big, friendly smile.

'I was waiting for you. What a pleasure to see you again. Come, I'm inviting you for lunch.'

Duroselle apologises to his colleagues, and follows Daquin with a sinking heart.

A tiny restaurant full of provincial charm. Astonishing, less than 30 kilometres from Paris. An elderly woman, of slight build and well-preserved, with a black choker round her neck (like my grandmother in a remote part of the Nivernais, more than 30 years ago, incredible), comes over and proposes coddled eggs or grated carrots. Two coddled eggs and a Beaujolais.

Daquin observes Duroselle. The look of the defeated. I've got him in the palm of my hand. Too easy to be any fun. So let's make it quick.

'I've come to give you news of the Moulin case.'

'I thought I wasn't ever going to see you again.'

'It's true, I promised. But there have been some new developments. First of all, the person behind Moulin's tax inspection, a man called Thirard, is well and truly a killer. But that's not all. He's also an international drugs smuggler. As a matter of fact, I've arrested him.'

'It's nothing to do with me.'

A strangled cry. Daquin thinks he can hear Duroselle's teeth chattering. He calmly finishes his coddled egg.

'That's not so certain. In searching Thirard's place we found a note about Moulin's tax inspection which mentions your name, and only your name.'

'What would you like as a main course, gentlemen? Rabbit or beef bourguignon?'

'Rabbit, that'll make a nice change. What about you, Duroselle?' He nods, no longer able to speak. 'Two rabbits please. I'll continue. If this note is made public, one way or another, your superiors will see it as the ideal way of getting you to carry the can for this unfortunate tax inspection ordered from outside. And they'll succeed. That is, unless we find the drug dealer's real accomplice, and that's where you can help us.'

A very mediocre cheese, a piece of chalky Camembert. Rural apple tart. I won't risk the coffee. A little plum brandy maybe?

'So Duroselle, you're not saying anything?'

'What do you want, you bastard?'

'It's very simple. I give you a name and an address. Christian Deluc, Quai d'Orléans, Paris. By the day after tomorrow, I want his tax records from 1981 onwards. And within a few days, you'll be beyond suspicion once and for all. You couldn't ask for more, could you?'

Lavorel drops in to see Daquin at the end of the day. It's the first time he's been to the Villa des Artistes. He feels ill at ease, this isn't his world. He prefers Daquin in his office, at HQ.

'Interesting, the diskette. On that day, A.A. Bayern's share price collapsed.'

'I'd gathered that.'

'Those shares were bought at rock-bottom prices by various financial companies based in Luxembourg and Guernsey. They were probably acting as fronts, but a long inquiry would be needed to find out who's behind them. When Pama announced its public tender offer, they immediately tendered their A.A. Bayern shares at the offered price and have thus more than doubled their money in the space of just a few weeks.'

'Is that illegal?'

'Yes, insider dealing. But it's common. It takes five years' investigation to get a suspended fine.'

'A bit controversial?'

'Not at all, chief. With all due respect, sir, I don't think you quite get it. These days, it's no longer a crime to make a fortune illegally. It's a proof of intelligence and good taste. Only losers stay poor in the '80s.'

'Let's get back to the subject, Lavorel.'

'If we look at A.A. Bayern, it gets even better. During the first two hours of monitoring, the price remained stable. Then it began to plummet, and finally collapsed. On inquiring further, the owner of thirty per cent of the capital suddenly sold everything. Does that ring any bells'

'Transitex?'

'Exactly. Only much bigger. The person watching the prices knew they were going to collapse that day, although there was nothing to suggest it. It looks like a forced sale, with the involvement of the person who saved that information onto the diskette. Madame Renouard, perhaps. You found it at her place, didn't you?'

'That's right. I say, Lavorel, how do you fancy a few days' holiday in Munich?'

Saturday 28 October 1989

Daquin, clean shaven in a towelling bathrobe, is sprawled on the sofa drinking coffee. Sonny Rollins, for a bit of rhythm while he lets his mind roam. Take stock of the situation. Not easy. Internal investigation: of no importance, for show. But the photos... Michel's murder... If I don't solve this, I may as well hand in my notice. I've already been semi-retired. A holiday... What do I have left? Romero and Lavorel. My inspectors. Daydreams for a moment. If I go, they'll go too. Lenglet was always suggesting I join him in the Middle East. The four of us would have made a good team. Too late. Notes that the memory of Lenglet is no longer painful. Gets up, makes a coffee and stretches out on the sofa again.

Let's go over it all again. Romero, Lavorel, and the Martian too. With them, there's one possible point of impact, the business with the chauffeur. That's solid. We simply have to choose the right moment to pounce. My trump card.

And then there's Annick Renouard. At this point, Sonny Rollins no longer fits the bill. Daquin puts on Thelonious Monk in concert in London and sprawls on the sofa again. Amazing Monk, discordant Annick. Image: Amélie's head on his shoulder, the smell of hash, our generation is a bit off the wall. Annick's sure of herself but she's afraid of me. Why? Use that fear? Daquin pictures Annick leaning forward, seductive smile, husky voice. This woman can stand on her own two feet. If I try to get past her by sheer force, she'll resist, and the outcome is uncertain. Michel, of course, Michel. I've got her. Daquin goes upstairs to get dressed.

Taxi to the clinic at Le Vésinet, a magnificent white nineteenth-century villa surrounded by gardens, trees and lawns interspersed with flowerbeds. A nurse shows Daquin up to the second floor, waxed parquet floors.

'How is she?'

'So-so.' A dismissive shrug. 'Drugged up to the eyeballs. She's going home tomorrow, but don't tire her out.'

'Don't worry.'

The nurse knocks on the door, shows Daquin in and leaves them. A small room, simplicity and comfort. Annick is sitting by the window looking out over the garden. She slowly turns her head, looks at Daquin, surprised to see him there. He's wearing a dark grey heavy corduroy suit with a round neck over a cashmere sweater. Not exactly the same man as in his office.

'Sit down, Superintendent, and tell me what you're doing here.'

'I've come to find out how you are...'

'I'm fine, thank you.'

Her face hollow and pale, her pupils like pinholes, her speech and movements sluggish. And fully in control. Daquin smiles at her.

'... and to talk to you about Michel.'

'I saw Inspector Bourdier yesterday.' Very curt. 'I told him everything I had to say. It's finished. I don't want to talk to you about him.'

'I've come to talk to you about Michel. Not the murder.'

'His life is none of your business.'

'It is, in a way. I spent a whole night with him, last week.' She stares at him fixedly, without budging. Maybe it hasn't sunk in? 'I had sex with him, if you prefer. He enjoyed it very much, and so did I.'

She closes her eyes, still sitting motionless, opens them again after a moment, and says in the same slow, confident voice, as if stating the obvious:

'I must have been wrong about you. You're not a rapist cop.'

Daquin is surprised. Feels like telling her that it is perfectly possible to rape a boy. Flashback: he's thirteen, it's the year his mother died. Strangely, he is unable to remember the rapist's features precisely. Just a moustache. The memory that is still etched in his mind today, just as acutely, is that of his own face, pushed down into the earth and the dead leaves, the taste of mud in his mouth, the smell of the earth, the suffocating sensation, the earth burning his eyes. Turns back to Annick. What experience does she have of rapist cops? Wait. Let it come out when she's ready.

After a while, she continues:

'Why do you say that?'

'So that you know you are not alone.' Daquin gets to his feet. 'I'll be off, you must be tired.'

'Thank you for coming.'

Week-end with his family in Saint-Denis for Lavorel. His wife is a primary school teacher and town councillor. She raises their two daughters aged five and three competently and efficiently. The three of them form an organised, united trio who greet him warmly when he arrives. But he always feels like a tourist in his own home. His true life is elsewhere, it begins somewhere around Quai des Orfèvres. Long may it last. A few phone calls to his friends in the Fraud Squad to find a contact in Munich.

Sunday 29 October 1989

It is very early in the morning when Daquin's phone rings. Annick's voice.

'Come to my place right away.'

An hour later, on the landing of the seventh floor, a glance at the closed door of Michel's apartment and Daquin rings the bell. The door opens. She's waiting for him.

In the main living room (a glance around, nothing's changed since the other evening, the feeling of being back in familiar surroundings), Annick, wearing navy blue slacks and pullover, very prim, leads the way and sits in one of the wing chairs, her arms on the armrests, upright, slow, an air of suspense created with minimal effort.

Daquin sits in an armchair next to her, and waits. When unsure, do as little as possible.

'I know who killed Michel.'

Ears pricked. 'I'm listening.'

'I want you to help me nail his killer.'

Daquin's antennae sense danger. Things are moving a bit too fast, the situation is out of control. Flashback: internal investigation, being sent on leave. Lavorel and Romero. I don't really have any choice.

'To do that, I need proof.'

She stares at him for a moment. Stock-still. No coke for several days, probably on medication.

'The murderer is a friend of mine called Christian Deluc...'

Daquin sinks back in his armchair. He feels slightly giddy. Runs his hand over his face. Me too, I thought Deluc could have had Michel killed. So what she has to say interests me. But it's no more than speculation. And as for killing Michel himself... What is she trying to drag me into?

'Apparently you know him?'

'A little. I met him once. Tell me how you reached this conclusion.'

'I came home this morning. And on the coffee table I found this cigarette case.'

Lying in front of Daquin is a metal case, strawberries-crushed-in-cream pink, beedies – Indian cigarettes. Those are the cigarettes Deluc smokes.

Unusual. You don't find them in that packaging in France. They come from Davidoff, in Geneva. This case wasn't here when I left. I found it when I came home this morning. I called the concierge who did the cleaning here while I was away, and asked here where she had found it. It was there, under the cushion of the wing chair.

Daquin opens the case. Half a dozen slim cigarettes, dark brown, carefully laid out, a cloying smell.

'Is Deluc a friend of yours?'

'Yes, you could say so.'

'So he's been here before?' She nods. 'Even if this case is his, he could have lost it at any time.'

'No. No way. Michel and I liked to keep the place neat and tidy, with everything is in its place.' Daquin remembers the meticulously organised studio. 'Michel cleaned the place thoroughly every day. If the case had been in the wing chair before Michel's death he would have found it and thrown it away. Or put it away. But it wasn't put away.' After a pause, she continues: 'Deluc came here last Wednesday. Not Tuesday, otherwise the case would have disappeared on Wednesday morning. Not Thursday, as nobody except the concierge came into the apartment after the police left. Deluc came on Wednesday afternoon, rang the bell, and Michel opened the door. Deluc sat in the wing chair. They had a drink, Christian smoked a cigarette. The concierge found two dirty glasses and an ash tray in the sink. They went into Michel's studio, and there, Christian killed him.

Daquin listens carefully. A memory is struggling to the surface. The murder was on Wednesday. Thursday evening, at the Élysée, rack of lamb, Château Carbonnieux, Deluc puts down his glass. '*Yesterday afternoon, a meeting of our working party to crack down on drugs*' And he repeated: '*Wednesday afternoon*.' Was he stating his alibi?

'Help me to understand. Did Deluc know Michel?'

'Of course. When I entertained, Michel did the cooking. All my friends knew him.' Abruptly, she leans towards him, grows animated, smiling provocatively. 'Michel and I made an odd couple, didn't we? We were very happy together, for more than ten years. Affection without sex. Happiness. Can you understand that, Superintendent?'

'From your point of view I can, but what did he get out of it?'

'I was his anchor. I made every conceivable freedom and pleasure possible in his life.' Her smile becomes more insistent. 'Don't tell me nobody's ever loved you for your dependability rather than for sex. Usually, in these cases, you take the sex too. We didn't have sex, and that suited Michel perfectly.'

Daquin sinks deeper into his chair with a half-smile.

'I've experienced that too, but it hurt. Let's get back to Deluc. Why would he have wanted to kill Michel?'

Now she's sitting upright again, remaining stock still in her armchair.

'I know Christian. I see him as disturbed, repressed and capable of anything. The type of person I wouldn't be surprised to learn one day turns round and shoots his entire family and then commits suicide.'

Lenglet's breathless voice echoes in Daquin's ears: '*a repressed lech, made you think of a fundamentalist Protestant paedophile.*'

'What do you mean?'

'Complicated relationships with women. He remarries at each stage of his career. First wife, on arrival in Paris. Second, on his return from Lebanon, and third on entering the Élysée.'

'Do you mind if I say that he's not the only person who sleeps his way to the top? And that it's not a crime?'

Another broad smile. 'I see what you mean, Superintendent, and you're right. But Christian doesn't sleep with his women.' Daquin raises an eyebrow. 'They've never made a secret of it. He's a laughing stock among the Paris chattering classes...'

'Charming. What about his son?'

'He's not the father. And it's public knowledge that he only gets pleasure from Perrot's girls.'

'Just because a man sleeps with whores, it doesn't mean he kills queers. Let's change the subject. Last Wednesday, why did you accuse Jubelin of having killed Michel?'

'I wasn't myself.'

'That's not a good enough answer, and you know it.'

'Jubelin and I have fallen out. We've crossed swords at Pama. The day before the murder, he asked me to hand in my notice. As he hated Michel and the life we lived — I think he was ashamed of it —, I was in shock, I didn't know what I was saying. I don't seriously think that Jubelin had Michel killed. I'm not being devious, if that's what you want to know.'

'If I find Michel's killer, whether it's Deluc or someone else, you'll tell me what you know about Jubelin.'

Again, she leans forward, the smile, turns on the charm.

'Our interests might well converge there.' A silence. 'I've already found his successor. Young, assistant manager of Pama's insurance arm for ten years, a graduate of the École Polytechnique and a Protestant. After Jubelin, an ambitious, unscrupulous self-made man, he's someone who'll offer a reassuring image and steer a steady course.'

Sincerity in her voice. It's probably safe to assume that she's not trying to protect Jubelin by giving me Deluc. Daquin runs his thumb over his lips.

'You have no proof against Deluc. But for reasons of my own, I'm going to pursue this line of inquiry.' He rises. 'It would probably be best if nobody knows you're back home. You never know. I'll be in touch as soon as I have anything.'

Take a walk through Paris, to think. Taxi down to the Seine, then Daquin walks home from the Pont du Carrousel via Saint-Germain-des-Prés and Boulevard Raspail. First point: my trump card is still Perrot's chauffeur. To be played first. Second point: I have no means of putting pressure on Annick Renouard, I simply benefit from a bit of sympathy for having briefly been Michel's lover. But is she really trying to find his killer, or is she using this murder to play some complicated game at Pama? There's nothing of the naïve young girl about her. He walks for a kilometre mulling over the question and concludes that she's probably in earnest. Third point: in any case, I have no choice, I have to play her game because, whatever happens, she'll give me Jubelin who may be as important to me as Perrot. I'll have to improvise as I go along.

He enters the Villa des Artistes. A shock. Rudi's there, sitting on a low wall, waiting for him. Stunning: black trousers, black leather jacket, belted, round neck buttoned up to the chin. Only a month. Another era. Rudi smiles at him.

'I've come to lock up my apartment and move out my things. I wouldn't dream of coming to Paris without dropping in to say hello. You're usually in at this hour on a Sunday.'

Daquin opens the door and they go into the house. Rudi, very much at home, takes off his jacket to show a beautiful orange-yellow shirt, and sits down on the sofa. Daquin disappears behind the counter, mixes two margaritas and waits to find out what this visit is about. They chat about this and that. Hundreds of thousands of demonstrators, Honecker's resigned, the Politburo's in tatters. Daquin admits he's been wrong about the GDR. Rudi tells him about his day-to-day life in Berlin, two trips to the GDR with a false passport, the excitement.

'And it's not over. The Communist world is falling apart and we are the ones who are burying it.' Daquin is still waiting. 'Mitterrand is leaving in two days for an official visit to the Federal Republic of Germany. And he's planning to go to the GDR in November.' Silence. 'The opposition in my country takes a dim view of this trip.' Still no reaction. 'Could you introduce me to a few people I could discuss it with? Purely to exchange information, of course. Friends of Lenglet's, for example?'

Sigh of relief from Daquin. Situation clarified, defined.

'I can.' Glances at his watch. It's already after one, appointment at the stadium at three. 'Tomorrow. But fair's fair. One of my inspectors is leaving for Munich tonight, on unofficial business. He doesn't speak German. Can you find a crash pad there for him?'

Monday 30 October 1989

After a night on the train, Lavorel finds himself in the café at Munich railway station, sitting between a worthy colleague from the Fraud Squad, a bespectacled fair-haired boy who resembles him like a brother, and a man in his thirties called Stefan, who introduced himself as the interpreter hired by Superintendent Daquin.

The low-down on A.A. Bayern, an insurance company specialising in the property and civil engineering sector. A good network that stretches from Bavaria to cover the whole Federal Republic of Germany. A family business established after the war, listed on the stock exchange in 1965, but the Muller family owns – or rather still owned – thirty per cent of the capital until recently, when Heinz Muller, the MD, sold all his shares in a single day causing the share price to plunge and paving the way for Pama's takeover bid.

'Does that sound at all odd to you?'

'Yes, but Muller is free to sell as he pleases. Then, he left the city with his entire family. No complaints, nothing. It remains to be seen whether the takeover bid is above-board, and that's a matter for the stock exchange authorities.'

He doesn't seem inclined to say any more, pays for his drink and leaves Lavorel alone with his interpreter.

'What do we do now?'

'Let's drop by Muller's place, on the off-chance.'

A large, very bourgeois apartment building. Entry phone. Stefan rings the buzzer. No reply. After a while, a young woman comes out of the building. Stefan approaches her.

'I'm a friend of the Mullers. I was supposed to come and see them but they're not answering my letters, nothing. Do you know where I can get hold of them?'

'No idea. They moved out suddenly, about a month ago. They didn't leave a forwarding address. We were surprised, it wasn't like them. They were always charming neighbours.'

At the reception desk of A.A. Bayern's head office, Stefan, with Lavorel still at his side, asks to see Heinz Muller. He is sent to see his secretary. A tall, square, rather heavy woman, around forty, friendly.

'I'm looking for Herr Muller. We made an appointment over a month ago. Yesterday I went to his apartment as arranged, but there was nobody at home. And his neighbours don't seem to know where he's gone.'

'Well neither do I. I've worked with him for ten years. And one fine day he informed me he was selling everything and leaving the company. The next day, he did just that. He didn't come in the following day, and I haven't heard a word from him. It's unbelievable.'

She seems very put out.

'Wasn't there a police investigation?'

'No. Why should there be? He's free to sell up and go off, even if it does seem absurd.'

'There must be a solicitor, banker, lawyer, someone who knows how to get hold of him?'

'Probably, but not the company's.'

Stefan quickly translates the gist of this for Lavorel, who pulls a face. Last try.

'What about you, did you notice anything recently, odd behaviour, something that might help me understand and give me an idea where to start?'

She hesitates slightly.

'There's something that bothers me. I haven't told anyone about it yet. Herr Muller is an upright family man. In ten years of working together, he never acted improperly.' Stefan, composed and earnest, translates at once for Lavorel who says to himself that he wouldn't venture to either. Perhaps a nutter like Romero would, but even he might balk. 'On several occasions recently, I heard him tell his wife on the phone that he had meetings and would be home late. I knew it wasn't true. One day, I followed him. He dropped in to the Europa Eroscenter before going home. I was very disappointed that he should be like that.'

Stefan takes Lavorel to the nearest café.

'This is beginning to get interesting. The Europa Eroscenter is notorious here. Its clientele is mainly businessmen, and it's run by an Italian, a guy called Renta, suspected by the police of being involved in a pizzeria racket, but they've never been able to nail him. A smart guy. Muller was perhaps in business with Renta. Wait here for me. I'm going to make a few calls.'

An hour later, Lavorel has eaten several sausages, drunk four beers, and is bored out of his mind. Stefan comes back, looking rather surprised.

'When he disappeared, Muller was about to be arrested for espionage for the Stasi. An anonymous informer, with evidence to back up his accusation. You've really stumbled on a big fish. By accident?'

Late that night, close to midnight, after having dinner together, Romero and Le Dem drop in on Daquin who's waiting for them, listening to jazz and reading. Le Dem stares wide-eyed as they enter the Villa. Glass roofs, ivy-clad walls, peace and quiet – it's a far cry from La Courneuve. No time to go on about it, get down to work straight away, sitting around the coffee table. Daquin does the talking.

'I've found out how Deluc made his fortune. He earned a decent living until 1981 but didn't seem to have a vast capital at his disposal. He rented an apartment in the 9th arrondissement. In 1982, he bought a one-hundred-square-metre apartment on the Île Saint-Louis. For the sum of around three million, using a loan from an offshore bank. At this stage, we don't know what the loan repayment terms were or who the people are behind the bank. The vendor was Perrot's property development company. In 1988, a year ago, after Mitterrand's re-election, Deluc bought a villa on Lake Annecy for just over four million. This time, the vendor was a non-trading property company behind which it wasn't difficult to find Perrot, and Deluc borrowed the money from the same offshore bank. To be investigated further. My conclusion so far is that Deluc had done his friend Perrot some huge favours, and not only the tip-off about the Bastille district in 1981. And it is very much in his interest to protect him, because if we manage to destroy Perrot, it's very likely Deluc will go down too. Another totally unexpected factor, and a bit of a surprise, Annick Renouard is convinced that Deluc murdered Michel Nolant.'

And Daquin gives them the gist of his conversation with Annick.

'What do you think?'

The response is rather sceptical.

'That's not all. Lavorel called me from Munich. The boss of A.A. Bayern is alleged to have been a Stasi agent about to be arrested, which would explain why he sold up and shipped out.'

Le Dem, who is not very clear about the Stasi, takes this information in calmly, but Romero grasps the full impact.

'Are you suggesting that someone at Pama has some sort of ties with the Stasi? Madame Renouard a Stasi agent... that'll give me something to fantasise about on my next holiday.'

'Don't despair. The source can't be checked. And even if the information is reliable, we can't do anything about it, we don't have the resources or the time. I told Lavorel to drop it and come back. He'll be here tomorrow morning. Now, tell me how far you've got.'

Romero sits up.

'The grocer told the concierge this evening that he'd be receiving a delivery some time this week.' A pause. 'I realise that this isn't earth-shattering, after what you've just told us...'

'No hesitation. We swoop on this delivery. It's now or never. What do you say?'

'We go for it.'

'Le Dem, you can still back out.'

'I'm beginning to like it.'

'Fine, let's do it. Now we have to get Dubanchet's team to keep them under twenty-four-hour surveillance and pounce when the concierge comes to pick up her supplies, not before. Leave the grocer and the concierge to Dubanchet's team, and you rush over and arrest the chauffeur with his pants down in the car park, if timing permits. Nab the girl who comes and gives him a blow job too. Lavorel's coming back tonight, so there'll be three of you to carry out the arrest. Then, interrogation in your office, at number 36. Plan thoroughly, Romero. I can't show my face, but I doubt the chauffeur will be too hard to crack, he's got too much to lose. And add some questions on Deluc. Which of Perrot's girls did he visit... on the day Michel was murdered, did anything unusual happen at Perrot's? Make it up as you go along, but you get the picture. Get Lavorel to write the reports, and tell him to drop anything you find out about Deluc. Above all, nothing must be mentioned that might connect him to Michel's murder. He must write it in such a way that it gives the impression that the chauffeur is giving us Perrot without being asked for anything in return. That will make later negotiations easier. Once the report has been written, hand it to Dubanchet. A quick call to keep me posted, and go to bed with the phone off the hook. I'll deal with the flack from Dubanchet and the chief.'

Monday 6 November 1989

Le Dem, in a swanky car, parked opposite Le Chambellan. Lavorel and Romero are walking slowly up Rue Balzac towards the Champs-Élysées. Perrot's car arrives, moving slowly, the chauffeur gets out and opens the door. Perrot alights and vanishes inside the restaurant. The car pulls away slowly then turns into the driveway to the car park. Just as the chauffeur picks up the remote control to open the automatic doors, Romero opens the passenger door, whips out his gun and presses it into the chauffeur's side. He stares open-mouthed at Romero and has the feeling that he's about to go under. I've seen this guy somewhere before...

'Police. Your dealer grassed. Open this door and drive slowly into the car park.'

As he lets out the clutch, Lavorel clambers into the back. They enter the car park and the chauffeur heads towards a space right at the back.

'Not there,' says Romero, 'this is your space here.'

The chauffeur obeys.

Romero searches under the seat while Lavorel keeps an eye on the chauffeur. His groping fingers come into contact with a corner of carpeting that has come away. He lifts it: the cold feel of plastic. He pulls out a bag containing four small doses. Holds it under the driver's nose and places it in his lap.

'You do exactly as we tell you and you'll come out of this better than you think. It's not your hide we're after.'

Romero and Lavorel get out and hide behind a car parked nearby.

'When the girl arrives, push the stuff as usual. But no blow job today, we haven't got the time.'

Another shock.

The girl arrives, the same one Romero saw from his hiding place last time. The moment she opens the door, the chauffeur holds out the sachet. Surprised, she steps back and bumps into Lavorel and Romero.

'Freeze. Police.'

Romero inserts two fingers in her trouser belt and pulls out five neatly folded five-hundred franc notes. Lavorel hauls the chauffeur roughly out of the car.

'Get moving, let's not hang around. We're going to Quai des Orfèvres.'

Pushed and shoved to the car park exit. Le Dem's waiting, parked at the entrance. Everybody piles into the car.

The chauffeur is sitting in Daquin's office, guarded by Lavorel, who is absorbed in making up a crossword puzzle. In the inspectors' office, the girl is sitting cross-legged on a chair, looking bored and blasé. Romero is standing, half leaning on a corner of the desk, while Le Dem, seated, looks unconcerned as he asks her name and civil status. She smiles at him.

'I'm not sure all this is entirely legal. Intrusion into a private residence, and the owner knows people...'

Romero interrupts:

'Wait, let me stop you right there. Don't you take that attitude, not with us. The dealer and the chauffeur's wife have already been arrested. He's going to cop it. We have several charges against him. And as for you, we can nail you for trafficking, because you were planning to sell the stuff to your work mates. Shut up and let me finish. Things don't look too good for you as far as Perrot's concerned either. He's involved in some highly irregular wheeling and dealing and he's got every reason to want to keep the cops away from Le Chambellan. How's he going to react when he hears that you brought the cops in with your small-time dealing? Do you think he's going to be pleased it's going to be splashed all over the papers that his luxury brothel is crawling with junkies and pushers? What do you reckon, is he going to give you a lawyer, or punish you?'

The girl thinks for a moment, crossing and uncrossing her legs. Shapely.

'This is the deal: you answer my questions, I won't take a statement, and I let you go. But watch it. I already know quite a lot. If I catch you trying to pull a fast one, no deal, and I come down on you like a ton of bricks. Do you understand?'

'OK.'

'How exactly does Le Chambellan's brothel operate?'

Little snigger. 'Why, does it turn you on?'

No time to finish her sentence. Romero, in a gifted imitation of Daquin's style (hours of training), gives her a resounding slap with the full force of his arm, without moving the top half of his body.

'That's enough. Last chance.'

She gingerly touches her cheek and the corner of her mouth. It's burning, but not bleeding. After all, what has she got to lose? In any case, she's blown it as far as Perrot's concerned.

'What do you want to know?'

'Who runs the place?'

'Madame Paulette in theory. Perrot actually. He comes by every evening at around six or seven o'clock. He checks everything, the girls' appointments, with which clients. Everything. He's only interested in the regular clients.' She falters a little.

Romero, standing behind her, taps her on the back of her neck.

'Go on.'

'We have to tell him exactly what they like, how they respond. He takes notes and gives orders. And he watches. He's installed cameras in all the rooms.'

Romero recalls the video lounge in Perrot's apartment, and the double-locked cupboard full of cassettes that the cleaner told him about.

'And of course, the clients are unaware of this.'

'Of course.' Condescending.

Romero ignores this and continues:

'Who are the clients?'

'All very respectable people, rich, influential. But we don't always know their names. We have dinner or go out with them. You don't just sleep with them, you've also got to be elegant, to be able to talk about the latest shows, exhibitions and all that. Madame Paulette takes care of our wardrobe and makes little cards to help us keep the conversation going. If a girl isn't up to the job, Perrot doesn't use her again.'

'Amazing. Do you know a man called Deluc?'

'Yes. He's a regular.'

'The name of the girl who looks after him?'

She shoots Romero a sidelong glance. A trick question or not? Let's get this over with.

'She's a transvestite.'

Romero and Le Dem, suddenly interested, manage to conceal their surprise.

'Continue. Tell me about her.'

'She's called Evita. She doesn't work regularly at Le Chambellan. Perrot only brings her in for Deluc. And she never goes out with him.'

'What does she look like?'

'Tall, about six foot I'd say, very dark, long hair, probably a wig. Hazel eyes, lovely breasts. Loads of make-up. Always wears short, tight dresses. She's certainly a knockout. She looks like one of the Crazy Horse girls.'

'Do you know how to get hold of her?'

'No. We've never spoken to each other. She arrives, goes and waits for Deluc in a bedroom, and then she leaves. Only, about ten days ago, there was a hell of a fight between her and Deluc.'

'Last Wednesday?'

'No, the Friday before. Things had barely got off the ground, it must have been around ten o'clock. Evita was with Deluc. There was the sound of shouting and breaking glass, Deluc was yelling. Madame Paulette called Perrot to the rescue. He locked himself in with them, and must have calmed them down eventually. But then Evita left, she had a nasty gash on her shoulder. We haven't seen her since.'

'What about Deluc?'

She thinks for a moment.

'I don't believe we've seen him either.'

'What are your working hours?'

'Any time, by appointment. But actually, we work mostly in the evenings and at night.'

'How many are you?'

'About ten.'

'Pay?'

'Do you really want to know? You'll be livid. Some nights we earn up to eighty thousand francs.' She's gloating, this is her revenge. Stupid cop. 'For Perrot, it's free, of course. He comes almost every night and does his workout with his live inflatable dolls.'

'Don't complain, inflatable doll. You are young, pretty and cultured thanks to Madame Paulette. You'll be able to set up as a professional woman when you get out of here. If Perrot doesn't get his hands on you... Le Dem, I'm handing her over to you. I'll be next door.'

'Aren't you letting me go?'

'I'm waiting to see what the chauffeur says. If it fits with your story, I'll let you go.'

The chauffeur really isn't showing off. Lavorel lets him stew in his corner without even glancing at him. He knows he's already talked too much and wonders to what extent his situation is compromised.

On that point, Romero leaves him in no doubt.

'It's going to be hard to limit the damage as far as you're concerned. Drug dealing, caught in the act.' A pause. 'Your wife was arrested today along with the grocer who supplies you.' The chauffeur fidgets in his chair, very ill at ease. 'And another charge of procuring.' He turns ashen. 'It's going to wipe out all your savings. Bye-bye that little bar-cum-tobacconist's in Lyon. Hello the nick. And yet you had a good job, well paid... when Perrot finds out you were pushing drugs to his girls on his premises and that you're a pimp, we're going to have to protect you. Are you getting the picture.'

'I am.'

'A good starting point. I'm offering you a deal. I'm interested in Perrot, not you. You help me, and I'll fix it so you get off with the minimum charge, just protective custody until it all blows over.' A pause. Romero smiles. 'And what's more, I'm offering you a chance to take revenge on this boss who sprawls in the back of the car, telephones in front of you, talks about everything, his private life, his schemes and makes you run his errands as if you were a robot, unable to hear, see, or understand, capable only of driving.'

'Have you been a chauffeur?'

'Yes, for my Superintendent.'

Lavorel raises an eyebrow. The chauffeur suddenly warms to Romero. At the same time he must keep his wits about him, see what's coming, how much he knows. And get a better deal as he goes along, if he can.

'What do you want to know?'

Romero fires questions about Transitex, Aubert, Thirard (with photos). Draws a blank all the way down the line. The chauffeur doesn't know them, has never heard of them. The Italians? Mori, Ballestrino? Yes, when they came to Paris, Perrot hosted them, parties at Le Chambellan, he pulled out all the stops. He often phones Ballestrino, in Milan. But briefly. 'Everything OK?' and that was all.

Lavorel and Romero exchange a look which the chauffeur catches.

'And a man called Deluc, do you know him?'

He sits up a little. Now's the moment.

'You don't know much you guys, you're groping in the dark. I'm prepared to help you, but it'll cost you a bit more. First, you've got to let my wife go. She was picked up at the grocer's by chance.'

It takes Romero an hour to arrange for her release. Meanwhile, the girl grows irritable and Le Dem starts playing cards with her. Lavorel goes back to his crossword grid and the chauffeur half dozes, pleased with himself.

When the questioning resumes, the chauffeur is so talkative that Romero can hardly get a word in edgeways.

Perrot handles considerable sums of cash. The transactions often take place in the car. Perrot leaves home in the morning with an attaché case. He asks me to stop the car en route, someone gets in, they talk about amounts, dates, rates. Then Perrot opens the attaché case. The chauffeur can't see what's inside, but of course they both count. The attaché case changes hands and the guy gets out before they reach Rue de l'Université.

'Bribery?'

'I'd say it was loans most of the time. I don't know the names of the people. Except one, a guy called Leccia, a film producer, who was shot dead in an underground car park two or three months ago. I saw his picture in the papers. I recognised him all right. Three months earlier he'd come to pick up his attaché case from the car.'

'Does the name Jacques Montier ring any bells?'

'The name, no. But if you showed me a photo... I've got a good memory for faces.'

'I know what it's like, from seeing them in the driving mirror, as if you're looking at the cars a long way behind, you end up photographing them.'

'Exactly.' Definitely a nice guy, this cop.

'We don't have a photo right now, but we can get one. Apart from the loans, does Perrot grease any palms?'

'I get the impression he does. Sometimes, I had to deliver attaché cases. Never saw what was inside: they were locked with a code. I can give you a list of addresses, but not necessarily the names.'

'A man called Deluc?'

'Him, yes, I know him very well. Once, I delivered an attaché case to his home. I handed it to him in person. He opened it in front of me, you know, keeping the contents hidden from view behind the lid. He took out a brand new five-hundred franc note and gave it to me to say thank you.'

'Very clever... Roughly when was that?'

'Some time around last summer.'

Lavorel gives a satisfied smile as he concentrates his mind on producing a brilliant fictitious version of the interrogation.

'And a man called Jubelin, did you see him often?'

'I didn't see him a lot, no. But Perrot phones him all the time. In business, apparently, they're as thick as thieves.' He falters.

'Go on.'

'One day, not long ago, on leaving home, Perrot calls Jubelin. He says: "A.A. Bayern is for today. Can you deal with it?" Jubelin says yes, apparently. Perrot adds: "Bid for Deluc and for me as you would for yourself."'

'Did Annick Renouard's name come up at that point?'

'No. I remember the details clearly because I thought it was a tip-off. The minute I was alone I called my wife before she left for work and she bought A.A. Bayern shares through our broker the same morning. I've followed Perrot's lead several times before, and it's always worked. Tip-offs for the races, too. Well, this time, it didn't work, the share price plummeted during the day.'

'Pity.'

Resigned. 'Perrot must have lost a lot more than me.'

'Changing the subject. Do you know one of Perrot's girls called Evita?'

'No. No Evita ever came down to the car park.'

'What about a transvestite?'

'Never seen a tranny at Le Chambellan.'

'Last Wednesday, did anything unusual happen? Anything at all, even a tiny detail.'

'It wasn't a little detail. That day, Perrot came back to Le Chambellan earlier than usual and I went and waited for him in the car park. After a while, I don't know how long, he came down with Deluc.' Romero feels a shiver run all the way down his spine. 'Completely out of it, Deluc. I wondered whether he'd been shooting up. And the three of us left to pick up his car.'

'Where was it?'

'It was parked in Boulevard Maillot. He was so shaken up that he wasn't in a fit state to drive. So I ran him home in his car while Perrot drove his back to Le Chambellan himself. The minute I was back, Perrot sent me to pick up a girl, outside the Brasserie Lipp...'

'What did this pretty young lady look like?'

'I didn't get a very good look at her. Very tall, with fabulous breasts. A blonde wig, I'm certain it was a wig, trousers, sweater, dark glasses and a scarf. She sat in the back, and didn't say a word. Nothing. Not even thank you when I dropped her off.'

'And where did you drop her off?'

'In Munich.'

'In Munich... Did Perrot send you there?'

'Of course. I dropped the girl off in the early hours at the station café where a friend of Perrot's was waiting for her. And I came straight back to Paris.'

'A friend? Who?'

'Signor Renta. An Italian who often comes to Paris. He's also a friend of Ballestrino's.'

Tuesday 7 November 1989

The chief is livid. He paces up and down in front of the window. Lying on his desk is the report signed by Lavorel, while Daquin, sitting in an armchair, watches him with a completely blank expression.

'It's unspeakable. I'm going to clean up the department, and I'm going to start now. With you...'

'I was on leave, Sir, remember, I haven't set foot in the place for a week.'

'... and your inspectors, who are nowhere to be found, by the way, vanished into thin air after their antics last night...'

'They called me in the night and I advised them to make themselves scarce for the next twenty-four hours. Let time do its work, as the saying goes.'

The chief was speechless.

'How can you...?' Daquin is so laid back that the chief is thrown. He sits down at his desk. 'What do you have to say in your defence?'

'In my defence, nothing. In my inspectors' defence, I can tell you that they carried out a sting, you've had the reports and so has the investigating magistrate. They had a search warrant and were working in cooperation with Superintendent Dubanchet's team. Dubanchet is delighted with the success of the operation. Regular deliveries of heroin from Holland, that's quite something.'

The chief takes this in. He's furious that he attacked Daquin without thinking of obtaining Dubanchet's support first. Embarrassing.

'Don't imagine for one second that I'm going to believe this was a coincidence. In this office, I asked you to lay off Perrot. One week later, your inspectors arrest his chauffeur on a minor dealing offence and he makes a whole series of accusations against his boss, spontaneously of course...'

'I haven't seen his statement.'

'Well I have. Bravo. That's devious.'

Lavorel, devious...

'The main thing seems to me not what you believe, Sir, but how you are going to handle the situation. Perrot is up to his ears in compromising deals, closer to the world of crime than that of big business, and people are beginning to talk. He's vulnerable, because he rose very fast, but he hasn't protected his rear. In other words, he's a danger, especially to his friends. It seems to me you need at least twenty-four hours to be able to cover the situation from every angle.'

At dawn, after a night on the road taking turns at the wheel with Lavorel, Romero parks the car two streets away from the Eroscenter and Lavorel goes over the plan they worked out during the night once again. A little stroll to the grand, classical-style apartment building. Tall carriage entrance, monumental staircase, red carpet and elevator. The Eroscenter occupies the entire first floor. You have to ring a buzzer to gain entry. On the upper floors, opulent apartments, two to each landing. On the ground floor next to the entrance, a pizzeria, closed at this early hour.

'We can't do anything until early afternoon. Let's go and have a slap-up breakfast. That'll keep us awake.'

4 p.m., Romero goes up, rings the buzzer, smiles at the surveillance camera. The door opens and he walks in with just the right sway in his gait. Nobody in the vast reception lounge other than a pretty hostess leafing through a magazine behind an airport-style desk.

'*Si parla italiano?*'

'No.

Relief. 'Français?'

'Of course. It's very early, Sir. We're not open yet.'

'I'm a cousin of Signor Renta's. I'm passing through Munich and I have to leave in an hour.'

'Signor Renta, that's different.' I should have guessed, there's a family likeness. 'What can I do for you?'

'Renta told me about a French transvestite who's just arrived...'

The hostess leans towards an intercom.

'Evita, a client for you.' A frantic whispered exchange follows. Go in, Sir, third door on the left.'

Big smile. No need to show the colour of your money. A cousin of Renta's doesn't pay. Romero walks down the corridor, third door on the left, opens it and finds himself face to face with Evita. She towers above him in her high heels. Very beautiful, and angry, that's for sure. Romero, a finger on his lips, signals her to follow him into the adjacent shower room. He turns the taps full on and says:

'In case there are any hidden mikes.'

She laughs.

'Are we shooting a spy film?'

Romero, irritated, feels a bit silly.

'It's no joke.'

'It doesn't look like one.'

'Did you see or hear anything in Paris that's dangerous for your employer, Perrot, or for his client, Deluc? Perrot sent you here. I don't know why you agreed to come.'

'Good money.'

'You have no idea. All Perrot wants to do is get rid of you. He and his buddy Renta are about to sell you off to Saudi Arabia and they're planning to send you there in two days' time.'

'To Saudi Arabia!'

Her initial reaction is to burst out laughing. Romero looks miffed. The second is to say to herself that after all she's here with no ID papers, her every movement is watched and it's beginning seriously to get on her nerves.

'Who are you, tall dark stranger and what do you suggest?'

Romero, bare-chested, wearing only his trousers, bursts into the corridor looking completely panic-stricken, just as Le Dem rings the buzzer and sprints into the reception lounge.

'Help, a doctor...'

'What's going on?'

'Come and see.'

The hostess races after him into the room where Evita is writhing on the ground half naked, groaning, foaming at the mouth, white froth covering her cheeks, filling her nostrils and streaming down her neck where the veins are swollen. Her eyes are slightly bulging, her wig askew and her make-up streaked.

Romero, frantic:

'I'm afraid it's rabies, I saw a rabid dog in Italy once, it was foaming like that.'

The hostess is trembling from head to foot.

'Rabies is dangerous.'

'Very, but I think we have a little time before she bites us. Help me with this sheet.'

He takes the sheet from the bed, wraps Evita in it, still frothing at the mouth, tight so that she is unable to move, sits her up in an armchair, hoists her up onto his shoulder and grabs his jacket on the way, forget the shirt.

'I'm taking her to the hospital.'

Strides across the lounge. Dumbfounded, the hostess trails behind. Le Dem holds the front door open. The two of them head down the stairs holding Evita's shoulders and legs. The girl upstairs starts yelling:

'Wait, where are you going...?'

Outside the building, Lavorel in the car, engine ticking over, everyone in, they shoot off at top speed. In the driving mirror, Lavorel sees two men rush out of the pizzeria.

Evita wriggles an arm out of the sheet. Lavorel hands her a bottle of mineral water. She drinks, rinses out her mouth, spits out of the window, wipes her mouth and straightens her wig. Lavorel takes numerous detours, there's not much traffic at this hour.

'We're going back to Paris, but not by the motorway.'

'Clever trick.'

'It's an effervescent powder for stomach ache, you're meant to put a little in a big glass of water. If you put a lot with just your saliva, it froths all over the place. When I was a kid, we would do that just before taking the métro in rush hour. We always got a seat and plenty of space around us.'

Wednesday 8 November 1989

They arrive at Daquin's place in the middle of the night. He's lying on the sofa, waiting for them. The four of them are like schoolkids on an outing. Evita has removed her make up in the toilets of a service station and has carefully combed her wig and wrapped her sheet around her like an ancient Roman toga with a great deal of style. The masculine face is showing through beneath the female features, she'll need a good shave. Le Dem is totally fascinated.

'Do you want to get changed while I make coffee?' Daquin asks her. 'I can lend you some clothes.'

Five minutes later, Evita comes back down, in a plain, baggy sweater, jeans, bare feet and short, dark hair. Standing with a cup of coffee in her hand, she looks them up and down.

'Nice bunch of males... This place has a manly smell. So, you guys are all cops... I'd never have guessed. Who's got a cigarette for me?'

Romero grumbles:

'Cut it out, will you. You don't smoke at Daquin's place. Besides, we're here to work.'

Le Dem, perched on a corner of the coffee table, stares steadfastly at his shoes.

Daquin kicks off:

'May as well come clean with you, since you agreed to come...'

Evita turns to Romero with a theatrical gesture:

'I didn't agree, this gorgeous Latino kidnapped me.'

'Maybe he did. We're interested in one of your clients, Christian Deluc. Can you tell us a little about your relations with him?'

'Are you asking me to breach professional secrecy? That's not something I do. I have very few carefully selected clients who pay well and in exchange, I guarantee them total discretion.'

'He's not exactly your average customer.'

'Give me one good reason why I should talk to you about him.'

Daquin smiles at her.

'Look at the audience you've got. Hanging on to your every word. What an opportunity!'

'That's a good reason, and I like you.' She puts down her cup of coffee, settles comfortably on the sofa, crosses her legs very high, her wrists on her knees, giving her words an air of solemnity. 'Deluc was a regular client for three years. Through Perrot, who made the appointments, paid and ruled everything with a rod of iron.'

'Was?'

'About ten days ago, he tried to kill me. So I decided to strike him off my list.'

Evita is enjoying being the centre of attention. She feels she's made a good first impression. Now she has to hone the part.

'We'd just fucked in a bedroom at Perrot's place. I was getting dressed when Deluc started acting crazy. He broke a big mirror that took up a whole wall of the room, grabbed a piece of glass with his jacket wrapped around his hand and rushed at me to stab me. But I'm used to having to defend myself, in my job... and besides, he's not very physical. I laid him flat pretty quickly. But he did give me a nasty gash on the shoulder.'

'Then?'

'There's no then. As soon as he went down, I left. I went home and I told Perrot that I didn't want any more appointments with that nutter.'

'What kind of client was this Deluc?'

'Very repressed. He always needed a little encouragement.'

'Meaning?'

'He smoked ice.' She sees the scene in her mind's eye. 'Special cigarettes which he kept in a packet of beedies, you know, those stinky Indian cigarettes. Maybe that's what it was that made him lose it? Poor grade stuff... Otherwise, no worse than any of the others.'

'Poor quality ice, OK, and we're not asking you who his dealer was. But behind the mirror in the room, there was a video camera, and that must have come as a bit of a shock to him, don't you think?'

Well informed, these cops. Careful. Emphatic wave of the hand.

'Absolutely. I was going to tell you about it. I found out about it at the same time as he did.'

Daquin smiles.

'We're not trying to make things difficult for you.'

Romero changes the subject:

'Do you think that after that fight he could have gone off in search of homosexual relations?'

Evita stares at him for a moment in silence.

'What planet are you on, lover-boy? What my clients want is a beautiful woman with big breasts and a penis. Some of them come as soon as they touch my cock. And they all dream of being screwed. So you see, homosexual relations or not, it's hard to say.'

'Let's go back to Deluc. And your departure for Munich, last Wednesday.'

'Perrot calls at about five or six, I'm not dressed yet. He tells me he's sending his chauffeur to collect me to take me to Munich for a month, for my protection. Initially, I refuse. I've always been self-employed. He insists.' She pauses for a while. 'Do you know him? He's not someone you really want to argue with.' Another pause. 'To be honest, he scares me. When he sees that I'm going to say yes, he talks about money. Enough for me to go partying in the Caribbean for three months. Three months partying in exchange for one month in prison, I'll take it. And he agrees to pay up front.'

'He didn't say why he needed to keep you out of Paris?'

'No, and I didn't ask. In my profession, the less I know the better. But I did think Deluc must have done something stupid, and that Perrot was keen that nobody should find out about his little sexual habits, his cigarettes or his outbursts.' She carries on with an enticing smile. 'As I know nothing, I'm not in great danger. But by the time the gorgeous Latino turned up with his Saudi Arabia story, I was sick of being locked up. I told myself, since Perrot paid in advance, three months' partying in exchange for one week of misery is even better. And the journey was great fun. Thank you, all of you.'

Daquin arrives at Boulevard Maillot in a taxi before the sun has even risen. It takes Annick a while to come to the door. Her features seem indistinct, lost in the mass of golden hair tumbling over her shoulders. She's wearing a midnight-blue towelling bathrobe that is too big for her. Michel's probably. Wants to caress her shoulder with his fingertips. Absolutely out of the question.

'Come in. I'll try and make some coffee.'

When she comes back into the big living room, Daquin, comfortably settled in a wing chair, starts talking straight away while she pours the coffee.

'I've come to settle the score with you. But first of all, I've got a few questions to ask you.'

'Go ahead.'

'Have you known Deluc long?'

She sits on the sofa, cup in hand, and gazes at him for a moment intrigued.

'I imagine you already know the answer?'

'Of course. Otherwise I wouldn't ask the question.'

'We were at high school together in Rennes, then in the same political group in May '68. We fought alongside each other, attacking the foremen with iron bars at the factory gates.' The sirens, the cops, the chase through the woods, falling… she smiles at him. 'Are you shocked?'

'Not really.'

'He played the charismatic leader, and I do believe I was in love with him.'

He runs over to her, she falls, not a hand out to help her, he carries on running. It was important to salvage the hard core of the revolution, he would tell her later. The hard core of the revolution. At nineteen. Until he let me down... Teenage heartbreak.

'I left Rennes, and I lost touch with him.' A silence. 'When we met up again in Paris, years later, we needed each other to extend our networks, him in business, and me among the socialists who had just come into power, and we became close friends again.' She falls silent, stares at him. He hasn't moved, tense, attentive. 'You know, I'm just like everybody else. I have memories. I live with them. That's all.'

'No, it's not all. My job is to listen to people. And when I listen to you telling the story of your provincial background, I'm struck by the emotional intensity that lies behind it. I want to know what there really is between you and Deluc.'

Annick lets herself go, her eyes closed, lost alone on the sofa.

'During a clash with the cops, Christian left me alone and I was raped at the police station.'

Daquin flexes his hands. This is the chink.

'I blamed him for what happened.' Her voice remains neutral. 'Then I pragmatically decided to put it all behind me, so that I could get on with my life, I papered over the cracks as best I could and I've survived.'

Daquin lets the minutes tick by without saying a word, without moving. Annick suddenly opens her eyes.

'For years, I refused to face up to the facts. And now, I admit to myself that ever since that night, I've hated Deluc, with every fibre of my being. And that makes me feel good.' Another lapse into silence. 'You're a very unusual man.'

Daquin rises, picks up the coffee pot, fills their two cups and sits down again in the wing chair.

'My turn now. For about twelve years, Deluc has been receiving large sums of cash from Perrot. 'Annick flashes back to the hard core of the revolution. 'In exchange for information and contacts. He probably didn't feel he was being bribed, at least at first, just that he was clever, powerful and resourceful. Then Transitex goes under and Perrot, who runs the whole business behind the scenes, is worried. Naturally, he goes to Deluc and asks him to have the investigation stopped. That was probably last Friday. That must have shaken Deluc, who thought Perrot was a risk-taking property developer, not a drugs smuggler. He discovers that it's not he who's using Perrot, but vice versa. A heavy blow to his puffed-up ego.'

'You seem to know him extremely well.'

'He consoles himself by smoking vast quantities of ice, which he's always got in plentiful supply in his famous cigarette case...' Annick shudders, '...and by fucking the transvestite he regularly puts through a routine at Perrot's.' Annick sits up, her elbows pressed to her body, without a word. Daquin smiles at her. A very charming person.

'Spare me your sarcasm.'

'Shall I continue?'

'Go on.'

'First violent outburst – that evening he nearly kills the transvestite. Then, between Sunday and Wednesday, Deluc has the photos of Michel and me having a good time in front of him. You can imagine how that shakes him up. He comes here, we've had confirmation that he was in Boulevard Maillot in the afternoon. To get Michel to talk to him about me so he can create trouble for me? To fuck him? I can imagine Michel's domestic slave side would excite him.'

'You can't talk about Michel like that.'

'I'm not talking about Michel, I'm talking about Deluc. In living room, he takes out his cigarette case and smokes a cigarette stuffed with ice to boost his courage. Result, he gets a hard-on. According to the transvestite, he couldn't get it up without a smoke. They probably began to have sex together. I expect Michel found the situation very amusing until things turned nasty. Deluc panics, bad trip, like with the transvestite. He kills Michel and goes and hides at Perrot's in a state of shock. He probably told him that he'd just killed Michel and Perrot took a certain number of precautions to protect him because they have very close ties and he needs him. There you are.'

Daquin rises, walks over to the bay window. The sun is up, autumn light, murky grey, maybe it'll snow. He turns to Annick.

'We have no witnesses. We've managed to trace the transvestite but she knows nothing that would be of any use in court. No proof either. No fingerprints, no clues. The cigarette case wouldn't hold up for five minutes. And as far as I know, Deluc has got himself a cast-iron alibi at the Élysée.'

'What do we do?'

'First of all, make me another coffee.'

Thursday 9 November 1989

'Hello, Christian? This is Annick.'

'Hello, how are you, my darling?'

'Better, thank you. I came back from the clinic this morning. I need to see you urgently.'

'I'm tied up all day.'

'This evening?'

'I'm having a dinner party.'

'Christian, it's really serious. And I don't want to talk about it over the phone. I found a file at my place that belonged to Nicolas, and it relates to Pama. I can't talk to Jubelin about it and you're the only person I trust.' Gives him time to think about what such a file might contain. 'Listen. I'll drive over this evening and I'll be outside your place at midnight. Come down and see me when your friends have left. It can't wait. Tomorrow might be too late.'

'All right. Midnight, outside my place.'

'Christian Deluc called me this morning. He wanted to see me, me and nobody else, he said. We've always been very close, ever since we were kids. He was tied up all day and had a dinner party at home this evening. As I was having dinner out myself with friends, we agreed to meet around midnight outside his apartment.'

Annick parks her Austin Mini right outside Deluc's apartment in Quai d'Orléans, just before midnight. Thanks to the cocaine, the chevet of Notre

Dame is very clear, close, and radiates a feeling of serenity. At midnight, she switches on the radio. An incredulous male voice comes on the air:

'*The East German government announced earlier this evening that from midnight, there would be free movement between East and West Berlin, and for the last hour we have witnessed small groups of young people converging on the checkpoints of the Wall. And now the gates of Checkpoint Charlie have just been thrown open and young people are pouring into West Berlin in their hundreds, in their thousands.*' The voice is choked with emotion. '*There is something unreal about the situation. The Berlin Wall is falling in front of our eyes.*'

Annick laughs until tears run down her face, she can't help it. Deluc appears in the driving mirror, walks over to her, opens the door and gets into in the passenger seat. Annick switches off the radio and wipes her eyes with her hand.

'So what's this all about?'

First, bait him. 'When I got home this morning I found a file that had been sent by post. A file Nicolas had put together and which he must have given to someone to take care of, asking them to send it to me if anything happened to him.' Apologetically: 'You know Nicolas, he was very romantic.'

'What was in the file?'

'Come here, and get a good look. Do you know that Jubelin has a secret fund at Pama?'

'If I didn't know, I had my suspicions.'

'According to Nicolas's dossier the money for this slush fund comes from drug trafficking via Perrot.' Annick, her head on her arms, resting on the wheel, seems devastated. Now he must be toying with the idea of getting rid of Perrot. She continues, without looking up: 'That's not all. The dossier also contains the transcript of a recorded conversation between Nicolas and Michel. Michel saw Perrot hand over a briefcase full of notes to Jubelin at my place and count them. He gives the date and the time. Christian, do you realise what this means? Nicolas and Michel are dead, and I feel as though I'm in danger.'

Deluc is lost in thought. Would it be possible to use this dossier both to get rid of Perrot and bury Michel's murder once and for all?

Now, now. Now or never.

'He came downstairs at around midnight and came and sat in my car, in the passenger seat. He seemed a little anxious and preoccupied, but that's all, and I wasn't worried. He started telling me that he was a man of conviction. What was I supposed to reply? I told him I'd never had any doubts and I let him talk.'

'He told me that he had just found out that Perrot was compromised in a drug trafficking scandal. I tried to reassure him by telling him that he had nothing to do with this business, but I couldn't convince him. Perrot had financed his apartment and his villa in one way or another, he told me, and had lent him money interest free to play the stock exchange and make a killing, as he had a few days ago with the takeover bid for A.A. Bayern. At that point, I could feel he was becoming increasingly depressed. He carried on talking and told me that he had tried to exert pressure to stop the investigation into Perrot without bothering to use any fancy methods, for fear of being tainted by a scandal. He didn't say what. In any case, it didn't work and he was convinced the whole thing was going to blow up at any moment and he couldn't bear the thought. He looked utterly desperate. He leaned on my shoulder. I think he was crying.'

Annick gets out of the car, as if seeking a breath of fresh air, takes a few steps along the deserted embankment, glances up at the windows of the apartment blocks, no lights on, and slips on a rubber glove while Deluc is still pondering the best use he can make of Nicolas's dossier. Annick walks quickly round the car, opens the door with her left hand, takes a revolver out of her pocket and thrusts the barrel under Deluc's right cheekbone. His eyes wide, mouth open, he doesn't have time to move a muscle. Annick fires. Deafening report, deep hole where Deluc's right cheekbone had been, his skull shattered, the back of the car is splattered with blood and pink matter, the back windscreen is in smithereens.

Paralysed for a second in a state of shock. How can it be so easy? Then, quickly, place the gun in his dangling hand which drops it, tear off the glove. And scream for help.

'At that point I felt stifled. I was anxious and tried to think of something to say to cheer him up. I got out to go for a little walk along the embankment.

Then I went back to the car. I wanted to suggest he came for a walk to Notre Dame with me. It's such a ...' she hesitates, trying to find the right word, '...serene place. You know what I mean? When I reached the door, I saw him through the window raise a gun to his head and shoot. I grabbed the door and opened it. I don't know why – a reflex – to help him, I was panic-stricken. I think I stopped the body from falling out, I can't remember. And then I started screaming.'

Friday 10 November 1989

A sleepless night reading James Ellroy's *Black Dahlia*. Unaware of time passing. At 6 a.m. Daquin gets up to make coffee and turn on the radio. A slightly hoarse male voice:

'*Last night, just before midnight, the Berlin Wall came down. The Germans can now move freely between East and West. Throughout the night, the people have been dancing in the streets of West Berlin. People reunited... thousands of Berliners spraying bottles of champagne in the streets... Right now, young people from West Berlin have just scaled the Brandenburg Gate, which has remained shut all night, and they in their turn are pouring into the Eastern part of the city.*'

Silent homage to Rudi. Perhaps regret that he hadn't listened more carefully to what he'd been saying. A feeling of weariness that is nothing to do with politics. With a pang, Daquin pictures Lenglet in his hospital bed wondering: '*What are we going to look like after the collapse of the Communist world?*'

The news ends. Not a word about Deluc.

That afternoon, when Daquin enters the chief's office, he walks into a gathering of the top brass all standing around chatting. They immediately clam up and everyone sits down, Daquin in the armchair indicated by the chief, who goes on the attack:

'You know about Christian Deluc's suicide, Superintendent?'

'Yes, Sir. Inspector Bourdier has already consulted me concerning Madame Renouard's declarations.'

'Well?'

'On a certain number of points they corroborate what my inspectors and I have discovered from other sources in the course of our investigation. And which we have included in our reports and interview transcripts. On other points, of course, we have no information.'

'How do you see the sequence of events?'

'From what point of view, Sir? I am still on leave pending the results of an internal inquiry. I don't think that the investigators will come across any professional misconduct on my part, if that is what you are asking me.'

The chief smiles.

'That's not what I'm asking you, as you well know. The internal investigation concerning you has been called off, as of now, and your leave cancelled. You are in charge of the Transitex case, and that is why I'm asking you what you think will happen now.'

'Everything that Perrot's mixed up in revolves around money laundering. Thirard seems to be behind the Berger and Moulin murders, even if it is difficult to find those who did it. I believe they're contract killers probably brought in from Italy or Germany. These two cases seem to be linked to the whole Transitex affair and therefore covered by my team. If we decide to extend the investigations to Pama, we should liaise with the Fraud Squad. All the rest is outside my remit. And Nolant's murder is a matter for Bourdier and the Crime Squad.'

'Deluc's suicide?'

'It is a suicide, isn't it? Not a murder...'

'Definitely. The investigation is already over, to everyone's satisfaction.'

'It that case, it has no bearing on my team's work.' With a smile. 'Nobody wants to complicate matters.'

'The chief of the Drugs Squad has just been transferred. Would you agree to take over in the interim, until the appointment of his successor?'

First of all: go back to my office. Regain possession of my territory. Daquin pushes open the door. He is greeted by a cheer that echoes down the corridor. Romero pops a cork, the champagne gushes out and fills the five crystal flutes waiting on the desk.

The four of them drink a toast.

'To us.'

The atmosphere of the locker room after the match, after a win, when the game looked uncertain for a long time.

On the second bottle, Daquin:

'Our work isn't quite done yet. There's one job left for us to do, and perhaps the most difficult. I promised Le Dem he could keep his horse with him when he left for Brittany. On making inquiries I found the horse belongs to the national stables and they won't sell it under any circumstances. We're going to have to steal it.'

Le Dem clears his throat.

'Maybe we could wait a little. I'd like to think things over for a few days before putting in for my transfer. If I could stay with you... I'm afraid I might be bored in Quimper or Pont-l'Abbé.'

'That calls for another drink, and besides, we have to finish this bottle.'

Another round. Le Dem raises his glass.

'When the cavalry drinks a toast, which is often, we say: "To our horses, our women, and to all who mount them".'

Riotous laughter.

The Last Kabbalist of Lisbon
Richard Zimler
£7.99

'An American Umberto Eco' – Francis King, *Spectator*

Richard Zimler's *The Last Kabbalist of Lisbon* is Arcadia's most successful book to date, having sold over 75,000 copies. To coincide with the 500th anniversary of the Lisbon Massacre, Arcadia are delighted to bring out a new edition of Zimler's gripping contemporary classic.

The year is 1506, and the streets are seething with fear and suspicion when Abraham Zarco is found dead, a naked girl at his side. Abraham was a renowned Kabbalist, a practitioner of the arcane mysteries of the Jewish tradition at the time when the Jews of Portugal were forced to convert to Christianity. Berekiah, a talented young manuscript illuminator, investigates his uncle's murder, and discovers in the kabbalah clues that lead him into the labyrinth of secrets in which the Jews sought to hide from their persecutors.

'An exciting mystery set in sixteenth-century Portugal. Abraham Zarco, a member of Lisbon's kabbalist school, is found dead with a naked young woman in a sealed room. His nephew, Berekiah, has to solve the murder' – *Daily Telegraph*

One Helluva Mess
Jean-Claude Izzo
Translated from the French by Vivienne Menkes-Ivry
£10.99

'A gritty Marseilles-set novel' – Maxim Jakubowski, *Guardian*

'Marseilles is no place for tourists.' This warts-and-all portrait of Marseilles, Izzo's hometown, looks at the effects wrought by unemployment and National Front racism on a large immigrant population. *One Helluva Mess*, the latest fast-paced Izzo thriller, features Inspector Fabio Montale, the Marseilles *flic* fond of pretty women, good food and drink – and solo fishing trips. What will his catch be this time?

Ugo, a childhood friend of Montale's, is shot by corrupt cops in Le Panier, a rough part of the port. Then Leila, a young *beur*, is found raped and murdered in a field. In the background lurk the Mafia and neo-Nazi thugs. Time for Montale to down a glass of malt whisky, and prepare for a tough inquiry . . .

'Izzo does more than provide a crime story; his book sheds light on the social and political realities of a troubled but romantic city' – *Times*

The Depths of the Forest

Eugenio Fuentes

Translated from the Spanish by Paul Antill

£11.99

'Fascinating modern Spanish baroque from an enterprising small publisher' – D J Taylor

Paternóster, a remote nature reserve in Spain: Gloria, a young and attractive painter, is found brutally murdered. A few days later, a female hiker dies in exactly the same way. Next on the list is one of the reserve wardens, shot dead at point-blank range while on patrol.

The Depths of the Forest is the story of a journey to the interior of an impenetrable and imposing landscape, but also into the secrets deep within each of the characters. What ties Marco, Gloria's lawyer boyfriend in Madrid, to his university friend Octavio, who leads a strange and disturbing life with an elderly landowner who has taken him under her wing and treats him like an adoptive son? Gloria appears to have attracted love and admiration in equal measure – from men and women alike. The woman who was her co-director at the trendy urban art gallery they owned together, and the passionate sculptor dividing his time between Madrid and a converted studio near the reserve – what was the true extent of their smouldering jealousies? These secrets make each of them a potential perpetrator of the crime and, at the same time, a victim of their own destiny. Nature itself becomes an underlying protagonist to form the background of a novel exuding mystery and tension.

'The tensions of the plot are wonderfully balanced with profound feeling for the imposing forest: explorations of the secret, haunted landscape accompany Cupido's search. The writing as a distinctive sensuality, and the murdered Gloria is fully recreated as a complex human being: an authorial feat rare in most crime fictions, where the victim is so often just a stooge for the investigator. A most welcome addition, not just to crime fiction, but to literature in general' – *Independent*

The Writing on the Wall
Gunnar Staalesen
Translated from the Norwegian by Hal Sutcliffe
£11.99

'Popular Norwegian series featuring private eye Varg Veum, an upmarket Scandinavian Philip Marlowe' – Maxim Jakubowski, *The Bookseller*

It was one of those days in February of which there are far too many, despite its being the shortest month of the year. February is the year's parenthesis. The tax forms have already been sent in and the tourist season has not yet started; there is nothing on the schedule. Greyish-brown slush lay in the gutters and the hills around the city were barely visible through the fog. Like the golden buttons on the waistcoat of a forgotten snowman, you could just make out the lights of the funicular up the hillside and the street lamps were lit even in the middle of the day . . .

In this crime drama detective Varg Veum's adventures lead him to a dark world of privileged young teenage girls who have been drawn into drugs and prostitution. This situation worsens when the local judge is discovered in a luxury hotel, dead and clad only in women's lingerie. Called in by anxious parents to look for a missing daughter and explain the judge's death, Varg finds clues that lead him only deeper into Bergen's criminal underworld.

'*The Writing on the Wall* is an intriguing reworking of an old idea, set in a sleazy teen demi-monde' – *Time Out*

Final Curtain
Kjersti Scheen
Translated from the Norwegian by Louis Muinzer
£10.99

'British début for a bestselling Norwegian crime writer' – Maxim Jakubowski, *The Bookseller*

Former actress Margaret Moss is not your usual private investigator. Fond of her vodka, divorced and living in Oslo, she supports herself and her punk daughter with routine assignments such as tailing faithless husbands and wives. The tempo picks up when her friend Rakel Winkelmann, the renowned actress, disappears and Rakel's sister engages Moss to look for her without involving the police.

She has very little to go on, but a visit to Rakel's cousin brings her into contact with a group of neo-Nazis. Other clues lead to a mountain resort and Rakel's telephone lover. There Moss meets up with truck driver Roland Rud, her modern-day knight in shining armour. Piece by piece she uncovers an intrigue with roots in the theatre as well as the outside world, and becomes a pawn in a fatal game . . .

'Author Kjersti Scheen sends Margaret across Norway in a hunt that turns up a gang of neo-Nazis, among other suspects' – *Daily Mail*

Because of the Cats
Nicolas Freeling
£10.99

Freeling is 'rather special' (Patricia Highsmith); 'marvellous' (Anita Brookner, *Spectator*); 'one of my favourites, continually interesting' (P.D. James); 'the best of all police detectives' (*Sunday Times*).

Chief Inspector Piet Van der Valk of the Amsterdam police has a teenage gang on his hands: they are coming into Amsterdam from out-of-town, and they are remarkably professional. They leave behind a trail of wanton damage, senseless brutality, and rape, and one piece of possible evidence – 'the cats won't like it'.

As usual, Van der Valk's approach to the case is both unorthodox and intensely human. He immerses himself in the lives of his suspects, and in the small-town atmosphere of the seaside resort in which they live, and cracks the façade of respectability behind which they hide. Under his obsessive probing the mystery is eventually unraveled, but not before there has been a final explosion of violence as the cats act to defend themselves.

'Nicolas Freeling's Inspector Van der Valk is one of the most distinctive, original and humane fictional detectives. Here is an author who is as much concerned with the impulses and motives of the human heart as he is with the details of detection. The combination of elegant style and the continually interesting narrative give his novels their special flavour, and I am delighted to find *Because of the Cats* – one of my favourites – in print again' – P. D. James

Rough Trade
Dominique Manotti

Top Thriller of the Year – French Crime Writers' Association

'The novel I liked most this year. Set in Le Sentier, the district of Paris where expensive clothes are made in sweatshops, it uses real events – the struggle by foreign workers to get legal status – as the setting for an extraordinarily vivid crime novel'
– Joan Smith, Books of the Year, *Independent*

'A splendid neo-realistic tale of everyday bleakness and transgression set in the seedy underworld of Paris. You can smell the Gitanes and pastis fumes of the real France' – Maxim Jakubowski, *Guardian*

'Combines the circumstances of a Turkish workers' strike, the globalization of the weapons and drugs trade and the commercialisation of sex: brilliant'
– Amanda Hopkinson, Books of the Year, *Independent*

The Priest of Evil
Matti Joensuu
Translated from the Finnish by David Hackston
£11.99

'Matti Joensuu is a serial novelist and a criminal investigator for Helsinki PD. *The Priest of Evil* centres on a fantastical priest who brainwashes teenagers into carrying bomb-filled backpacks. Joensuu, who believes the police officer's 'ringside seat' on society can lend prescience, says "the priest believes there is only one way to think. So do suicide bombers and superpowers"' – Maya Jaggi, *Guardian*

There have been a strange succession of deaths at Helsinki tube stations. The police are baffled: nobody has seen anything and the tapes from the CCTV show nothing.

Detective Sergeant Timo Harjunpää of the Helsinki Violent Crimes Unit has seen more than enough of the seamier side of human nature in his career, but the forces of evil have never before crossed his path in such an overwhelming fashion. It emerges that his adversary is a deluded but dangerous character living in an underground bunker in the middle of an uninhabited Helsinki hillside.

'Matti Joensuu – a scholarly cop who might get along better with Morse than Rebus – has emerged from a long silence with a ninth novel about Inspector Harjunpää. He's still arson and explosives expert on the Helsinki force' – Boyd Tonkin, *Independent*